ABOUT THE AUTHOR

After many years as an actor in film and television Phil moved into writing and producing feature films, series and single dramas for TV and radio, documentary and animation.

In 2017 he published his first novel and has just completed his third – all standalone crime thrillers.

Through his company, Funky Medics, he produced and wrote animations and books for the UK, Europe and US on health education.

Originally from Haverfordwest in Pembrokeshire, he now lives near Cardiff.

Visit: philrowlandswriter.com

Published in Great Britain in 2021
By Diamond Crime

ISBN 978-1-8384026-3-1

Diamond Crime is an imprint of Diamond Books Ltd.

Thanks to Greg, Jeff, Steve and Jen

Book design: jacksonbone.co.uk
Cover photograph: Deleece Cook
and Nicholas Kwok – Unsplash

Also by Phil Rowlands
Siena

And coming soon to Diamond Crime
Time Slip

For information about Diamond Crime authors
and their books, visit:
www.diamondbooks.co.uk

single cell

A psychological thriller

PHIL ROWLANDS

PROLOGUE

HMP Hill Sutton

Stan Walters, Senior Night Shift Officer on B Wing, opened the slider on the cell door and glanced in. A small light, high above the door, threw a shadow over the large and loudly snoring shape in the small bed. It was one of the only two, fought-over, individual cells on the run. The other fourteen were shared.

Stan closed the slider. It was the same routine every night. He listened outside each one and looked into every other, so, on the four rounds during the shift, each cell was checked twice, not strictly by the book, but good enough for him. He tried to be considerate and make as little noise as possible on the metal walkways. He was glad he'd worn his own boots tonight and not the heavy leather sole-and-steel toe cap standard issue that made soft steps tricky. His feet always ached in those too. Anything that could ease the pain was worth the bollocking if anyone gave a shit what he wore.

Tonight, for some reason, the shift had seemed to go on for ever, even with happy feet. But this was his last round and by four thirty he had reached the sixteenth and final cell on the wing. As he pulled back the slider and glanced in he was thinking about home and snuggling up to his wife's warm and sleepy body, and hoping the kids didn't wake up before they had a chance for a bit of a cuddle.

In the far corner of the cell he could see a pair of feet dangling above the floor.

'Fuck!'

* * *

Frank Clarke, serving a fifteen-year minimum sentence for the murder of a young woman with severe learning difficulties, was found hanged in his cell at Hill Sutton high security prison at four-thirty a.m. on July 24th

He was alone. The man who shared the cell with him, Ralph Bateman, was in the infirmary after a severe asthma attack the night before.

Clarke's death was reported to Assistant Governor Giles Lawson at four-forty a.m.

Lawson informed Prison Governor, Gerald Wright, of the death at four forty-five a.m.

Later, Lawson coordinated the investigation into the death with the Inquiry Chair, Assistant Chief Constable Patrick Duggan of the West Yorkshire Police. On September 15th, the Inquiry into Clarke's death returned a verdict of suicide.

September 16th
Zoom meeting, London
Charles Stanley Moncrieff sat in front of a wall-wide screen in a small private room at the headquarters of CSM, his multi-national corporation, in the City of London. His mobile, lying on the arm of his chair, buzzed quietly. He glanced down at the caller and held up his hand to the person who was speaking. 'I have to take this.'

The five others present in the video conference were Sir Simon Bartenson, a university professor, Lady Anne

Evan-Dyer, a hotelier, Cynthia Orbanon, an MP, Sir David Amebury, the head of a large global consortium, and Sir Roger Alsopp, a high-ranking police officer. They watched and waited as Moncrieff listened. It was a diverse and eclectic gathering, with a unified purpose.

After a couple of minutes Moncrieff smiled, said 'Thank you,' and cut the call. He looked up at the faces on the screen. 'It went as I thought it would. We can now move on.' He paused. 'I think we should finish there for today. Thank you all for your time.'

The goodbyes were said and Moncrieff leaned back in his chair, closed his eyes, and breathed deeply. He had been sure of the outcome but there was a moment of relief that it had progressed as seamlessly as he had expected. It had been trickier than most and had required a little lateral thinking.

CHAPTER ONE

Six months later
HMP Hill Sutton

Giles Lawson watched as a thoroughly pissed-off Bryn Morgan, the officer in charge of E Wing, left the office, shutting the door hard behind him.

Giles had just given Morgan an official warning, following an alleged assault on a prisoner by one of his team. He had some empathy with the man, given the reasons behind the incident, but he had to follow the strict guidelines. The suspension of the junior officer involved was automatic, despite the extenuating circumstances, and culpability also touched whoever had been in charge on that shift. There would have to be an independent inquiry into the assault. In the current climate of responsibility and shifting blame, the prison service was under constant appraisal by a mass of public and private bodies and individuals. That sort of scrutiny might, in time, create a mood for positive change, but Giles knew it would only happen if the right people at the top had realistic solutions and targets and, more importantly, a real sense of the core problems. They had to understand what the underlying causes were and find sustainable ways to deal with them. Rushing through unworkable measures only wasted time and money.

With a little effort Giles managed to push away this depressing reality. He pulled open a drawer in his desk and took a cigarette out of the 'office pack' stuck at the back behind his keys and wallet. He looked at it longingly, then sighed and put it back. He only allowed himself three a day and he'd had two already: one in the car on the way to work and one at lunchtime in the smokers' retreat outside the staff canteen. That left him with one for tonight, if he could sneak it in without being caught by one of the three feisty women in his life who were determined to keep him healthy and behaving responsibly. Then, with a sinking feeling, he remembered that he and Patty were going out to eat with some old friends of hers. The Barratt-Thompsons were non-smoking, organic home-made wine-drinking, and vegetarian bordering on vegan, not to mention lascivious and constantly lusting after each other. As always, it would be an evening of terminal boredom edged with the discomfort of watching the couple touch, tease, tickle, and tell tales about their stinking-with-cash chums. Patty never seemed to mind, but he always came away amazed that he lasted the night without screaming 'Fuck off!' as they prattled away. As a distraction, he would try subtly to take the piss out of Tarquin until, invariably, an icy look from Patty chilled and shut him up.

His objective and generous appraisal of the couple was that Katrina Barratt-Thompson was a snob and Tarquin, a pompous, irritating little shit. But Kat was an old Oxford pal of Patty's and she had introduced her to the woman who owned the design agency where Patty was now a creative director. So, he put up with them.

Giles knew that there would definitely be no chance for a ciggy after the meal, so he decided to have it now. He checked his door was shut, opened the window, took the cigarette out again and, quickly, lit it, drawing the smoke down deeply. The fiercely enforced indoor smoking ban only enhanced the pleasure. It was a wonderful and simple moment of lone protest and pleasure.

The telephone *brrred* gently. The subtle tone was one of the Governor's antidotes to noise stress, but almost impossible to hear if you weren't sitting on top of it.

'Lawson!'

'Giles, are you in the middle of anything?' It was his boss, Gerald Wright.

'No. Just finished.' Giles blew the smoke guiltily away from the phone.

'Good. Five minutes of your time, right away, if you don't mind!'

Yes, I do, so fuck off, Gerald.

'On my way.' Giles put the phone down, took a deep drag on his cigarette, then dropped it into his mug. He rose, opened the window, waved the remnants of smoke away, and went out.

Gerald Wright's office was similar in size to Giles' but had none of its 'patch up and paint' feel. It was newly renovated with a taste and care that was in stark contrast to its bleak and severe surroundings; no danger of the money for that little improvement being redirected. Its wall-length window overlooked the solitary confinement wing where the child murderers, abusers, and rapists were separated from the 'normal cons' for their own safety. Wright's large comfortable chairs, tiled floor, and stylish glass and steel desk were a million miles away from the claustrophobic and sparsely furnished dens of the inmates, where drugs, violence, and sexual coupling relieved the monotony.

He pulled himself back from his musings as Wright, a tall, hairy, thickset man in his late fifties, came into the room and eased his long frame into one of the oversized chairs. Single, but married to his job, his idea of relaxation was football, choral singing, and twitching – birds, not facial tics, although there was an occasional flutter in his right eye when he was on the boil about some perceived slight or threat to his authority.

His voice was deep and edged with the flat tones of his Mancunian roots. 'Sorry about the wait, Giles! Bloody parole boards. Right, first off… anything you want to talk about?'

Where to start, Gerald? I've got piles like bits of broken glass, my family treats me like I'm from a different world, I feel old, a sense of time wasted, and I don't get nearly enough sex and wouldn't have the time or energy for it even if the offer was made.

'Frank Clarke…' began Giles, but Wright quickly stopped him.

'For Christ's sake, Giles, how many more bloody times, there's nothing there, drop it. It's a waste of time and energy. Clarke topped himself, end of story.' Then his face softened into a grimace and he smiled. 'Sorry, didn't mean to be so sharp. It's been a frustrating day. Now, what about the match against Wandsworth? I thought if we put young Stevens from D Wing in the centre…'

That evening, Giles lay in the large Victorian bath, his head just above the water that was almost at the top of the curved enamel sides. It was his favourite room in the house, furnished from months of him and Patty scavenging around second-hand shops and scouring local newspapers to find exactly what they were looking for or, with a bit of creativity, could make work for both of them. The hours of scraping, cleaning, swearing, and fighting had all been forgotten in the hazy shadows of time. This bathroom had become his respite from the insanity of his daily life. He wrapped himself in the wonderful sound of Carmen ringing out from the four ceiling speakers. He had put them in over a weekend of DIY delusion, trying to ignore the crackle they made when he tried them out. Patty, without telling him, had had it all redone when he was at a European Prison Safety conference in Amsterdam. She thought he didn't know but he did and it was fine by him. He knew his limitations and even just a week of patchy sound had begun to irritate him. This way he could enjoy the illusion that the mellifluous perfection was all down to him.

He got out of the bath, dried himself, wrapped the towel around his waist, and necked the warm remains of his beer. Then he flopped onto the old armchair that he had to fight Patty to keep in the bathroom, closed his eyes, and began to doze.

A loud hammering on the door almost gave him heart failure. Through the pounding in his chest he heard his daughter, Sally, telling him that Mum said they had to leave in fifteen minutes.

'She said to get your wrinkled old arse out of the bath and, if you're not down in five minutes, you'd better have died or she'll kill you.'

'That's no way to talk to your father.' She'd gone by then though, and he was talking to himself… again.

He sighed and looked in the steamed-up mirror at his misty reflection, went to wipe it then stopped. Clear reality would only depress him. He pulled the plug out of the bath, rubbed a cloth around the sides, then unlocked the door.

Later a shadowy outline touched the edges of his memory as he helped himself to a second plateful of nut roast. It was obviously the stimulation of Tarquin and the Diva's diet. He thought hard, dug deep and almost found it.

Parole… it was something to do with parole… Christ, what the hell was it? Suddenly it was there, or a fragment was. Bateman. It was about Ralph Bateman's parole. He had…

'Are you all right, Giles? I know it must be a shock to the system, all this healthy tuck, but you seem to have slipped away from us.' Tarquin Barratt hyphen Thompson's languid drawl sounded as though each word just managed to avoid getting tarnished by the one before it.

'Yes, sorry, I'm fine, just remembered something that's been bugging me for weeks.' He tried to edge a hint of sincerity into his voice. 'I'll have another glass of your rhubarb and peach wine, if I may, it's very good.' He felt Patty glaring at him from across the table and smiled weakly at his host, who, after a brief pause, brayed loudly.

'Very good, thought for a moment you might be taking the piss. Not everyone's cup of tea, or rather glass of plonk, hah, what?' Katrina joined in the donkey serenade, draping herself over Tarquin and kissing his neck with absolute joy at his rapier wit. Giles snorted a laugh. Thank God they'd think it was with them. He tried to control himself as he caught Patty's eviscerating look but it just made his giggles unstoppable.

It was nearly eleven when they arrived home. The Barratt-Thompsons, whatever the occasion, retired early and rose early, bright, satiated, and ready for all the fun the new day would bring.

Giles, feeling the large amount of wine he'd drunk to get through the meal and badly needing a pee, started to get out.

'Why are you always so bloody rude?' asked Patty coldly.

Giles held her look for a moment, trying to think of something to say that would get him off the hook, but the wrong words were out before he was able to stop them. 'I don't like them, they're condescending, sickeningly healthy and, worst of all, disgustingly rich, and, even more unforgivable, bollock-squeezingly boring.' He saw anger and hurt in Patty's face and still didn't stop. 'I'm sorry, she's an annoying little rich girl and he's a prize twat.'

'Fuck off!' Patty got out and slammed the door. Giles sat there for a moment. Shit, had he really said all that out loud? It should have been confined to his thoughts. He had been hoping for a bit of passion to brighten the evening, but his little moment of tipsy truth had just blown any chance of that tonight… and probably for the foreseeable future too.

Giles stood in the kitchen, holding a bottle of brandy. It was three-quarters of an hour later and things had calmed down. There'd been loud silence and a few harsh withering looks as he tried to find other ways and words to take away the sting. Patty mostly ignored his attempts, except for the odd snort of derision. Then she had left the room and Giles thought she'd gone to bed. He was waiting for her to throw down the old sleeping bag he was given when banished from the bed for saying the wrong thing at the wrong time or even, when he was trying to be witty and wise, the right thing at the right time in the wrong way. But on this occasion, it didn't happen. She had come back with her hot water bottle, filled the kettle, put away the things their two girls had left out, and then poured milk into a saucepan, taken out a jar of dark chocolate powder, and put a couple of spoonfuls into a mug. She was still strong and scary but now silent too. He wasn't sure which was the most unnerving.

He waved the bottle and tried to put warmth into his voice. 'Brandy, sweetheart?'

'What?'

Obviously, he had spoken in a whisper although it had sounded normal to him.

'Do you want a brandy?'

'No.' She held the mug up then turned towards him. 'Sorry. No… thank you!'

That was a good sign.

'Okay, but I'm going to have one.' He was about to follow that with 'as you obviously weren't making anything for me' but thought better of it and took a deep breath. 'I'm really sorry I said what I did about the Barratt hyphen Thompsons. They're not as bad as I made out and the nut roast was good, even if the wine was shit and I wish I hadn't drunk so much of it… or had a fight with my beautiful wife. The blame is all mine and I deserve whatever punishment you wish to inflict.'

Patty almost smiled. 'Shut up.' She took a saucepan off the stove. Giles moved quickly away in case it was to be used as a weapon but she poured the milk into the mug and stirred it. 'They don't have one.'

'Who doesn't have what?'

Patty hard-eyed him for a moment. 'A bloody hyphen!' She took a deep breath. 'Oh, for Christ's sake, let's give it a rest for tonight. I'm exhausted. If we want to have a good scrap, we'll both be more capable tomorrow.'

Giles smiled. 'Trowels at dawn by the rose border. Kate can be my second, you can have Sally.'

'That's not fair. Sally won't wake up until twelve and she has no idea what a trowel looks like.'

They looked at each other for a moment then laughed.

The good thing about Patty was that although she was terrifyingly direct with her considered and immediate responses, in the right situation, she was just as quick to move on. She would revisit the past, but only if it was pertinent to the present.

Giles went over and kissed her head. 'I'm really sorry, sweetheart. I've had a shit day. I know that's no excuse, but I do love you to bits and I promise I shall try very hard next time we meet the B hyphen-less T's. I didn't really mean what I said about them. Well, perhaps just a bit of it. But it was wrong of me and they are your friends, so I should just grow up and behave, whatever I think.'

Patty gave him a shut up now look. 'Sorry.' He moved closer to her. 'I know I don't deserve it and it's not a special day and I was a dick tonight, but is there any chance of a cuddle while you're still awake?'

Patty softened, touched his cheek, and he realised she'd probably had more to drink than she should've had to drive home. 'You'll have to wait until my lenses are out and my vision blurred enough to pretend that you're someone younger and more attractive.'

Giles curled his top lip. 'Of all the eyes in all the world, I have to end up with yours.'

Patty smiled and winked. 'Here's looking at you, kid!'

CHAPTER TWO

Giles went to the open door of his office. 'Jill, if anyone wants me, I'm not here.'

'Right, Mr Lawson!'

Her default response, no matter how difficult or facile the task! She was a fantastic PA: she covered his back and made sure his life ran smoothly. He did sometimes wish though that she'd turn on him and they could have a good old shout at each other, but it would be more about getting rid of his frustrations than anything else. However, it wasn't going to happen, and, on balance, that was probably for the best.

He shut the door and started going through the statement taken from Bateman.

Bateman had been 'involved' with Clarke since he moved into the cell several months before his death. After it, he was inconsolable and deeply disturbed. It brought on another, almost fatal, asthma attack.

Giles brought Bateman's case history onto the screen and read through it. There was something he had seen in the file that was scrabbling at the edge of his mind. Something that didn't feel right! He knew it was here somewhere. Then, suddenly, he found it. He was looking at the parole dates when it jumped out at him. Shit, that was it. Why hadn't he clocked it before? It was the timing.

Bateman had been paroled two months after Clarke was found hanged in his cell. But it was too early a timeframe for any parole consideration. He had been serving an eight-year sentence for sexual assault and wasn't eligible for a Board interview until the following June, at the earliest. It had been brought forward by nine months! That wasn't unheard of, but was unusual enough to warrant another look at the reason behind the decision. He pressed the button on his phone. 'Jill, can you find out who chaired the September parole board?'

'Right, Mr Lawson.'

'Thank you!' He leaned back in his chair and tried to put some perspective into his thoughts. Why was it important? If it had been then surely someone else would have brought it up. It wasn't his first suicide! There must have been five or six in his time in the prison service. But was he being obsessive about Clarke's death? It was possible that there really was nothing suspicious in Bateman's case, that it was just what it said it was: an early release on medical grounds. Was Gerald right? Giles was always willing to listen to the views and instincts of others and act on them if they were a better option. The last feedback from the yearly assessment by the officers and management was that he was fair and easy-going, but hard on discipline and in making sure that all rights, including those of the inmates, were not abused.

But something about this had been niggling at him for months, although the heavy pressure of work had forced it to the back of his mind. However, it kept floating around the edges of his thoughts and occasionally slipped out in actual words, like it had with Wright yesterday. But then when he tried to really focus on what was bugging him about it, the more distant it became; until last night, when a light had flickered briefly.

It was one small positive thing to warrant the existence of Tarquin and the Diva.

His phone buzzed.

'Mr Lawson?'

'Yes, Jill?'

'Sir Leighton James chaired all of September's Boards.'

'Thank you.'

'Right, Mr Lawson.'

Leighton James QC was a brilliant barrister, but particular and prickly on form and protocol. Giles had come up against him on several occasions and they had a grudging respect for each other.

He brought up the Board applications for September. As usual, the system was incredibly slow. No matter how much was spent on updates and faster up and download speeds, it never seemed to change. At last the file appeared and he scanned through it to find the reasons for bringing forward Bateman's appeal, There were only two; (a) he had been a model prisoner and (b) the Board felt that the general state of his mental health as well as the frequent asthma attacks, particularly the severity of the last one, could only be worsened by further incarceration.

Pompous farts, why couldn't they use simple language?

The Board had recommended a release on licence and Bateman had left the prison on the first of November.

Giles then read through the prison doctor's and psychiatrist's reports. They both supported the Board's decision. It made sense as a whole but Giles' gut was playing up again. It just didn't feel right; he knew that he was going to have to mess around with it until he either found something he could hang his doubts on or was satisfied that there really wasn't anything there to find.

He opened the file on Clarke and, for a moment, studied the strong face and hard eyes, then looked out of the window at the darkening sky and clouds.

The loud buzz of his mobile had woken him from a dreamless sleep. He fumbled for it, trying not to disturb Patty as he got out of bed. 'Lawson!'

'It's Walters, sir, sorry to wake you but I'm afraid there's a bit of bother down here. Frank Clarke's topped himself.'

'Oh, shit. I'll be right down. Have you told anyone else?'

'Only Dr Stevenson, she was here on a call-out.

'Good, ask her to meet me in my office and get the body to the Fridge as quickly and as quietly as you can.' He checked the time on his phone. 'I'll be there before six.'

'Right, sir.'

His thoughts were interrupted by Jill's voice. 'Mr Lawson, Father Satorri is here.'

He had forgotten Peter was coming over this morning. 'Send him in.'

'Right, Mr Lawson.'

* * *

Sidney Pargeter sat in the corner of the library repairing books. Over the last two years of his three-year sentence for burglary, from eight-thirty to five-thirty each day, he passed his time in the same way and, more or less, he enjoyed it. He was forty-eight, a small-time thief who had been in and out of prison for most of his adult life. He was short and fat, with greasy hair, a gammy leg, and foul body odour. Not the most popular guest at Her Majesty's Hotel. He was, not surprisingly, a loner, and being practically invisible to the other inmates overheard a lot of their prison chatter. Anything he thought important he passed on to the librarian or Mr Carter, one of the friendlier screws, and some of it had proved useful so he had received a few subtle privileges. The one that meant the most to him was keeping his job in the library even though it was a coveted position and was usually passed around.

For the last six months, though, ever since he'd overheard two of the cons talking about the way Frank Clarke had died, he had kept things to himself and was in a continuous state of panic. From what he'd heard, Frank hadn't topped himself, it was done for him. The thought that he knew what had happened terrified him! As always when he was like this, he sweated profusely, smelt worse than ever, couldn't sleep, and experienced anxiety attacks. It was too big, this, not just a bit of nicking or dope dealing. If they only suspected he'd heard something then they'd bloody make sure he didn't talk… ever. He had to try to get away from here to another prison before it was too late.

* * *

'Giles, my boy, how are you on this dark and dangerous morning?' Peter Satorri had been born in Neath in South Wales, the son of an Italian father and Welsh mother. He was fifty-one, stocky and fit, with dark good looks and deep brown eyes that seemed to search into your soul. He loved good food, wine, and single malt whisky, and was probably the only truly selfless man that Giles had ever met. He was popular with the prisoners. He understood and cared for their particular problems and, although Catholic, was available to anyone who had need of him. Over the five years they had known each other the two men had become good friends and shared the same sense of the ridiculous, and a love of opera.

'Good, and you?'

Peter smiled 'Terrific, just spent half an hour with Billy Thomas and his guilt over not being there to provide for his just-born seventh child, and the other six, for another eighteen months. He wondered if the Church had any emergency funds that might be able to help out until he can start earning again. It's the same conversation we've had for the last two births and when he was out briefly, between numbers six and seven, his way of providing was to break into a care home and manage to lock himself in the wheelchair room!'. Peter laughed. 'Not his wife's fault, so I said I'd go and visit her. The poor woman is thirty-two, looks fifty, and deserves a bit of pastoral care and attention.'

Giles smiled, opened his desk drawer, and took out a bottle and two glasses. 'Can you spare half an hour? I'd like to talk something over with you.'

'Only if it's juicy, I haven't had a good confession for weeks. Pour away, Giles, I am all yours.

CHAPTER THREE

Professor Sir Simon Bartenson was looking out of the window of his study on to the campus of the University of Hull. He was sure there were many worse places to live and work. It was a pleasant site with lots of green areas, bushes, trees, and a mix of neo-Georgian, Edwardian, and contemporary buildings. He had enough freedom and space outside his academic brief for all the innovative and exciting research he could wish to explore. He had little interest in anything like that, though. He hadn't published a paper, either jointly or singly, for two years, and had given up the lucrative international lecture rounds that he had done since his first Chair at Cardiff when he was in his thirties: he also kept refusing the sort of academic opportunities that had once energised and driven him.

It meant nothing now.

He was only fifty-three but had aged considerably over the last few years. What was left of his hair was grey, his face was worn with deep lines, he had lost weight, and looked fragile and drawn. Since his divorce from Tilda, he had become more reclusive, spending his spare time either in his rooms at the university or his small apartment in a new city centre block. He also had a small boat moored at Whitby that he would live on during the long summer break, moving around the coast in short hops, hoping to find the solitude and peace he craved.

Tragedy sometimes drew people together but with him and Tilda it had had the opposite effect. So, when out of the blue, he had been offered the Chair at Hull he had accepted. It would give them the physical distance they needed. He thought they would keep in touch but they hadn't. It was as though they could retain some sort of life in their own small worlds but to share the torment would be too much. They had been married for twenty-five years and it had been a good and loving partnership. They'd always allowed each other space for their different interests and friends. They had empathy, honesty, and closeness between them, discussing and deciding together everything that impacted on them and their daughter, Jessica.

Then came the worst thing that could ever happen. Jess was murdered and their safe, comfortable, middle-class world shattered. They had been so torn apart with grief and guilt that their relationship fractured beyond repair.

He turned back into the room and looked at the picture of Jess on his desk. Strikingly pretty, she had a mass of ginger curls and her green eyes sparkled with fun. The photo had been taken the day she started at the Royal Academy of Dramatic Art. It was a dream come true that was to lead to an unimaginable nightmare. He missed her desperately and, in the deepest shadows of his darkness, raged at God and the humanity he had once believed in and trusted. Jess and he had been as close as a father and daughter could be and whenever they found time in their busy lives they'd met. She had fallen in love a year before her death. Although nobody would have been good enough for his little girl, he had loved her happiness in the relationship and was there to comfort and support her when it ended because of her intense focus on acting. Her man was a medical student and their lives and needs untangled.

Simon knew the hurt would go. There was time for love when she had established herself, and she had such talent, personality, and passion that he was in no doubt she would succeed. Would have succeeded…

The ring of his mobile broke his train of thought. He took it out of his old leather briefcase. 'Simon Bartenson.'

'Simon, it's Charles Stanley. Thursday evening. I'll let you know the time on Wednesday.'

'Fine.'

'Are you all right?'

'Yes, sorry, just a little tired.'

'Good!'

The phone went dead. Simon put it on his desk and picked up the photograph. 'Is it right, sweetheart? I'm not sure anymore that it is.'

In his office on the twenty-fifth floor of the CSM building in the financial heart of the City, Charles Stanley Moncrieff placed his mobile on his desk too. There was something in Simon's voice that troubled him. He had a growing feeling that the man's strength and commitment were being worn away by his grief. He understood totally, they all did, but it couldn't get in the way of what they had to do. Of all of them, the brilliant and precise academic was the most vulnerable and seemed disturbed by the ongoing work of the group. That was not good. He had to keep it all balanced, with everyone focused and committed to the same path. He would talk to the others individually about Simon and then have a quiet word with him before they all met on Thursday. Moncrieff was a persuasive, tenacious, and determined man. He knew he would find a way to resolve it. It was unusual for him not to get what he wanted.

A small, subtle light flashed on the panel built into his desk. He looked at his watch and touched the light.

'Yes, Penny?'

'The Foundation trustees are here.'

'Give me five minutes then send them in.'

He picked up his mobile and pressed a number. It was answered almost immediately. 'David, it's Charles Stanley.'

* * *

At Hill Sutton, Giles sat on the edge of his desk. 'So, what do you think?'

Peter Satorri looked at him for a moment 'Look, I don't want to knock your powers of intuition but it all sounds a bit of a stretch to me. Have you talked it over with anyone else?'

'Well...' Giles smiled. 'I did mention it again to Gerald but he wasn't too impressed.' He spoke with Wright's flat Mancunian tone: 'For Christ's sake, Clarke topped himself, end of story.'

Peter smiled. 'Not bad, but Eddy, the nonce, does a better one. What about running it past Patty?'

Giles went to the window and looked out. 'Haven't had the chance yet. Our talk times seem to work different shifts. We hardly get time for the practicalities, let alone anything like meals together, family chats, or just being cosy in front of the telly.' He turned back to Peter. 'Will you help? With Clarke and Bateman?'

'Let me think about it.' He drank the last of the whisky. 'What I will do for now, though, is listen out for any talk about Clarke's demise. My priestly presence doesn't seem to stop them, even if it's about stuff I shouldn't or wouldn't want to hear. Mostly I ignore it, but now I'll see what I can pick up.'

Giles smiled. 'I couldn't ask for more.' He lifted the bottle. 'One for the celestial road?'

'No thanks, I'd better be off.' He stood up. 'I'm giving a talk on "faith in yourself" to the AA. Wouldn't do to arrive pissed. Thursday still on for Carmen?'

'Yes.'

'Good, I'll pick you up about six.'

'Perfect.'

Giles walked him to the door. Peter touched his arm.

'Try and make time for each other so it doesn't get to be a problem. It might just creep up on you.' He stopped by Jill's desk. 'Jill, my sweetheart, if only I were a little younger and more ungodly, who knows what stories we could share.'

Jill smiled. 'Right, Father!'

Giles shut the door and sat at his desk. Peter always surprised him. He had a way of inching into deep areas where you'd tried to fold things away, things you didn't want to admit or were trying to avoid facing. Perhaps telepathy was a priestly perk. Worth a fortune if you could run courses. But he was right about him and Patty. So why not start now?

He unplugged the charger from his mobile and pressed a number. It rang twice and was answered.

'Hello, gorgeous.'

'Giles, anything wrong?'

'No!'

He felt a moment of irritation. Why the hell should there be something wrong for him to want to talk to her?

'Giles?'

'Sorry, Pats, Jill's just going off early.' She wasn't. Why did he say that? He started to follow that thought through but pulled himself up. Just get to the point. 'Are you free for dinner this evening? I know a little place that is very discreet, good food, good music, and quiet corners. How about seven thirty for eight at Gino's?'

She laughed 'Sounds good to me. Hope you're paying, and not out of the joint account. Will you have time to sort the girls out first? I won't be able to get away until seven.'

'Yes, I'll see you at Gino's then. Love you.' He ended the call and went to the door. Jill was frowning at something on the screen of her old desktop.

'What's up?'

She glanced up at Giles. 'This is getting worse. It takes for ever to do anything and now text is disappearing too. Do you think the new one will be here soon?'

'I'll chase them tomorrow if you remind me.' He headed for the door. 'I'm going over to the library and then home about six. If there's anything that can't wait before then, give me a call.'

'Right, Mr Lawson.'

Giles went into the library and looked around. He saw Sidney Pargeter concentrating hard on a large book, caught the eye of the duty guard, and pointed towards Pargeter. The guard walked across to him.

'Pargeter!'

Pargeter twitched wildly as though an electric shock had coursed through him.

'What's the matter with you, man? Mr Lawson wants a word.'

Pargeter stood up and closed the book, a large graffiti-covered Atlas of the World that he was trying to patch up.

'Jesus, you stink. Go on, move.' The guard pointed towards Giles.

'Right you are, sir… and I can't help it.'

'What?'

'The way I smell, it's...'

'I don't want to know.' The guard walked off and Pargeter hobbled across the room and stood in front of Lawson.

'Yes, sir?'

Giles turned his head but the smell followed and curled round with it. 'Isn't there anything you can do about that?'

'No, sir, it's a medical problem, I wash and use deodorant but it don't seem to make any difference.'

'Oh.' Giles eased further away from him. He held up a book with the pages written over in large black letters. 'Do you have any idea who's scribbling on these books?' Over the past few months, graffiti, words and pictures, had started appearing in several of the larger books. 'The Governor sucks pigs' and ''Lawson's old lady is a Coprophiliac'' were two of the more literary examples.

They must really have scoured the internet for that last one. Where had it come from? Maybe it wasn't one of the prisoners. Perhaps he should use it in a question at the monthly staff versus the inmates' quiz night and see who answered first. Those nights were another of the Governor's relationship-building projects that, despite the perks of tea and cakes, had the opposite effect.

Pargeter looked puzzled. It didn't improve his looks greatly.

'I don't know nothing about that, honest I don't.'

Giles couldn't bear it much longer. The smell was slowly wrapping itself around and choking him. 'Well, keep your eyes open. All right, you can go.'

Pargeter looked uncomfortable. 'Mr Lawson… I, ah…' He trailed off.

'Yes?'

Pargeter looked at the floor. 'I… ah…' He started to shuffle backwards. 'Ah… it's nothing, Mr Lawson. Sorry.'

He scurried back across the room to the safety of his table.

Giles turned to the guard. 'I've got to get some air!' He went out of the library and made his way outside for his daily check on the prison gardens. There were some beautiful old roses being nurtured by a green-fingered serial killer who had promised him some cuttings.

* * *

Sir Roger Alsopp, Chief Constable of West Yorkshire Police, had called the meeting for five-thirty p.m.

There had been a number of abductions and violent rapes of teenage girls over the last year. All had the same MO and were thought to be the work of the same sick bastard. A week ago, he had struck again, but this time had gone much further and a fourteen-year-old Muslim girl was dead. She had been beaten, raped, and her breasts hacked off. She had bled to death. Her body had been found in a small park by two eight-year-olds who would never be the same again. Alsopp wanted the killer caught before he found his next victim.

'Bob, what are your lads doing? There must be someone out there who knows something; he'd have looked like he worked in a fucking abattoir. If we don't wrap this up soon, we're going to have a lot more grief from the media and the public. People are scared shitless. If we're not careful, we'll get amateur vigilantes cutting the balls off every sex offender they can find. And some of the agitators in the Muslim community are winding up bad racial feeling and trying to get people out on the streets. We need to stop that before the far-right mobs get involved and it explodes into full-scale riots. We should have had the bastard by now.'

Chief Superintendent Robert Davies held Alsopp's accusing glare calmly. 'We're checking out a report of an attempted rape in Bingley. A social worker was calling at a block of flats when she saw a man trying to drag a young girl under a stairwell. She pulled him off her and the girl got away, but he then attacked this woman. However, she's ex-military and more than he could handle, so he ran off, but she thought she'd cut his face badly by hitting him with a half-full five-litre paint pot. She was very together, didn't give chase, and reported it as soon as he'd gone. The team should have covered the area by now.'

The phone rang.

'Alsopp.'

'Sir David Amebury for you, sir, he couldn't get through on your mobile. I told him you were in a meeting, but he said it's important.'

Alsopp hesitated for a moment 'Put him through, Laura. Bob, would you mind? Let me know as soon as you hear anything.'

'Right, sir!' Davies got up and went out.

'Yes, David, what can I do for you?'

'We need to get together. Is Thursday alright for you?'

The door opened and Davies stuck his head round.

'Just a minute, David. What is it, Bob?'

'They've got him, sir! And on their way in. I've got a medic coming. She broke his nose and cracked his cheekbone but he'll be okay to interview after he's patched up. More than the shit deserves.'

'Is the woman all right?'

'More angry than anything else! She helped find the girl he'd attacked and was able to calm her down.'

'Who's the duty doc?'

'Jeff Calderbank.'

'Good. Ask him if I can have a word before he goes and let me know as soon as they arrive.'

'Right.' Davies went out.

'David, can I call you back, something's come up?'

'Of course. Make sure you keep Thursday free!'

Alsopp put down the phone. He picked up the framed photograph on his desk. It was of a young woman at a university graduation, smiling, proud and happy. He looked at it for a long moment then put it back, got up, and went to the door.

CHAPTER FOUR

'Would you like a drink, Daddy?' Sally was there as Giles opened the front door.

Kate came around her, kissed him, and took his arm. 'You look tired.'

It was the first time they had said more than a few words to him for days. He could hear 'Nessun Dorma' ringing through the house. The two girls were looking adoringly at him. It was unnerving.

An image flashed into his mind of the two of them running to meet him. It must have been their third or fourth birthday. They had been born an hour or so apart, Kate the elder. Their faces were full of excitement and joy at seeing him. He had run towards them, tripped over the dog and hit the ground hard with his nose. It wasn't broken but had bled profusely and they had been helpless with laughter.

He wondered what his fate was to be this time. They were seventeen and pretty. Kate had her mother's nature: a selective memory, saying what she meant, hard on stupidity, but with a big heart. Sally followed him: untrusting, grumpy when tired, but with a forgiving nature and an infectious laugh.

He let them lead him into the kitchen, which was a warm, safe space used both for meals and serious family chats when they all had time. Over the last few months they very rarely did, and it wasn't much more than a crossing point as each ran to whatever was taking up their lives.

Kate eased him into a chair. 'Can I get you a sandwich?' She smiled sweetly.

'What do you want?'

Sally smiled at Kate. 'Don't be so suspicious, Daddy! It must be working with all those poor misguided souls. It's a wonder we haven't been scarred.' She handed him a drink.

Shit, two 'Daddies' on the trot. It was going to be a big ask! He had to go in hard first. 'You've got one minute to tell me what you want or your allowance stops for the next month.'

The girls glanced at each other and Kate sat down opposite him. 'Well, if you put it like that, there is one little thing…'

Sally took over. 'Next Saturday, there's a weekend boat trip, before the hard work on A levels starts. It leaves on Friday and is back Sunday morning. Mr Clare and Mme Sevrin are coming to make sure there's no depravity.' She took a deep breath. 'It's eighty-five pounds each.' She and Kate waited, poised, expecting a negative response and prepared to launch a second attack.

'All right.' He smiled.

'What?' Surprise filled his daughters' faces. Giles tried not to look smug. He and Patty had already talked about it and agreed that they should go. He loved their reaction, though. It was worth the money just for the rare moments like this when he threw them off balance and came out on top.

'But Mum said...' Kate started.

Giles interrupted her. 'Just goes to show how strong and persuasive your dad can be. Now, my darling daughters, I am going to have a bath and then meet your mother for a romantic dinner for two at Gino's. So, you can cut the bovine excrement and become your sweet selves again.' Giles got up and went out.

Sally looked at her sister. 'Bovine excrement?'

'Bullshit!' said Kate.

'That's my girl.' Giles smiled to himself and went up the stairs.

He arrived at Gino's at seven fifteen and sat in the small bar. It was a café-type Italian restaurant that was popular, as much for its atmosphere as its food. They had found it a couple of years ago and now tried to eat there at least once a month. It was owned by Marco Gioscelli, and he had become their best friend since they had brought Peter there for a birthday meal. He now always insisted they have a complimentary bottle of wine, personally selected by him. Giles was convinced that Marco hoped their friendship with the priest would buy him a little celestial clout when the time came.

He started thinking about Frank Clarke again and poured himself some wine from the small carafe he had ordered to keep them going until Marco's bottle arrived. He was sure Bateman was the link. Clarke, although he had known him for only a few months, didn't seem the type to take his own life. He was a hard man who mixed little and it was odd he and Bateman had become close. Still, prison sometimes forged bizarre relationships. Clarke didn't try to mix with anyone but Bateman and there must have been speculation and gossip amongst the prisoners when he died. He knew that if there were anything to find out, it would be from them. Not that they would tell him, but perhaps Peter could get something out of them. If Clarke had been killed: who had done it and why? There were no signs of a struggle.

'Have you been here long?'

He realised that Patty was standing in front of him.

'No.' He stood up, kissed her, and gave her a hug.

Patty smiled, pulled away and sat down. 'Girls all right?'

'Yes, they're fine, a little off-balance after their easy victory but I loved it.' He looked away from Patty as Marco arrived, He was a contented and charismatic man with a rich baritone voice and a soft and sensual accent that Patty loved.

'Patricia, you look beautiful.' He kissed her on both cheeks and embraced Giles. 'Good to see you, Giles, the table is ready, I have a wonderful wine for you tonight, an exquisite Turandot, and a quiet corner for romance.'

'If only the food were as good,' said Giles.

'Ha!' Marco walked ahead of them into the restaurant. Giles let Patty go first.

* * *

Sir David Amebury's portfolio of companies included residential property, restaurants, high-level security, and a chain of exclusive luxury car outlets across Europe and Asia. He had made his money in 'arms and men' contracts in a variety of countries and regimes, mostly officially, but some, particularly in the early days, sat on the very edges of legality. He had been lucky to get away with it and got out at the right time, using the huge wealth he had accrued to diversify. He was now, outside of his corporate entity, a highly respected and much-lauded security consultant for corporations and governments around the world.

Tonight, he and his wife Julia were getting ready to attend a charity dinner at the Mansion House. They were patrons of the 'Find a Family Foundation', a charity that placed orphaned children from around the world with families where they would be safe and cared for. They had been married for thirty-two years and were still as much in love as they had ever been. The murder of their son Charles had bound them even more tightly together. They had shared the agony and recovery and their understanding, insight, and support for each other was what had carried them through their darkest times. After that terrible tragedy there was nothing that could ever test their relationship as fiercely again.

David couldn't envisage life without her. He watched as she put on the gold lion earrings he had given her on a visit to Africa twenty years ago. Feeling his eyes on her she turned and smiled at him.

'What is it?'

He went over and kissed her.

'Nothing, just thinking how beautiful you are and how much I love you.'

'Sounds like senility setting in!' She smiled gently at him and touched his cheek. 'Now let me finish or we're going to be late.'

* * *

Two hours later, Giles tilted the bottle towards Patty's glass and said, '"Did you know I'm utterly insane?"' It was a 'who said what in which film?' game which he sometimes dropped in suddenly and unexpectedly. It could be irritating but Patty and the girls usually just responded and then carried on with whatever they were doing or saying.

'You tried that one last week, Christian Bale in American Psycho, and no thank you, I'll be asleep if I have any more. You'd better go easy too. I might have plans for you later, if you're very good.'

'It can't be December already!' When they were together on their own like this it was warm and easy. He leaned over the table and kissed her.

'What was that for?'

Giles sat back in his seat. 'I don't always appreciate you.'

'No, you don't.' She kissed his cheek. 'I'll go to the loo and send Marco over with the bill.' She moved out of the alcove and crossed the room, stopping briefly to speak to Marco as he served at a table. Giles watched her. She looked gorgeous, classy and calm, and he felt a surge of love that surprised him. He emptied the bottle into his glass, feeling that some of the stress of the past days had eased just by being here with her. It had been a wonderful meal and the wine was everything Marco had promised. Patty was always fun to be with when she was relaxed, as she was tonight. They both were. It was a long time since that had happened. She made him laugh, and they talked easily about their workdays, a film that they wanted to see, and an art show Patty had been to with a girlfriend. She also told him a story about Katrina Barratt Thompson at Oxford that made him think he should look a bit deeper and not just see what was fluttering loosely on the surface.

It would be great if it could always be like this. And, if he was honest, he was probably more to blame for why it wasn't and for the way it was at home. Certainly, over the last couple of months he had been more tense, had a shorter fuse and got annoyed over the smallest things the girls did wrong. Sometimes they couldn't do anything right. Patty was more balanced with them. They knew where they stood with her, but he was either silly or cross and seemed, recently, to have lost the ability to find the right level of love and discipline. Probably it was just work stress. If it was, he should leave it there, be more the dad the girls needed and find space for more quality time with Patty. It would be good for all of them.

He saw her heading back to their table as Marco arrived with the bill.

* * *

'Dad,' Sally shouted as Giles opened the front door, 'Uncle Peter phoned and asked you to ring him if you got home before eleven. He said it was important.' Giles looked at his watch. It was five to eleven. He searched his jacket for his mobile and after a moment of thinking he'd left it in Marco's, found it on the shelf by the door.

He scrolled through to Peter's number and tapped it.

'Where's Mum?' Kate appeared alongside her sister.

'Putting the car away.'

'No she's not!' Patty shut and bolted the front door. 'Peter, it's Giles.'

'Did you have a nice time with the man from the prison?' Kate asked Patty.

'Can you shut up for a minute?' Giles shouted.

'Oh, I like a strong man.' Sally giggled.

'So do I,' said Patty 'but for now I have to make do with your father.' The two girls laughed.

'Oh, very funny! Sorry, Peter, my family are being witty again'.

Peter laughed. 'How was the meal?'

'Lovely. Marco sent his warmest to you.'

'A gentle hint, it's been months since I was there. Anyway, think I might have something…'

Patty went to the bottom of the stairs. 'I want to talk to you two before Dad finishes his call.' She went into the kitchen. The girls exchanged glances, smiled at Giles, then followed.

Giles focused on what Peter was saying '… I tried to get hold of you, but you were in a meeting. It might be nothing but I thought I'd mention it. I talked to Sidney Pargeter.'

'The body that launched a thousand smells.'

'Yes, poor bugger. Well, he's not one of my usual supporters and I've hardly said two words to him, but he cornered me in the library and asked about confession, whether it was just between him and the priest? I told him it was. He said that something had happened that was very bad and he needed to tell someone but he couldn't trust anyone else. He seemed to be terrified. Mind, with his particular problem, I would think he'd be eternally safe from any sort of physical attack. I said I'd take confession from him.'

'When?'

'Tomorrow morning at ten-thirty.'

'Look, I know this is tricky for you, but if it is Clarke he's on about, will you try and persuade him to talk to me?'

'I wouldn't have rung if I hadn't already decided to do that. Now, I'm sorry but I have a tired body that needs to be put in a warm bed.'

'And you a man of celibacy!'

'Get off the phone, Lawson. We'll speak tomorrow.'

'The Lawson coven well met at nearly midnight.' Giles poured himself a brandy and sat at the opposite end of the table to the three of them. 'Is the defence allowed to make a statement before sentence is passed? Or are you open to bribes?'

'Shut up, Giles!' said Patty, 'the girls and I have something to say.'

Giles curled his lip. 'I don't like dames with big mouths.'

'It was James Cagney in the film where he threw his breakfast over his wife. Now just listen, please, Daddy,' said Sally.

'Daddy' again, must be important! 'Sorry. Go on.'

Patty took over. 'This is the way it's going to be. We've all been a pain in the arse over the last few months and it stops now.' Straight to the heart of it without waffle: one of Patty's skills that Giles envied. 'We all grow up and behave like adults. No more stupid arguments or point-scoring. Agreed? Kate? Sally?' The girls agreed in unison. 'Giles?'

He was about to say something that he thought was witty but sharp looks from the three of them changed his mind. He smiled, sincerely, he hoped. 'Agreed.'

'Good. Now go to bed, you two.' Kate and Sally kissed them both and went out. Patty got up and walked slowly over to him. 'Right, Lawson, get upstairs and get your clothes off.

Giles lay curled tightly into Patty's back, his left arm around her, his hand cupping her breast. He was warm and safe, sleep hanging around the edges of his consciousness. His thoughts jumbled in and out of focus and finally landed on Peter's call about Frank Clarke and Pargeter.

'Leave it 'til tomorrow, Lawson,' Patty said sleepily.

'What?' Giles mumbled.

'You just went away. Now either go to sleep or...' She reached back and felt for him. 'Well, that didn't take long!'

'Surprised me too. What do you suggest we do with it?'

Patty turned and rolled on top of him.

CHAPTER FIVE

Giles arrived at work early. He had a pile of stuff to do and needed to catch up on some of the constant updates to the guidelines on the treatment of prisoners by management staff as well as the officers on the wing floor. It was one of his less than welcome duties as DG to analyse, report, and act upon what academics and politicians theorised about without any useful experience. He was convinced that most of them learned all they knew from liberal documentaries or left-biased newspaper articles on abuse of prisoners. Although most of the guidelines were impossible to put into practice as they were, he usually managed to find a way to manipulate them into a middle ground that would be at least workable and get Wright off his back. He was on his second batch of the day when his mobile rang.

'Lawson.'

'It's Bates, sir, there's a bit of a crisis down here. Reg Bird has tried to top himself by stuffing something down his throat and we can't get hold of a medic.'

Oh, for fuck's sake, just what he needed.

Giles rushed out. 'On my way.'

There were three of them in Bird's cell: Giles, Bates, and a young trainee, Rees, an almost unintelligible North Walian, who had just come into the Service. He was in a panic and useless.

'See if you can see where the doc is, Rees,' Bates said as he pushed him out of the cell. Bird was having difficulty breathing, trying to pull air in through his nose. He was on his knees and slowly changing colour. 'Looks like he's got something big lodged.' Brilliant piece of deduction from Bates.

Giles grabbed Bird, pulled him to his feet, stood behind him. 'I'm going to try and get whatever it is out of you, so try and relax, Bird.' Stupid thing to say to a choking man but he didn't want him struggling more than he was already.

He put his right hand, thumb in, under Bird's breastbone, just up from the belly button, joined it with his other hand, and pulled hard in, repeating the movement in short bursts. It seemed to go on for ever but suddenly Bird coughed and opened his mouth, and Bates could see something blue coming out of his throat. One more thrust and cough and there was more of it. Bates reached out, held Bird's chin, kept his mouth open and managed to grab it. As Giles gave one more thrust, he pulled hard and suddenly it came out and it was clear. It was a J-Cloth.

'Jesus Christ!' Bates laughed. 'Must be easier ways to do it!'

Giles helped Bird back onto his bed and he lay there, gasping for breath.

'Probably needed a deep clean after what he's had in his mouth, bit excessive though, gargle with a mug of canteen tea would have done the trick!' said Bates. Giles tried not to laugh but failed.

Rees stuck his head back in. 'Orderlies are on their way, sir.'

'What?' Giles didn't have a clue what he'd said.

Bates translated. 'Beginning to get the hang of his accent now, think he said the orderlies are on the way.' Rees nodded. 'Brilliant bit of business that, Mr Lawson, saved his life.'

Giles smiled, brownie points were always welcome, particularly from senior men like Bates. He leaned down to Bird. 'You should be fine now. Dr Stevenson's in today and she'll check you over and arrange for you to see someone to talk over what put this into your head. I'll have to have a word too when you're up to it.' He stood up. 'Make sure the doc knows he's in the Infirmary, Mr Bates.'

As he went on to the walkway, one of the cons shouted from his cell door. 'Swallow all right, is he, Mr Lawson? Only we got a date later and I wondered whether I'd have to make other plans?'

Giles was confused for a minute then realised what he meant. 'Shut up, Bryce, or you'll be in solitary for the next week!'

Walking back to his office Giles met Gerald Wright on one of his 'catch and reveal' trips into the dark end of the prison, to check on treatment and welfare. It was a regular and pointless exercise. As soon as he left his office, the grapevine would pass the word, so nothing was ever found wanting.

'Glad I caught you, managed to arrange a match with Bronzefield in late May. Thought you could OIC and referee it. You know Daisy Spring, the DG there, don't you?'

Giles did. He got on well with her but when pushed she was tough and, after spending three months working on an Equalities in Prison Board with Wright, not particularly fond of him or his methods of steamrolling his initiatives through by bending policy and getting high-level support. She wouldn't be happy about this at all. 'You sure that's a good idea, Gerald?'

'Why?'

'Apart from it being a women's prison?'

Wright glared at him. 'So? Bit of gender integration is good for the morale.' He tapped Giles on the arm. 'Give you something other than Clarke to think about. Inter-prison football was your idea, wasn't it?'

Yes, but only between male prisons. And even that was something he always regretted, particularly as he wasn't really interested in ball games of any kind and he had to cope with the violent reaction by some of the more deranged players when fouled or in disagreement with a referee decision.

'It was.' Giles watched Wright walk off. He'd find a way to derail it. Was sure that Daisy hadn't agreed willingly and would be happy to stitch up something with him. Then he remembered that he'd promised to talk to the kitchen about putting on a greater choice of vegetarian meals and snacks and hurried off. He'd just have time to get that over with before they started the food scrabble and he had his meeting with an artist who was creating a mural with the art group and having a tricky time enthusing his helpers. Then there was the lunch meeting with Ruby Stevenson, but that wasn't until one thirty, so, with a bit of luck, he'd have time to prepare for that too.

Sidney Pargeter sat apart from the twenty or so other men waiting outside the 'priest's hole', the wing name for the room Peter used to take confession. The door opened and a large man with a tattoo of a jellyfish covering his face came out. He was holding a Bible and there were tears in his eyes. 'Next.' he said. There was a communal sigh of relief as Pargeter got up and made for the door.

Inside the small room, Peter Satorri pondered, as he always did, on why it was only when all else failed that God was given a chance and expected to come up with the goods. He opened the drawer and was just taking out a bottle of single malt when there was a knock. 'Damn!' He put it back and closed the drawer. 'Come in.'

Pargeter limped in, closing the door behind him. Peter indicated a chair near the slightly open window. 'Sit over there if you don't mind and push the window open a bit more.' Pargeter did and glanced at the window. 'What can I do for you?'

Pargeter slumped in the chair and looked at the floor. 'You said that anything I told you was just between you and me?'

Peter crossed his fingers. 'Of course.' he said.

'I want to move to another prison, it's not safe here.' He picked nervously at a scab on his neck.

'Why do you say that?' Peter leaned forward and looked closely at him. Apart from the rancid smell, Pargeter was sweating profusely and looked strained and exhausted.

'I… uh…' he looked at the door and dropped his voice so that Peter had to lean even further towards him. 'It's about Frank Clarke.' He paused, swallowing hard. 'I think he was killed. I don't know who by, but I heard something.' Pargeter was beginning to shake 'I'd been to the bog. I had the runs and was coming back when I heard it.' He looked up quickly at Peter then lowered his head again. 'It didn't make sense until I heard them saying that it would look like Frank topped himself. Then I got scared. What if they'd seen me?'

Peter gently interrupted. 'What exactly did they say?'

Pargeter cleared his throat nervously. 'I was passing the cleaning store when I got this bad pain in my guts and stopped to see if it would go or if I'd have to make a dash back. Anyway, all I heard was someone I didn't recognise say, 'After the second screw's round. Bateman's in the infirmary. It'll look like the sick bastard topped himself.' Then I had a really bad pain and must have made a noise because he stopped. I didn't wait to see if they came out, just ran as fast as I could to the bog and stayed there until Mr Carter come to find me because he knew I was having problems with my guts. When Clarke was found the next day...' He stopped suddenly as though this waterfall of words had taken all the strength from him. There were tears running down his cheeks. He looked up at Peter. 'Please help me, Father, I'm shit scared. I've got to go somewhere else. Please.' The pathetic sight of his suffering disturbed Peter deeply because he knew that he couldn't help. A fallible priest! That would upset the Papal Father.

He got up and walked around the desk. 'The only thing I can do is make a recommendation to the Deputy Governor, but that means you'll have to tell him what you've just told me.'

'But you said that anything I told you was a secret!' Pargeter was almost sobbing.

'So it is. However, if you want to move to another prison then Mr Lawson must have good reason to recommend it to the Governor. I can arrange for him to see you tomorrow if you want.'

Pargeter grumbled but finally agreed to the meeting.

* * *

Cynthia Orbanon put down her mobile, unlocked a drawer, took out her private diary and wrote '8 p.m. A' in Thursday's space. In Friday's there was one word: 'Grace'. It didn't seem possible that it was the fourth anniversary of Grace's death. She must remember to phone Hugh about their annual wake. It was the only time that they allowed the intense anger that they still felt about her murder to surface. It was their yearly purging. It also refreshed memories of the fun and free spirit of her life as they drank copious amounts of her favourite Bollinger. It seemed strange that, apart from this once-a-year time, she and Hugh hardly saw each other. But then there was no reason to, really. There were no children to hold them together, no one to dilute her little sister's memory, and nothing in common except the death of someone they both loved. Still, Grace remained locked in her heart and thoughts and drove her on.

She shut the diary and put it away. Grace and Hugh's wedding had been nearly twenty years ago. When the longed-for children didn't come, they decided to do what they could to mix pleasure with a little altruism by spending three months each year at a children's home and school in India. One of Grace's college friends was a member of the charitable trust that ran it. Grace taught the little ones English and Hugh coached the boys and girls in cricket and football. It had seemed to fulfil their need and they had decided that in a couple of years they would sell up their wine business, move there permanently, and build a house near the campus. That dream had been taken away when Grace was killed, and Hugh hadn't been able to face going there alone. He threw himself into work and when he'd eventually sold the business last year, he'd made more money than he could ever spend. He had married again, but the deep hurt and rage was with him every day. As it was with her! She felt the tears start to come and quickly forced them away.

Cynthia had been an MP for fifteen years and was slowly moving up the ranks. She had held a couple of junior ministerial posts in Opposition and now, in Government, she was at the Treasury and had been promised a promotion to Education in the next reshuffle.

There was a knock at the door and Sophie, Cynthia's PA, came in and put some papers on the desk. 'Your meeting with the Chief Whip is in fifteen minutes. Do you need the Lawrence report?'

Cynthia smiled at her. 'No thanks, but will you book lunch for two at the Grange for one-thirty on Friday and make sure the rest of the day is clear, please.'

* * *

Ruby Stevenson was in her early thirties but looked younger, with short dark hair and smiling eyes. She had been the prison medical lead for three years and had a good rapport with the inmates, seamlessly deflecting their attempts at seduction with wit, cheek, and a quick, sharp response. Most of them adored her and would have jumped in hard if anyone went too far. She and Lawson had an easy working relationship and together they had made several innovations to ease the present untenable structure of prisoners' lifestyle and health care, after finally persuading Wright that, if it worked as they thought it would, it could become a standard uptake across the Service and therefore another positive notch in his profile.

They tried to get together every week for a quick update and once a month met over a picnic lunch in Giles' office to sort out any problems and assess progress with on-going or new initiatives. Today, it was the results of cholesterol tests on a sample of hundred men in mixed age groups and use of statins. Giles also brought up the subject of Bateman and the recommendation of the Parole Board. He said it was for a five-year review of parole percentages, one of Wright's pointless political exercises. Ruby commiserated with him, took a few moments to search her memory, then said that she had examined Bateman before the Board and that physically, apart from his asthma, he had been in reasonably good shape. He had eaten little since Clarke's death and was underweight. There was a trace of dope but no hard drugs. She had felt that his problem was a psychological one, as did the shrink, and that it might possibly become worse the longer he was in prison. That obvious thought had seemed to be the major deciding factor in the Board's recommendation. She paused for a moment.

'I had a feeling though that Leighton James had already made his mind up about the parole.'

'Why?'

'He didn't want any detail, just our recommendations, but it isn't as simple as that… usually they'd dig a bit deeper.' She smiled. 'I guess we were nearly at the end of a full list and he was keen to get to lunch.

'Or a lucrative brief.' Giles didn't push her any more on it and, as they finished the food, they went over the timings for a series of talks and podcasts on STDs.

Just before she left, she briefed him on Bird, who was recovering in the infirmary. He hadn't said much, except that he was fed up being everybody's tart. She'd arranged for him to see a psychotherapist. He wanted to know what the chances were of him being moved to somewhere a bit easier where no one knew him. Giles would see what he could do but it might take a while to organise. Ruby was popping in to see him before she left.

'Tell him I'm on it,' said Giles. She smiled at him and left.

After he'd cleaned up the remains of the meal Giles phoned to make an appointment with Chris Harby, the prison's psychiatric lead, but he was away on leave for the next two weeks. He arranged a time for the Monday following Harby's return and was just starting his weekly sport report for Wright's 'Active Body, Active Mind' initiative, when his mobile rang.

'Peter, any joy?'

'Sorry I haven't got back to you before, but it's been a particularly sinful week in the Glee Club and I've only just given the last one a bit of a celestial rub down. I did, however, have an interesting chat with our aromatic friend and, though reluctantly, he'll share his thoughts with you tomorrow and reveal what he knows. I'll give you all the guff tonight. I've got to dash to a meeting with the boss, earthly one that is… I hope.'

'Can't you tell...'

'Sorry, boy, must go.' The phone went dead. Lawson looked at it in irritation, then put it down and pressed the intercom.

'Jill, can you come in a minute, please?'

'Right, Mr Lawson.'

* * *

Lady Anne Evan-Dyer was preparing for a meeting in the Blue Angel Hotel, situated in a small street off Mayfair in central London. It was the flagship of her Blue Boutique Hotel Group, a small high-end chain that was becoming a standard for quality and security and so attracted a wealthy and celebrity clientele.

She had taken over the running of the hotels after her husband Paul had been killed by a man who was trying to steal his car. It was two days after her fortieth birthday and hours after she was told that she had been awarded an MBE for the charity work she did with young widows. Paul had been given his knighthood some years before for services to young entrepreneurs.

Once she recovered enough to have any enthusiasm and energy to plan anything, she had channelled all her anger and grief into the business, although the violent and senseless murder had given her a deep and aggressive longing for a justice system that punished those who'd given up their right to humane treatment. The man had been caught a couple of months after the killing and sent down for life but had died from a heroin overdose a year after he began his sentence. The death was retribution of sorts but didn't seem equal to her loss and suffering. So, needing something to bring a balance back into her life, she took over the running of the hotels and it helped. The anger was still there, but she managed to focus on the positive and slowly move on.

When she could make the time, she visited racecourses all over the country. She had loved horse racing even before Paul had died, but a couple of years ago had decided to get more involved and bought two three-year-olds who were now beginning to win races. A year ago she'd met another owner, Mohammed El Faroud, at the Lambourne stables where he also had his horses. They started going for dinner after races and it had progressed from there; they now had an easy, warm, and passionate relationship, with no expectations on either side. For Anne, it was just good to share things with someone again.

* * *

A couple of hours later Giles had finished all he needed to do to catch up on the health reports when the phone *brrred*. He let it ring. Where the hell was Jill? After a moment, he picked it up. It was Leighton James' secretary. She said the barrister could give him half an hour the following Monday but wanted to know the agenda. Giles explained that he was doing a review of parole board procedures and wanted to pick his brains. They arranged a meeting for two-thirty. He put down the phone and looked at his watch. It was three-fifteen. He was chairing, in Wright's absence, a Governor's staff meeting at four and it was too late to delegate the job. He poured a coffee from his 'Coffee Worker' and sat in his recliner chair. Neither provided by the prison. He'd brought them both from home for those brief moments when he found time to stop and take a breath. He felt his eyes closing. God, he was tired! He was getting too old for multiple bouts of sex in a single night, but it had been worth it. Their lovemaking had always had an element of the ludicrous and laughter shared space with lust. They had been closer the last couple of days. Perhaps things would balance out again. Once this Frank Clarke thing was off his mind, he'd suggest they take a holiday, just the two of them.

He must have dozed off then, because the next thing he knew was Jill shaking his shoulder and telling him that he had five minutes to get to the meeting.

* * *

Charles Stanley Moncrieff looked down at Sarah Jane, her body at last free from the tubes and machines that had kept her alive but not living. Her beautiful face seemed relaxed and after so much suffering she was at last at peace. In his mind he could see her eyes, bright and intelligent, strikingly blue and full of the joy of being young. He bent over and kissed the cooling lips.

'Goodbye, my darling angel.'

He was alone in the room and for a moment the overwhelming loss felt like a great and suffocating weight. With a huge effort he managed to drive it away. The time would come when he would give in to the grief, but for now he needed the anger at her inconceivable death to drive him forward. He walked to the window and looked out over the lake and the acres of woodland that surrounded the mansion. The gardens, stark with winter, were being turned over ready for the first breath of spring. It had been a happy house once. Sarah Jane, orphaned when his student daughter died in childbirth with the father's name hidden in her heart, had filled the rooms and smoothed away the rough shell of his loss. Now she was gone too! He felt old and numb, frozen and locked out of the normality of family life. He had only one use for his vast wealth now. Revenge! It gave him strength as he looked for one last time at her silent, empty form and then went to the door. He would have to tell Sarah's grandmother, his first wife, Jacinta. She would be devastated but would understand. He wasn't sure that she would have been able to make the choice he had made but he knew that they would share the emptiness of life without her and she would respect him for making the decision.

'You can come in now, we're ready.'

He stood aside as the two nurses went in. The doctor stopped for a moment.

'I've made the arrangements. We'll take her to the chapel.'

'Thank you,' said Moncrieff and watched as the door closed behind him, shutting out the agony of seeing her still and lifeless face. She would be from now and always only in his heart and mind.

* * *

Giles left the prison at a quarter to five. It was already dark and cold as he started the five-mile drive home. The meeting had been, as usual, pointless, with nothing new to report and no innovations on practice discussed or suggested. He wasn't sure what purpose these meetings served, as very little ever came out of them except a litany of moans and meanderings on pay and overtime. It was yet another one of the Governor's recipes for 'a happy team is a good team'. He was glad to be on his way home and looking forward to a glass of red, a bath, then a quick meal and the trip to the opera with Peter to stimulate his mind and relax his spirit.

He also decided, that when Wright got back, he would have another go at him about Clarke, this time with what he hoped Pargeter was going to say and Peter's back-up, it might be enough to re-open the inquiry or at the very least get Wright to consider it.

He arrived home at five-thirty, leaving him enough time for a longish soak in his haven before the girls came home and threw the peace off balance. However, there was a note from them on the kitchen table saying they were meeting some friends and going to the movies but would be back by ten-thirty and they hoped he'd had a nice day. That wasn't like them. What did they want now?

He checked for messages on the landline. There were four for Patty. Nobody ever phoned him or the girls on it anymore. Some of Patty's friends still used it though, mainly those who lived out of town where the mobile service was patchy. Perhaps they could save a bit of cash by cancelling the contract and just using mobiles. The signal they got in the house was good enough, he thought, and at that moment, his phone beeped. It was a text from Peter cancelling the opera visit and saying that he would be happy to let them feed him at around nine p.m.

Giles didn't mind much. He was exhausted anyway and would probably have fallen asleep. He took a cold beer from the fridge, put on Madame Butterfly, and went upstairs.

CHAPTER SIX

The large old house was situated in an isolated part of the Cotswolds and was surrounded by three acres of dense woodland. There was a high-security fence around the perimeter and only one way in or out.

A small army of guards patrolled whenever the farm was used. Each time the team on security was new and sourced from an agency used by high-profile clients whose identity was known only by the couple who ran the operation. It was probably the most secure organisation in Europe. The guards were paid well, helicoptered in and out, and knew nothing of where they were, what went on in the house, or who was there. A state-of-the-art US military system also protected the house and its land.

By five-fifteen everyone had arrived and was seated around an ornate Georgian table. 'Before we start,' said Amebury, 'I would like to pass on my deepest sympathy to Charles. Sarah Jane's life support was switched off today.'

'I'm so sorry, Charles,' said Cynthia Orbanon.

Moncrieff looked drawn. 'Thank you, Cynthia. Her health had deteriorated over the last two weeks. There was no other choice. She is at peace now. I will miss her deeply, but her death has increased my resolve in what we are trying to achieve. So, as David is chairing the meeting today, I'll hand over to him.' He glanced around the table. Lady Anne Evan-Dyer, Simon Bartenson, and Sir Roger Alsopp gave their agreement.

* * *

Pargeter sat in his cell, trying to take his mind away from the fear that was burning through him. He was trying to read a book of poetry, borrowed from the library. He read very slowly, working out the meaning word by word. Sometimes, when he had persevered and it was almost clear, he could escape to a place where all around him there was love, beauty and freedom, the opposite of the shadows in which he lived his life. He had never read any poetry before he worked in the prison library. He found the short lines easier to understand than the blocks of text in ordinary books.

Tonight though, his concentration was shot, the words jumbled in and out of focus and meant nothing. He was sweating and his arms itched like mad. He rubbed his hand and wiped a spot of blood away. As usual, at dinnertime, he had been pushed around in the food queue and must have caught his hand on something, scratching it deeply enough to bleed. He gave up on the poetry. Perhaps there was something on television to distract him, and he would be safe enough with the screws around.

Peter had arrived just after nine and they were sampling an expensive bottle of wine that had been given to him by a grateful parishioner. He had told Giles what Pargeter had said and they were discussing the best approach when Patty came back from checking the food. 'Let's eat, boys.'

Pargeter was going down the stairs when he suddenly felt dizzy. He stopped for a moment and leaned over the rail, waiting for his head to clear. After a moment he felt better and straightened up again. Then a tremendous pain enveloped him and, as he started to fall, sunshine and trees flashed through his mind until it closed down. His body collapsed over the low handrail and bounced onto the safety netting above the level below.

Peter was in the middle of a long and involved story about a defrocked priest who ran a burlesque club in Rhyl when Giles' mobile rang. He answered. 'Yes, hang on.'

He glanced at Patty 'I've got to take this. There's a problem at work. I won't be long.' He got up from the table. 'Wait until I get back.'

Peter watched him leave the room. 'How are things?' he asked Patty.

'We're getting there. The four of us talked and listened like adults for once. We agreed we all had our faults and that we need to be a little more caring, a bit less self-indulgent and childish, learn to give and take and find a space in our busy little lives to spend proper time together. Simple!'

'Piece of piss.' Peter smiled and filled her glass, then topped his up and tapped hers with it.

Giles came back into the room.' 'Pargeter's dead!'

'What?' Peter put his glass down.

'He was on his way down from level three when he went over the rail. He was dead by the time they got to him. I'm going to have to go over there.' Giles picked up his keys from the worktop 'I'm sorry, sweetheart.'

Peter stood up. 'If you don't mind, Patty, I think I'll go with him.'

'Of course not! Come again soon.'

'I will.'

'Love you, Father.'

'You too, darling girl.'

'Peter!' Giles shouted.

Peter kissed the top of Patty's head and she hugged him. 'He doesn't know how lucky he is.'

Patty watched him go and picked up her glass. The girls could have the rest of the risotto when they got home. She glanced at the clock, got up, covered the food with foil and topped up her wine. She'd watch that documentary on Picasso's ceramics she'd recorded months ago.

Peter got into the car and Giles reversed out of the drive, turned on to the road, and accelerated. He slapped the palms of his hands on the steering wheel as they picked up speed. 'Shit! Shit!' Someone must have got to him. It's too much of a bloody coincidence.'

Peter touched his arm. 'Let's wait and see. There's no point in you having a seizure. I'm not trained. Look, he'd got himself worked up into a terrible state. It's possible his heart gave out. Although it is a bit too tidy.'

'What's going on, Peter?' Giles glanced at the priest. 'If I am right about Clarke, then why was he killed? And, more to the point, who did it. If the old man won't help, I'll have to go above his head and speak to Pat Duggan.'

'Talk to him again first.' Peter looked out of the windscreen. It was beginning to rain heavily and there was a close crack of thunder and a flash of lighting. 'Lovely night for it though.'

* * *

Ruby Stevenson was lying on the recliner, Giles was behind the desk, and Peter was sitting on the floor, his back against the wall. Giles put his mobile down. He'd phoned Gerald's PA to find out if he was going to be there in the morning. 'She said he's in tomorrow early a.m., that she's only paid to be his PA until five-thirty, and that she has a life too, so she'd appreciate it if I'd just fuck off and leave her alone. My words, not hers, but the intention was the same. Any thoughts yet, Ruby?'

She looked at him for a moment. 'Well, it's certainly possible it was a heart attack. He was overweight, had respiratory problems, and, from what you say, was very stressed. Has he got any relatives?'

Peter shook his head. 'None that I know of, poor bugger.'

Giles looked at his watch. It was almost midnight. 'There's nothing more we can do tonight. See if you can get the post-mortem moving first thing.'

Ruby smiled. 'I'll see what I can do.' She got up. 'I'll call you as soon as I know anything. Night, both.'

After she left, Giles walked around the desk and stood over Peter.

'Ready?'

'I think I'll sit with him for a bit. Help him on his way. At least it's cured his freshness problem. I'll stay over in the duty room and pick the car up tomorrow.'

'You're a hell of a guy, for a priest. So long, Father.'

'James Cagney to Pat O'Brien in one of the Boystown films! Go home, Lawson.'

The two men smiled and Giles left. Peter closed his eyes and leaned back against the wall for a moment, then stood up, turned the light off, and made his way to the mortuary.

CHAPTER SEVEN

The next morning Giles overslept and didn't get to work until eight thirty. Jill wasn't there but he found a message on his desk from Wright saying he wanted to see him as soon as he got in. Christ, what time had he done that? Fuck it, he could wait for him to have a coffee!

The phone rang. 'Giles, get over here now,' Wright said sharply and ended the call.

How the hell did he know I was in? He touched his mug gently. 'I'd better leave you for later then, my precious.' Imitating Gollum was his favourite embarrassment for the girls when they had friends round, particularly boyfriends. He was proud of it.

'That was good, sounded just like him.'

He jumped and saw Jill standing at the door. He smiled at her, 'Was it?' She seemed stressed. 'Are you all right?'

'I've only just got here.' She was normally in by seven, a good hour before him. 'Jack wasn't well, so I borrowed his car, but it broke down, I had to wait for the RAC to come and tow it to a garage and then get a bus.'

'It's alright, just sit down, relax, you can have my coffee, I haven't touched it. I'm going to see Mr Wright. I should be back by ten at the latest.'

'Right, Mr Lawson.'

'Go straight in, Giles,' Deborah, snake protector of the inner sanctum, hissed at him, as she sat coiled behind her desk.

'Thank you, Ms Willet. Sorry about disturbing you last night.' Somehow her first name never seemed an option. She ignored his apology.

He knocked on the door and went in. Wright was sitting behind his desk, jacket off, sleeves rolled up, the cold seeping through the open window. His glare wasn't welcoming and it was bloody freezing. Giles shivered and shut the door. 'Sorry I wasn't here when you got in. I expect you've heard about Pargeter?'

'I had a few words with your Welsh friend when I arrived.' Wright's hard eyes and tight face made the room feel even icier. 'What is it with you, Giles? Have you just got a problem with Clarke, or is it anyone at Hill Sutton who dies? People do it all the time. Sometimes even in prison. And most are not victims of conspiracies. Dr Stevenson thinks it probable he had a heart attack.'

'Pargeter told Father Satorri that he had...'

'Yes, I know, he told me. Can't you get that man out of your head? Obsessions are dangerous things, Giles. It was suicide. He topped himself. That's it. Nothing more and nothing less! As for Pargeter, wait for the autopsy.'

Giles felt his anger starting to bubble and tried to contain it with a reasoned response. 'If there is the slightest doubt about Clarke's or Pargeter's death, in my mind, or anyone else's, surely that warrants consideration. Pargeter knew something and Father Satorri will make an official statement of what he said he'd overheard about Clarke's death. He doesn't do that lightly but feels that in the circumstances it's warranted.' He paused briefly. 'I really think it should be looked into again.' Wright's eye was beginning to twitch. 'I've already made an appointment to see Leighton James on Monday and I intend to speak to Pat Duggan today.'

Wright's face reddened as he exploded at Giles. 'You will do no such thing. Whatever happens in this prison is my responsibility! I decide, not you, and if or when I consider there is something to question, I will do it. How dare you go behind my back to James? I won't allow any contact with him or approaches to Duggan…'

Giles lost it too. 'Who the fuck do you think you are? You're acting like some despotic headmaster. It's not smoking in the showers we're talking about. It's two deaths that I believe are suspicious and it is my responsibility to pursue them as I think fit. I don't understand...'

Wright rose to his feet, his voice booming. 'I will not have...'

Giles stood his ground and continued. 'Unless of course you have something to hide.' Wright was now apoplectic, his eye fluttering uncontrollably. 'I'm not going to let this go, Gerald. I will chase around as many corridors as I have to, and, if I think I have something substantial then I will go to anyone who will fucking listen to me, with or without your permission! Is that clear enough for you?' He stared at Wright who leaned over his desk so that his face was inches away from Giles.

'I am your superior and while you are still at this prison you will do exactly what I say. If not, I am quite willing to accept your resignation.'

Giles held his almost manic gaze. 'No way. If you want to get rid of me then you'll have to sack me and that's not going to be easy, and I do realise that I have signed the Official Secrets Act. I don't see any point in continuing this.' He turned and walked to the door, half expecting Wright to throw something. Nothing hit him and he opened the door and went out, leaving it open.

Wright watched him leave then went to the door. 'Deborah, I don't want to be disturbed.'

She looked concerned. 'Yes, Mr Wright. Is everything all right?'

'Why wouldn't it be?' He shut the door, sat down at his desk, and took out his mobile. His hand drummed impatiently on the table as he waited for an answer.

'Alsopp!'

* * *

Giles was back in his office. 'Well, would you tell him I called, please? Giles Lawson, Deputy Governor at Hill Sutton prison. He's got the number. It's important I reach him as soon as possible. Thank you.' He put down the phone and lit a cigarette, his third in a row. Talk about burning bridges. Shit, shit, shit!

Jill's voice came through the intercom. 'Mr Lawson?'

'Yes, Jill?'

'Sir Leighton James' office rang when you were out, but I had to go over to stationery...'

Giles interrupted. 'What did they want?' He wasn't in the mood for rambling.

'Sorry, Mr Lawson, they've had to cancel your meeting on Monday. I asked about another appointment but they said that he'd had to go out of the country and they didn't know exactly when he'd be back. They'll arrange another time when they know his movements.' She sounded hurt. He instantly regretted the sharpness but it was too late now.

'Thank you, Jill. I'm sorry too. I shouldn't have snapped at you. I didn't sleep well and just had a set-to with the Governor.'

'That's all right, Mr Lawson. Can I get you anything?'

A bit of time travel to reset the last hour would be nice.

'No thanks.'

What the hell was happening? It seemed he was the only one, apart from Peter, who gave a shit about the deaths. And why was Gerald Wright so vehemently opposed to looking at Clarke's death again? Wright's explosive reaction was excessive even for him, although Giles' own knee-jerk response had almost certainly exacerbated it. Before he did anything else though, he needed to put his thoughts in some sort of order. Talking it through with someone outside of the prison would help. Patty would have been 'no bullshit' ideal but she was on a course today. And she would have been less than impressed with the considered and adult way he had reacted to Wright. Her voice echoed in his head: 'You really are a dickhead, Lawson.' Still, that little truth would keep until later. He picked up his mobile and called Peter.

'Will you be at home for the next couple of hours?'

'Yes. Come over. I'll make us lunch.'

'Sounds good, thanks.'

Giles put the phone into his pocket, got his keys and wallet from the drawer and went into Jill's office.

'If anyone wants me, you've no idea where I am or when I'll be back.'

She looked surprised. 'Right, Mr Lawson.'

Peter stood by the worktop in the kitchen of his flat opening a bottle of wine. Giles sat at the table with the remains of lunch and looked around the large, comfortable, and cluttered room. The style was all Peter and not at all priest-like. Whatever that meant – stark and austere with a chill of self-denial? Whatever sort of picture that created wasn't the reality of Peter's home. His was a place in which to relax and feel at peace. The apartment was on the first and second floors of a large Victorian house. The upper level had bedrooms, dining room, and bathroom, the lower, a huge kitchen with a range cooker, walk-in larder, and massive wooden table, and a book-and-music-cluttered room which was the beating heart of the home. It was where Peter worked, read, wrote, and listened to music at deafening pitch, locked into his Dr Dre headphones, a fiftieth birthday present from Patty. It was, apart from his beloved bathroom, Giles' favourite place of respite. It was a warm and safe space and a sanctuary from an outside world where the messy side of life sometimes made monsters of what was good.

Its magic was working, and the tension of his fight with Gerald was slowly slipping away. Like his flat, Peter eased troubled souls. It was his irreverence, reason, and calm.

'Bring the glasses.' Giles followed Peter into the study. As the priest filtered Bruch into the background, Giles poured the wine, threw a couple of logs on the fire, and dropped into one of the old overstuffed armchairs. Peter sat opposite him.

'Something is rotten in the heart of Hill Sutton and old Claudius behaves in an odd and aggressive way, not helped by your vociferous attack on his gentle words. Reasonable enough in the circumstances but guaranteed to get a strong reaction.' He poked the fire, releasing a flurry of sparks. 'Any news from Ruby yet?'

'No.'

Peter thought for a moment. 'When I was sitting with Pargeter I had a few thoughts. Firstly, the only one who could realistically have any idea of what might have happened that night is Bateman. Something that occurred before he was taken to the infirmary or something Clarke said in the days before his death. It would be good to talk to him. Was Pargeter killed because he knew too much? If he was, then the stakes have gone up and someone needs to take a serious look into it.'

Giles had finished his wine. Peter went to pour him another. He covered his glass. 'No thanks.' He paused for moment. 'I think it's possible that Clarke was killed for some reason and that Bateman was, at the very least, a party to it. I also believe that Pargeter did hear something and is dead because he talked to you and was going to speak to me. Surely there's enough 'too much of a coincidence' in all that to at least open a discussion. But my little push gave Gerald such a hissy fit that he wants to shut it all down and get rid of me. Why?' His head had started to throb again and he was tensing up. 'What do I do now, Peter? I can't just drop it.'

Peter looked hard at him for a moment then smiled. 'I've got an idea.' He went to the iPad on his desk. 'This is going to take me a few minutes, so why don't you ring Jill to see if there's any fallout and find out the name of Bateman's probation officer and anything else about him that might be useful. You won't get a signal in here so use the landline.'

Giles picked up the phone and dialled. It was answered almost immediately.

'Jill, it's Giles…'

Giles finished the call. Jill had told him that Wright wanted to speak to him as soon as possible and that Patty had rung because she couldn't get him on his mobile. He asked her to check on the name of the probation officer while he was on the phone. She came back puzzled. She knew that Giles had been looking at the file but, apart from the date of the release, there was nothing there. It had disappeared. She'd check if it had gone into another folder and see if there was a hard copy and ring him if she found it or anything else that might be pertinent.

'Thanks, Jill.' He was just about to end the call.

'Mr Lawson, I think Bateman came from Jersey. I remember seeing in the file that his home address was in St Helier.'

'Are you sure?'

'It stayed with me because it's where we went on our honeymoon.'

'Thanks! See if you can get me a time to see Mr Wright.'

'Right, Mr Lawson.'

Giles filled Peter in on the call.

'It'll be interesting to see how Gerald reacts, but in the meantime, I know someone who it might be worth running this past. Valerie Loring. She's an investigative journalist at the Sunday Chronicle with lots of experience in these sorts of things, a tenacious digger and, once she's hooked on something, unstoppable. She's instinctive, unpredictable, and can't be bullied out of anything she believes in. It's won her equal amounts of praise and pissing off people. She's also no-bullshit straight. I met her ten years ago at the funeral of a mutual friend, Connor, who was a photojournalist. He'd been killed in a car crash days before he was ready to file a major story. It concerned a high-profile corporate banking head behind child trafficking from Catholic orphanages around the globe. He was rich and powerful and had thought he was untouchable. He was eventually arrested but with his wealth and contacts, bailed. He was shot dead the week before he was due to appear in court. Other high-profile people involved were uncovered, tried, and given long prison sentences. Since then, several of them have either taken their own lives or died. There were suspicions that some of the deaths were not what they seemed, but nothing was found and eventually the noise died down. Val had finished Connor's story and made sure it was published. I'd put her in touch with a bunch of widely spread colleagues in the Church who weren't afraid to talk to her. We became good friends. Why don't you make some fresh coffee and I'll see if I can reach her!'

In the kitchen, Giles found the coffee and spooned it into a large cafetière. Peter had one of those taps that gave boiling water instantly. The couple who'd sold him the apartment had left it there and he loved it. Giles was always jealous but knew that the three and a half thousand pounds it cost was way out of his reach, and even if it hadn't been, Patty would have thrown it out as lunacy.

He filled the cafetière and waited for it to settle and steep. The sense of peace he had found momentarily started to fade again as his mind spun through what had happened in the last few hours. One thing was crystal clear: he had handled the fight with Wright really badly. Although he'd had tricky moments in the past with him, he hadn't ever blown up like that before. He was truly pissed off with himself that he had lost it. Of course, Wright deserved it, but he should have kept focused. It was the only thing that would usually help ease around the Governor's stubbornness and bullying attitude.

Peter came into the kitchen. 'How do you fancy Turandot at Convent Garden followed by a meal at a pricey restaurant with a night at the Inn on the Park thrown in, all compliments of the Chronicle? Val will meet us for breakfast on Tuesday morning. I told her just enough to spike her interest. I think you'll enjoy meeting her, she's a bit special!'

Giles smiled. 'Great, that's a positive at least!' He looked up at the old station clock on the wall. 'I'd better give the coffee a miss and get home.'

'Okay.' Said Peter, 'ring me over the weekend and we'll sort out trains. Be good to get an early one then we can have more of the day in London. Give my love to Patty and the girls and try to relax. Things will look different with a bit of objective and professional focus.'

They reached the front door and Giles opened it.

'Thanks for letting me whinge on and being a voice of reason.'

'All part of the service, even for heathens like you.'

Yet, as he drove home, Giles couldn't stop the demons wriggling, and he began to feel a darkness slipping over him. It was unthinkable for Wright to be involved but, if he was, what the fuck did that mean? Bateman's early release, Pargeter's death, and now the missing digital files suggested that Clarke's 'suicide' had good reason to be revisited. If the answers didn't stack up then a new inquiry should, at the very least, be considered. If he was killed, who had done it? Was it personal for the killer, and if not, then who had wanted him dead and why?

Giles decided that the first thing he had to do was to talk to Pat Duggan. He knew that was really going to piss Wright off but, given the present state of their relationship, that was irrelevant. He also wanted to get to Bateman. He was sure he was key. But how could he do that? They had no recent address and needed to contact his probation officer. If Jill was right about Bateman being from Jersey, then he could be there? It was a starting point anyway. Perhaps Valerie Loring would be able to help find him. She probably had the right sort of contacts and, if she did think it was worth looking into, with a story at the end, she might be willing to help.

It always intrigued him that Peter's eclectic and surprising friends seemed happy to go to any lengths to try and do what he asked of them. Mind, he had probably done the same and more for them. He began to wonder how involved and proactive Peter had been with the Catholic orphanage exposure.

Wrapped in his thoughts and not really concentrating on the road, he didn't see the large green van pulling out until it was too late.

'Fuck!' The impact threw him hard against the tightness of his belt, winding him. Luckily the airbag mechanism was broken and didn't inflate. A huge bald raging Shrek, a tattoo of a scorpion crawling over his neck and chin, got out of the van and stood looking at him through the window. Shit, this was all he needed.

'You fucking twat!' Not a good start.

'Oh, shit!' Sensitive, reasonable, balanced were all words that didn't touch it. Giles reluctantly got out and walked around the car. There didn't seem to be much damage, a few scratches and a couple of broken headlights. The van was only dented slightly.

He tried to look complicit, ready to share the blame. 'I'm sorry, but you just pulled out. I know I should have been aware of you…'

Shrek looked down at him, growling like a warthog. His breath smelt like one too and Giles tried to turn his head away, but the face was so close he couldn't do it without a nose collision. Don't headbutt me, please! He took a deep breath. 'Look, it was an accident and if we do knock for knock it'll save a lot of trouble for both of us.'

The man pulled his head back and Giles thought his moment had come. At least it would get rid of his problem with Wright.

'It's a firm's van and you hit me, you fucking arsehole, so, it's down to you. Isn't it?'

Giles, after what he felt might be his last breath, nodded.

'Now give me your insurance details so I can phone it in and then I won't have to hurt you.'

'All right, move back a bit then.'

The ogre growled, but moved, and Giles slipped away from him, opened the passenger door, and looked for his insurance stuff. He couldn't find it. It wasn't in the door or on the shelf. Then he remembered he'd put all the details in his phone when the electrics were playing up and he couldn't shut the window properly.

It was nearly two hours later when Giles got home. He and Shrek had eventually exchanged insurance details, their chat concluding with an, 'In future keep your eyes open, you fucking wanker!' from the tattooed monster. The little bump must have done something more serious than he thought and the car wouldn't start. He had had to wait for the AA to ferry it, and him, to his local garage, a couple of miles from home. God, what a shit day! At least he had the house to himself. He poured a large brandy and was just sitting down, wondering whether he could risk a cigarette if he sat by an open window, when Patty and the girls walked in.

'You haven't forgotten you're taking us to Conlock Quay tonight?' Sally said as she put the top slice of thick sourdough on a huge Marmite and peanut butter sandwich. She cut it in two and passed one half to her sister. 'We've got to be there by seven thirty.' Giles took a moment to think about how he was going to explain but his face was there ahead of him. Sally glared at him. 'If it's a problem, Johnny and Josh said they'd pick us up.'

Giles sighed. 'Well, it wouldn't have been, except that I had a bump in the car and the lights aren't working... or the car. The AA dropped it off at the garage and I had to wait for a lift home.'

Patty smiled at Sally. 'I can take you'.

Kate got in on the act. 'No, it's all right, you stay and look after him. I'll ring Johnny and you get the bags down,' she said to Sally. 'And thanks, Dad.' The two girls got up and powered out of the kitchen.

Sally glanced back at him. 'Are you all right, Dad? You weren't hurt, were you?'

Giles smiled bravely. 'No, sweetheart, it was only a scratch.' Sally had gone. 'Just needed twenty stitches.'

Patty came over to him. 'What happened?'

'It's a long story and there's more to tell you about than just the bump. That was nothing really. Can we talk when the girls have gone?'

'Mum, can we borrow yours and his Barbours?' Sally's voice slipped sweetly round the door.

'His?' Giles started to get up.

Patty pushed him back in his seat. 'Leave it, Lawson.' She shouted back through the door. 'As long as you don't ruin them.'

'We won't! Can I have your red scarf too?'

'Only if you look after it.' Patty went across to the freezer and looked in. 'We need to stock up again. How about one of Katrina's vegetarian cottage pies?'

'Is that all there is?'

'It is.'

'And I thought today couldn't get any worse.'

'Don't be pathetic, Giles, it won't kill you.'

He wasn't convinced.

After the girls had gone, they talked. Giles emptied the last drop in the bottle into Patty's glass.

'I wanted to talk to you about it before but there was always something else that got in the way and, I suppose, I wasn't sure where I was going with it. I knew you'd want a clear picture and not me just creating chaos. I nearly told you at Gino's but I didn't want to waste the evening with me talking work and you pissed off with me for doing it.'

Patty looked ready to jump in but she didn't and, distracted for a moment, he struggled briefly to get back on track. 'Pargeter suddenly dying the night before he was going to talk to me and then Wright blowing me out like that only fed the fire. I know I didn't help by reacting the way I did with him, but it certainly feels like he knows more than he was going to tell me. I even thought, for a moment, that the bump I had today was to frighten me off in a not too subtle way.'

She didn't look convinced.

'Does any of this make sense?' Was that a completely pointless question? Was it? He wasn't sure now.

Patty looked at him for a moment. 'Do you really think there is a conspiracy about this man Clarke, with

Gerald Wright at the centre? You know that when you start obsessing about something you disengage and run with whatever scatterbrain reasoning comes into your head. So, it could be that you and your theory just got in the way of a bad day and you kicking off was the final straw for him.'

She stopped and Giles could almost hear the reasoning as she turned it over. That was positive, anyway.

'I think you should talk to Duggan and then it's down to him to decide if there's something that needs looking into.' She paused again. 'And if Peter thinks it's worth running it past this journalist friend of his then do that too. It'll be an objective eye at the very least.'

Giles stretched and his neck clicked. 'Yes, you're right.' He leaned over and kissed her head. 'I won't mention it again, at least not tonight.' He moved towards her again. 'Let's make the most of the girls being away.'

Somewhere in the house a mobile rang.

'That'll be them saying they've arrived.' Patty got up. 'God, I shouldn't drink before I eat, I feel pissed and…' she looked at her watch, 'it's only half past eight. I need food. I'll put some pasta on, can't wait for the pie.'

That was at least a little ray of sunshine in this dark day, he thought, but, for once, he didn't say it out loud.

CHAPTER EIGHT

Monday morning was one of those bright, crisp late winter days that made Giles feel refreshed, energised and ready for anything that fate might throw at him.

As he sat on the top of the bus that took him from the end of his road to the train station, squashed against the window by a large woman with a dog on her lap, his mind fluttered around the weekend. It had been fantastic, the most fun they'd had for months. They hadn't talked any more after Friday about Clarke or Wright. Giles had promised to try and put it out of his mind and, much to his surprise, he had. The time alone, without the girls, was great: loving, warm and cosy. He'd forgotten just how much they enjoyed each other before the pressures of working life, teenagers, and tight budgets took its toll. They'd gone for a long walk by the river on the Saturday, then had a cream tea and went to a five-thirty showing of an old movie they had seen on one of their first proper dates. After, they'd had dinner in the most expensive restaurant they could find and that night made love as though it was the first time, then slept, drained and exhausted, in each other's arms. Even the girls, when they arrived back on Sunday morning, seemed to have forgiven him for being their father.

* * *

David Amebury was in his car on the way into the office. Mostly he drove himself but this morning he was in the back of his chauffeur-driven Jag, working on a deal that was to be completed that day. His private and secure mobile rang. He answered it.

'Roger, is there a problem?' He listened intently then thought for a moment, his eyes cold and hard. 'Contact everyone. Eight p.m. tonight at the farm! No excuses. They have to be there.'

* * *

At the station, Giles browsed the paperbacks and magazines in WH Smith while he waited for Peter. He started to read Private Eye, decided to buy it, then picked up a Guardian as well, went to the self-service till and used the Apple Pay app on his new iPhone. The girls and Patty had bought it for his last birthday. He'd brought it instead of his work phone because of the paranoia that Wright would somehow be able to hack in and listen or monitor his calls and texts and probably pinpoint him in London.

He had just worked out how to use emojis too and was sending Patty a text with a smiley, a hug, a floating heart and a kiss, when there was an almost indecipherable announcement that the Northern Rail service to London Euston was running thirty minutes late; they were sorry for the delay and for any problems the late running might cause passengers. It was said as though it was the first time it had ever happened!

Patty replied quickly with 'xx stay focused'.

Peter arrived, slipped his arm around Giles' shoulder, and led him off in the direction of the new Caffé Nero on the other side of the concourse.

'Time for a coffee and a muffin and then you can share your weekend of passion and Patty with a sad and celibate man.'

In his room at Hull, Simon Bartenson dropped his phone onto the chair and wrote eight p.m. A on today's space in his diary and then cancelled his tutorials for that afternoon. He was exhausted. Sleep had eluded him for most of the night with rolling pictures of the past and sharp nightmare fears gripping him. When he did manage to doze, he jerked awake after a few minutes, shot through with horror and agonizing remorse. What in God's name had made him agree to be part of it? The insanity of his grief blinded his humanity and reason. There was only one thing he could do to stop this madness. He had to let them know he was finished with it. Tonight. He would tell them tonight. The sudden, surprising relief of having at last made that decision calmed and centred him. By the time his first tutorial of the day arrived, he was able to concentrate on the student completely and give the guidance she needed to attain the high mark she deserved for her dissertation.

* * *

On the journey to London, Giles and Peter created a timeline of events and listed everything that had happened from Clarke's death to Friday night's fun with Shrek and the green van.

1. 24th July – Frank Clarke found hanged in his cell.
2. 15th September – Inquiry returns suicide verdict in record time.
3. 25th September – Ralph Bateman released on parole.
4. 23rd March – Sidney Pargeter dies after arranging to meet Giles the next day.
5. 24th March – Wright explodes and Giles leaves. Giles' files on Bateman disappear from his and Jill's computers. Possible attack on Giles by Shrek to warn him off.
6. Bateman might be in Jersey.

Then they made another list of points that this raised:

1. When they did manage to contact Bateman's parole officer, would the man know where he was?
2. Bateman was out of his cell on the night Clarke was found hanged. Was his asthma attack real? It would have been easy to fake when you had a history.
3. Was it too much of a coincidence?
4. The speed of the Inquiry verdict plus Ruby Stevenson's feelings about Leighton James's decision.
5. Wright's quick and disproportionate anger over Giles contacting James without talking to him first and the barrister then cancelling their meeting.
6. Bateman's parole was much too early.
7. Could what Pargeter overheard be trusted?
8. Was Pargeter's death the day after he talked to Peter too much of a coincidence?
9. Why was Wright so adamantly against Giles looking into the death again? As Deputy Governor, he had a right to question anything that he felt needed more clarity or investigation.

10. If Bateman had gone to Jersey, why had he not told his parole officer or switched to one on the island? If he'd gone AWOL and was caught, it would mean him going back to prison.

11. Was the van incident chance or something more?

By the time they arrived at Euston it was early afternoon and they hadn't come up with any positives, only a few vague possibilities to chase around.

There were more armed police at the station than usual and it always surprised Giles that he accepted it as the norm now. He supposed that to this generation it was. There had been several severe security alerts in the capital over the past weeks and the increased activity reflected what was happening all over Europe. On the station concourse there was a small group of Extinction Rebellion activists with a variety of placards.

They checked into their hotel overlooking Regent's Park and then took a cab to Covent Garden, and wandered through the Piazza, stopping to watch a fire-eater and a harpist play to a small but loud and active audience. It was getting chilly and the daylight was fading fast. Faint seams of sunshine still tried to tease through the grey and rolling clouds, but they soon disappeared as the shadows of early dusk took over. As it got colder, they went for coffee at what was once the place where James Boswell and Samuel Johnson would meet and discuss the politics and gossip of the late 1700s. Then in a pub they had a beer and a sandwich to keep them going until their meal after the show before joining the queue to get into the Opera House.

* * *

In the Cotswolds, the meeting was about to start. They had all arrived at the farm by seven-thirty and at eight they took their seats around the table. Moncrieff called the meeting to order. 'First, let me thank you for coming at such short notice. I realise that for most of you this might have caused a major disruption to your day but David and I felt that the inconvenience was warranted. We have a problem. It is not insurmountable but needs decisive and prompt action. The last removal that was facilitated at Hill Sutton is being questioned. So far, we have managed to contain it. That, I fear, may only be a temporary measure! More investigation might raise difficult questions. It shouldn't, but we need to stop it now to make sure there are no repercussions. So, what I want from you tonight is agreement on instigating preventative action. What form that takes can be left to Roger, David, and myself. By the limitations we set down we need a majority vote. Does anyone have anything to say before I ask for a show of hands?' He looked around the table.

Simon Bartenson raised his hand. He looked tense and troubled.

'Yes, Simon?'

'What exactly do you mean by preventative action?'

Amebury answered. 'As Charles said, that need not concern you. All that matters is that our work continues. All of us have suffered greatly at the hands of these vermin, and if society will not fulfil its moral and legal obligations, then we must. Nothing should be allowed

85

to stand in our way. We are fighting for the right of every individual to a life that is free from the spectre of violent sexual abuse and murder. You, Simon, know the depths to which these creatures will go.' He paused for a moment then his voice hardened, his eyes locked on him. 'Remember what Jessica must have suffered in the weeks she was locked in that room. The pain of torture, the humiliation of rape, her body desecrated…'

Simon Bartenson threw his chair back and stood there shaking, tears streaming down his face, his body tight with agony. 'No!' It was a howl of torment. 'Jess, forgive me! I tried to find you.' His body shook uncontrollably. Cynthia Orbanon put her arms around him and held him until the shaking had subsided. Her voice, when she spoke, was calm and authoritative and broke the shock that had gripped the others at Simon's collapse.

'I think, David, that enough has been said. We should break for a while to collect our thoughts.' She looked around the table then back at Amebury. 'I will not tolerate this aggressive bullying again.'

She led Simon from the room. David Amebury looked around the table.

'I'm sorry I had to do that, but the memory of our pain is not enough. We must feel and utilise its power. Individually we are fragile and will fail. Together, our combined strength can ensure that we will be able to continue to make a difference.'

When they reconvened, there was a unanimous decision to authorise action. Simon had calmed down. Amebury apologised to him and he had accepted it but didn't say that he was done with it all. He decided he would wait until he got home and was more in control, then he would write to Amebury explaining his reasons for leaving the group.

* * *

Turandot had been a wonderful, all-encompassing relief from reality. Giles and Peter were lifted to such heights that by the time they sat down to eat at Joe Allen their reason for being in London had for the moment been eclipsed by the exquisite music and magic of Puccini.

By the time their food arrived the restaurant was packed. Joe Allen was a busy after-theatre haunt of West End performers, their friends and guests, with a smattering of civilians loitering amongst the gaggle of creatives and social players. Peter's irreverent takes on the C-list poseurs around them had Giles in hysterics and they suffered glares and glassy looks for the fun they were having at their expense.

They left the restaurant at midnight and had a couple of large brandies in the hotel bar before going to bed. As Giles was cleaning his teeth, looking in the mirrored walls of the bathroom and thinking he wasn't that bad for his age, he realised that he hadn't phoned Patty, or thought about work or Frank Clarke. Tired and more than a little pissed, he decided that Patty wouldn't look lovingly on being woken by him rambling and Clarke could wait until morning to be exhumed again.

CHAPTER NINE

Peter and Giles were sitting on the hotel terrace overlooking Regent's Park. It was a beautiful day, but with a chilliness that took the edge off the strong early morning sun. Peter's journalist friend, Valerie Loring, had arrived a couple of hours before and, over breakfast, they had told her everything. Peter was now giving her a snapshot of Gerald Wright. Giles watched her as she listened with both hands wrapped around her coffee mug. She was small and friendly, with short spiky hair and a husky smoker's voice. During their story, she had interrupted them with sharp probing questions and made notes on her iPad. Her relaxed confidence and the way she listened, her eyes holding whoever was speaking, encouraged trust and openness.

Giles realised she was now looking at him, questioningly.

'What?' He was caught off balance.

'Are you comfortable with telling me all this?'

'Yes, of course.' He was hot with embarrassment at being caught not listening but watching and analysing her.

Peter smiled at him. 'Giles has spent too long searching through minds much darker than his own and has a focus that masks his true feelings. So, forgive him and tell me, sweetheart, what do you think?'

Loring took out and played with a cigarette and poured some more coffee into her mug.

'This Bateman guy seems to hold the key and if he is in Jersey, I might be able to find out where and if he associates with any of the local villains. I've got a contact at the Bureau D'Etrangers who owes me.' She thought for a moment. 'Don't you know someone in St Helier, Peter? Some rich lawyer or barrister?'

Peter looked at her in surprise then smiled. 'Good God, Val, did I bore you with all that? Must have been a long and wet evening. You're right.' Peter leaned back in his seat and smiled. 'Stephen Caron is one of the reasons I became a priest. He's very bright, hugely successful, never allows a weakness in those he deals with but has a large and good heart and a wine cellar to entice even the most abstemious Papist. He's a polymath with fingers in many pies and has gathered a great deal of wealth over the years. His main job though is as an expensive but sought-after criminal barrister, or was the last time I heard from him. I've threatened to interrupt his revels many times with my priestly presence and the austerity of the Catholic canon. Perhaps this might be a good time to make that threat a reality.'

Loring laughed. 'Sometimes, Father, you talk utter bollocks.' She glanced at her watch. 'I'm sorry, I have to go.' She finished her coffee, packed her things away into a large and battered soft leather bag, and got up. 'I'll see what I can dig up on Bateman and call you.' She smiled at Giles. 'You might well have something.' She shook hands with him, kissed Peter, turned and smiled at them as she went through the door into the main restaurant. 'Thanks for the coffee.'

'Well, now that Val is on board, I think we deserve a treat.' Peter called for the bill. 'There's a Monet exhibition at the Royal Academy. Let's cleanse our minds with a touch of genius before the night train stimulates us with its comfort and exquisite cuisine.'

They caught the seven o'clock train and found a seat in the dining car. The food was mediocre but edible and the wine was reasonable. Giles was relaxed and almost at ease as it sped through the night.

'Why don't you and I go over to Jersey together?' Peter said, as the waiter bobbed and rolled with the train, clearing the remains of the meal. 'It might be good for you to get out of the way for a bit, and if we do find Bateman, a bit of known authority might give him the urge to talk. I'll ring Stephen when I get home and Val will fix it for us to see this guy from the Bureau. One of them will know if he's on the island.'

'You're enjoying this, aren't you?'

Peter smiled. 'You know, strange as it may seem, I think I am.'

Giles arrived home just before midnight. There had been an hour's delay outside Derby and a long wait for a cab at the station. The house was in darkness. He went in quietly, locking up behind him, felt along to the kitchen, then gently shut the door and put on the light. On the table there was a sandwich and a note. He made a hot chocolate then sat down and looked at the bit of cereal box Patty had written on.

Lawson, your inconsideration is limitless! Why didn't you phone? Gerald Wright wants to get hold of you, by the throat from the sound of him. I've had a hard day so don't wake me.

Shit, he had forgotten to phone her again. He started to eat as his mind went through the positives of the meeting with Valerie Loring. She had taken him seriously. He was beginning to be sure that Clarke and Pargeter's deaths really were connected. And Bateman? What would they find out if he was in Jersey? Would he talk to them? If he was involved, that didn't seem likely. He finished the sandwich and the chocolate and was suddenly hit with tiredness. He washed the plate and mug, turned the light off, and crept upstairs, avoiding the creaky bits on the old steps.

The next morning came far too soon and Giles, still tired and muzzy with a headache that threatened to explode into a migraine, was tetchy and tired. Patty had woken him with a cup of tea at six thirty and shown little interest in his decision not to go to work and even less in his apology for not ringing. He tried to go back to sleep but the cacophony of the family's breakfast and preparation for leaving the house kept him awake. Why did it all have to be so loud? He was about to shout and stamp his foot when peace was restored as his three mad women left to go about their daily business. He was just slipping back into a doze when the ring of his mobile drilled into his head. He reached over and scrabbled around the bedside table until he found it and answered. 'Lawson.'

'Good morning, Giles, and how are you on this beautiful day?'

'Exhausted, grumpy, thick-headed, and once again bottom of the Lawson popularity poll. Apart from that, I'm wonderful.'

'Good. It will teach you to respect the sanctity of marriage and fatherhood. Now, listen. I've spoken to Stephen and we can visit and stay with him. He's going to have a bit of a sniff around too. Meanwhile I've got us a lift to Jersey on Friday morning with an old pal who has a four-seater plane and too much money, so...'

Giles interrupted. 'Peter, I can't just flit when I feel like it, Patty will probably disembowel me.'

'I'm sure you'll manage. I'll pick you up at eight on Friday morning.'

The line went dead. Giles threw the phone onto the bed. He had the strangest feeling that now he had shared his suspicions, things might soon slip away from the little control he imagined he had.

* * *

In London, Valerie Loring was at lunch with Isaac Joseph, owner of Fact magazine. He was trying to get her into bed and print, in that order. She had no problem dealing with the first, but the second was more difficult. He was offering an open brief and much more money than she was getting now, plus the recognition a major heavyweight monthly would bring. Joseph was around forty, two stone overweight, with millions, possibly billions, in the bank. He was South African, had clawed his way from poverty to the top of the wealth heap, and was probably the most ruthless bastard she had ever known.

The reason Valerie was at La Coquille today with Joseph was because Nigel Davidson, Managing Editor of the Chronicle, had a personal quest to destroy him. To that

SINGLE CELL

end, he would encourage any liaison that might get near enough to Joseph to pick up solid evidence of misdoing or scandal. It didn't matter whether it was business or on a more personal level. Corruption, money-laundering, even underage sex would all be welcome. It was the last thing she wanted to do but Davidson was obsessed with the man. When Loring told him about the invitation, he saw it as an opportunity of getting her close enough to have a chance of discovering something incriminating about the 'odious twat'. Davidson would pursue it until he struck gold. Then he would destroy him.

Loring thought Joseph too smart to let slip anything that might weaken his position. Although Davidson was a bit of an arse, he mostly gave her a free hand and rarely played the heavy boss. So, this time, to keep him happy, she accepted the offer. She didn't disagree that Joseph needed taking down, but her energies could be used in a far better way than sharing time and space with the little toad. Sadly, it was also her thirty-fourth birthday and, although there was no one special in her life, she could think of loads of people with whom she would rather share it. She'd even take Davidson at his most arsey.

'So, what do you say Val… Val?'

Joseph was leaning across the table towards her. She tried frantically to focus on what he had said.

'Sorry?'

'A little token! It is your birthday, isn't it?'

How the hell did he know? Well, of course he would. His pack of ferrets would have bagged every usable snippet of her life before he approached her, anything that could be used to tip the balance. It was what she

93

had done with him, except that had just been her rifling through his mostly locked-down bins, and she wanted nothing from him!

He gently placed a delicate Cartier watch in front of her that would have gone a long way to paying off the mortgage on her Battersea flat. For the briefest of seconds, she was tempted, but the price was too high!

'No thank you, Mr Joseph.'

'Why ever not?'

She looked at him for a moment.

'Because then you would expect me to sleep with you.'

Joseph laughed loudly. 'You really are the most exhilarating woman I...'

Valerie slipped back into her thoughts, one part of her brain scanning for any titbits of interest or something that needed reply, whilst the remainder thought about Giles Lawson and Peter and what they had told her. It was a trick she had perfected over years of being bored shitless by people who had little she wanted or needed to hear. Only occasionally did it let her down, as with the watch, just now.

As Giles and Peter had unfolded their suspicions yesterday, she had felt that tingle, that almost visible fluttering in the stomach, when she knew that this had the potential to be a story worth the pain.

* * *

In the City, David Amebury opened his office door. His PA, Carly, looked up.

'Yes, Sir David?'

Amebury smiled at her. 'Anything pressing?'

'Not until your meeting with Mr DeRigers at one thirty.'

'Good. Anybody needs me urgently, I'll call them back in an hour.' He shut the door, picked up his mobile from the desk, and keyed in a number. 'Charles, it's in motion.'

* * *

Giles spent the day making arrangements for his trip. He told Jill that he would be away until the following Wednesday or Thursday and then organised Mike Florence, his deputy, to cover for him until his problem with Gerald was sorted out. The garage said his car wouldn't be ready until the end of the week but promised to deliver it and pop the bill and the keys through the door if nobody was home. He bought some flowers and a silk jacket for Patty and a DVD boxset of Game of Thrones for the girls. What a pathetic little man he was, bribing his family to be nice to him and let him go away without any harsh words!

Just as Giles was poaching eggs for lunch, Peter called.

'Val is on the move and has arranged for us to meet her Bureau D'Etrangers contact.'

'So, she's really up for it then?'

'Seems like it. Can't chat, got a date with Bobby Grant on D Wing, who wants to confess his sins and come over to the dark side.'

Giles laughed. 'Sounds like fun. Make sure he knows that it's only you that gets to wear the dress.'

He spent the afternoon lying on the sofa, listening to Verdi's Otello and trying to piece together everything he could remember about Bateman. The house phone was on message mode, his mobile on silent, and his thoughts tumbled and fell as the music washed over him. As he sank deeper into the music a memory surfaced. It was something that had happened a few months before Clarke's death. Clarke had badly hurt another prisoner who had beaten up Bateman because he refused to deal some crack for him. Although he didn't play tough, Clarke was, and because of his strength and size, wouldn't have been a pushover if he'd been attacked, even if there had been more than one of them. He would have broken bones before they managed to overpower him and that would have been messy, loud, and noticed. It would have needed someone he trusted to get close enough to do it. Bateman was the only one in a position to do that. He had to be connected. Giles tried to remember when Bateman was taken into the infirmary. Was it the same night? He should remember but couldn't, and as he got drowsier it was harder to focus on anything. Then he made the mistake of closing his eyes and his musings slowly faded and disappeared.

The next thing he heard were the twins coming in from school and arguing loudly.

* * *

Ralph Bateman looked out of the window onto a narrow street. Being stuck in this small dark room was worse

96

than being in prison. He had hardly been out of the small fisherman's cottage since he'd arrived in Jersey over four months ago. One good thing though was that his asthma, apart from a couple of mild attacks, was behaving. It was probably because now he rarely missed taking his medication. His mind slipped back to the night he had faked the attack that got him into the infirmary. After he'd sneaked back to the cell, killed Clarke, and gone back to the ward, he was given something that they said would keep him out of it for a couple of days; make sure no one suspected him. He didn't know what it was they'd injected into his leg but it was powerful. He'd been in and out of consciousness for three days and thought that he was being seen off too. He wasn't though, and they were right to do it to him because nobody had doubted he was ill and so there was no question of his involvement in the death. When the Enquiry had finally come up with the suicide verdict, he knew he'd got away with it. They, whoever they were, had promised him a change of identity and a new life in Australia or New Zealand. So far though nothing had been offered and when he took a deep breath and asked about it the answer was always the same, 'You have to be patient. It will happen soon but only when they're ready and everything is in place.'

Their understanding of 'soon' seemed very different to his. He was fed up with his own company and even when the two guys looking after him were there, they didn't really talk to him. Occasionally they allowed him out when it was dark but only if accompanied by one or both of them, like the night they'd taken him to a restaurant in the old port.

Outside the cottage he was never on his own but one time he had managed to escape for a few hours. It was a meal trip with just Marcel, who was the friendlier of the two and that made him just about bearable. When Marcel was on his phone and had lost interest in him, Bateman went to the toilet and managed to open the window and climb through it. He wasn't sure what he was going to do, just wanted to be on his own, perhaps find someone who'd help him. He went far enough away from the restaurant to feel safe and then hit the gay bars, cadging drinks at first and then ending up on the beach with a guy he'd picked up in the second or third bar and who had paid for everything from then on. He couldn't even remember whether he had enjoyed the sex or not. In fact, he remembered very little except that when he had been found he was on his own. Marcel had punched him in the face and then dragged him into the sea, holding his head under the water until he thought he was going to drown. Then he had taken him back to the cottage and the two of them had beaten the shit out of him. He was in agony for days and thought he might go blind in the eye Marcel had put his boot in. Eventually though, apart from a red spot, it got better. Once he was able to talk after the beating, they had questioned him for hours about the man he had been with, but he couldn't tell them anything. He'd had an asthma attack after that but surprisingly it hadn't lasted. After they stopped the questions, he had been locked in his room for three weeks. He hadn't tried to escape again. If there was a next time, they promised to kill him, and he believed them. Recently they had relaxed things a bit and only shut him in there when they went out.

In his heart he wished he had never been pushed into the killing, but the chance of freedom and money to someone who had nothing and no hope for the future was more than he could resist. He had even enjoyed the relationship with Clarke. In a funny way Bateman had begun to feel fond of the strong, silent man who never spoke when they had sex but cried when he reached orgasm. He had even said that they should find someone else to take him out, but they painfully persuaded him that making any more suggestions like that would be a serious mistake on his part. He had no choice but to do what they wanted. He knew that it was either no Clarke and a new life or the end of his own miserable existence.

He'd worried that, at the last minute, he wouldn't be able to do it but, in the end, it had all been too easy. He had come back from the infirmary and after they'd had sex the big man fell into a deep sleep as he always did. He had injected him with something to keep him from waking up. It had then been simple to tie the torn sheets around his neck and haul him up with the help of one of the infirmary orderlies. Whatever the drug was, it had disappeared by the time they did the post-mortem. After that, he had enjoyed a certain respect from the few prisoners and screws that were involved. He still felt a twist in his gut every now and then about his betrayal of the man who had protected him. Hopefully, as time passed, that would go or fade enough for him not to think about it. He had to leave the past behind when his new life began.

He heard the outside door open and then the key being turned in his lock. 'Did you get some beers?' He stopped as Marcel came in with a gun in his hand. 'What the fuck are you doing?'

Marcel was calm. 'I'm sorry, but it's not my decision.' He smiled as though it was all going to be all right. After all, it was only death getting in the way.

'For Christ's sake...'

The gun coughed twice, punching two holes in Bateman's heart. His face took on a look of amazement and he crumpled to the floor.

* * *

That night Giles made them dinner and, despite things being a little tense between him and Patty, they all watched a couple of episodes of The Crown on Netflix. The presents had of course helped him rise to almost acceptable in the good dad and thoughtful husband stakes. The only problem with Patty's was that he wasn't too hot on shades of colour and the jacket was the wrong green. She had, however, really liked the style and would change it at the weekend or live with it. He had left it until the girls had gone to bed to tell her what happened on the trip to London and about the planned one to Jersey. She surprised him by thinking it a good idea. If they found Bateman then at least they would know one way or another. It would make her life easier too as she had a rush job to get done by the weekend and would have to work early and late to get it finished in time. The girls could look after themselves for once. She also humoured him by agreeing to tell whoever might be interested that he was going on a fishing trip to the Lake District. Anyone who knew Giles at all would know that was bullshit. He had never wanted to fish in his life, let alone spend days trapped with relentless enthusiasts boring him shitless.

* * *

In the road outside their house, Sean Hallam, still and shadowy, in a car parked close enough for him to see but far enough away not to be noticed by the family, watched as the light went out. He stretched and sighed. His eyes felt scratchy and his back ached. He was getting too old for all this. He would stop soon. Choose to go rather than have to because he was past it. Perhaps this would be his last one. He smiled at that thought, started the car and drove slowly down to the end of the road before tuning the radio to BBC World Service and speeding up.

* * *

Roger Alsopp looked at his watch. Eleven fifteen. Time to call it a night. He was exhausted. He had returned an hour ago from a North West Crime Prevention Committee in Manchester. The drive back had taken him much longer than it should after an accident caused chaos on the motorway. It had been a long, hard meeting with the bloody politicians once again getting in the way of a strong crackdown on violent crime. He and the Police Commissioner were fighting a losing battle against political pressure that wanted to push forward a policy of understanding and psychiatric rehabilitative investigation. They had cited the case of a twenty-three-year-old labourer who had killed a severely disabled pensioner and then tried to burn her house down. His father had abused him as a child. He had left school at sixteen, had thirty-two convictions for theft, regularly beat up his common-law wife, and their two-year-old child had been subsequently taken into care. A suitable choice for compassion! Jesus Christ!

He breathed deeply. Getting angry with them wasn't going to help. He had to play the politics game and hope that he could find a way of manipulating them into applying a bit of reality in their analysis. His mobile rang. He took it out of his pocket, recognised the number.

'David.'

'Sorry it's so late, Roger, but I wanted to run something past you tonight.'

'Okay?'

'Our Jersey connection has been broken. Charles was in full accord. I felt strongly that we had to treat it with some urgency and act without a majority vote.' Amebury paused. 'The other matter is in hand too. The same firm will handle the new contract. Agreed?'

'Agreed.' He stopped at the knock on the door. 'Just a minute, David. Come in!'

The night shift Inspector stuck his head around the door.

'What is it, Jim?'

'Sorry to disturb you, sir, there's a bit of a panic on, a hostage situation on the Endersley Estate. A guy is holding his wife and two children at gunpoint. The ACC's in

Manchester but leaving there now. Superintendent Paul is on his way as OIC until he arrives. Mr Duggan should be there in an hour.'

'Thanks, Jim, I'll go over now on my way home. Ask someone to bring the car round, please.'

'Right, sir.' He went out, shutting the door.

'I'll have to talk later, David. Do whatever you think is best.' Alsopp cut the call and hurried out of the office.'

* * *

It was six-thirty the next morning. Giles was having breakfast when Peter rang and told him that their flight to Jersey had been changed to that morning. He'd pick him up in about forty minutes. They had to get to the airfield by eight-thirty. The friend flying them was on a tight schedule.

The girls had left at six as there was a school trip to Stratford and Patty, after dropping them off at the bus, was going to start on the rush job before anyone else came into the office. They had decided that he should be up and about as well and he had made them all breakfast; trying to load up on the brownie points. It worked and they all kissed him before they left, although Patty's little peck meant that he still had some way to go before he got into serious credit with her... or she might just have been distracted by her day ahead.

Giles had a shower, threw some clothes into a bag, searched for his iPhone charger, which he found in Kate's room, and his wallet, which was in the kitchen under the paper. His passport, for some reason, had been put in the cutlery drawer. He left a note on the table and was waiting outside when Peter drove up.

Ten minutes after Peter picked up Giles, Hallam arrived in a van with a plumbing company logo on the side, checked that Giles' car was still there, and stopped in a different spot to the last time, a bit further away and opposite a cul-de-sac. He wore a black beanie hat and his work jacket collar was turned up with his face partly hidden. He'd had to change a flat tyre on the way and was later than he'd intended. He poured some coffee from a flask, then opened a packet of ginger nut biscuits, took one out, dipped it, and got it into his mouth before it went too soft. He was settled in for the day and turned up Today on the radio. It was seven-twenty.

* * *

Giles and Peter landed in St Helier just after one and were met by Stephen Caron. He was a large fat man in his late sixties with a thick silver beard and a shaved head. He hugged Peter tightly.

'Let me breathe, for God's sake!'

Caron let him go, moved back and studied him.

'Jesus, it's good to see you. You're looking a little fatter than the last time, but then aren't we all.' He laughed joyously, deep and loud. 'And you must be the prison guy.' He held out a large, surprisingly soft hand and took Giles'. 'Good to meet you, my friend. If your man is on the Island then we should know by the end of this afternoon.'

'Really? How?'

'Time for all that later.' Caron put an arm around each of the men and walked them towards the exit. 'Unless my saintly friend has changed much for the worse, I think a little liquid stimulation will help us to focus our minds.'

Nice subtle arrival, thought Giles, as the chortling Father Christmas pushed them through the doors into the sunshine of Jersey.

Giles, Peter, and Caron were sitting in Bar Suisse. It was six o'clock and Giles was beginning to feel pissed. They had been drinking all afternoon and he was the only one on which it seemed to have any effect. Stephen had first taken them on a tour of St Helier in his scarlet Bentley. He gave them a rundown on the low life of Jersey as they went. There didn't seem to be anyone or anything that he didn't know about and he certainly appeared at ease around the diverse criminal fringe, or so it seemed to Giles. Peter had told him that Caron had been one of the most respected criminal investigation lawyers in France before he moved his business to Jersey. He had started investing his money in land there years ago and now he owned a good deal of property and dabbled in any little schemes that might keep age and boredom at bay.

Caron listened carefully as Giles and Peter told the story from Clarke's death up to the present, occasionally asking them to repeat something. When they had finished, he sat very still for a moment, then got up and told the barman to look after his friends. He asked them to excuse him and went out.

'How did you get to meet him?' Giles asked. Peter smiled.

'It's a long, long story, boy, involving the theft of some priceless and sacred artefacts from a little church in Provence that I looked after for a while. I'll tell you the whole tale one day but enough for now to say he recovered them all for us. We didn't question how he'd done it.' He laughed 'I'm also the only one ever to drink him under the table. It only happened once but I don't think he has ever quite forgiven me.' He topped up the glasses. 'If he is here, then Stephen will find him.'

Fifteen minutes later Caron came back into the bar. 'Well, we know where Bateman was, but he's not there now. The house was rented for a year and it had another couple of months to run. It was deserted and there was nothing there to tell us anything. The place had been given a serious cleaning. An old guy who lived opposite said he last saw someone go in yesterday. Apparently two men moved in about three or four months ago and he had seen both of them at various times and thinks that, once or twice, he caught sight of someone else, always at night, but he couldn't be sure whether it was a man or a woman. He gave us a pretty good description of the two he'd seen clearly though. One I didn't know, probably someone from the French mainland, but the other is Marcel Bonnere, not a pleasant man. He's hired muscle and his only loyalty is to whoever pays him the most. I thought he'd left the island after he was incriminated in the murder of a guy who had raped and killed the seventy-year-old mother of a Jersey-born Marseille gang boss.' He smiled at the look of horror on Giles' face. 'An even dirtier world, Giles, than your prison.' He called for the bill. 'For the moment, there's nothing more we can do, so I'll take you to my house while we wait for more news.'

He clapped Giles on the shoulder. It was like being hit with a mallet. He might be fat but there was a lot of muscle there too. 'Things are moving, my friends. I think the game is on'.

CHAPTER TEN

Simon Bartenson was in turmoil. What in God's name was he going to do? He was drowning in the knowledge that he had become part of the evil he had been desperate to destroy. He still craved revenge and didn't want anyone else to suffer as he had, but this was too much. He was struggling blindly to find peace for himself and his darling Jess, their spirits bound in suffering by the profanity of her death. He had welcomed the biblical requital of an eye for an eye, but he could now, in no way, accept the killing necessary to protect the monster they had created. It had to stop. He had to stop it, whatever the consequences. His life was merely a bleak existence as it was and, sometimes, he welcomed oblivion. He would write it all down from the very start then, if anything happened to him before he could tell it to anyone, the story would still get out and the killing would be stopped. He would do it tomorrow and send a signed hard copy to his lawyer to keep safe. He would tell the others of his decision to quit and give them the option of shutting down before he went public. It would put him at great risk but that was of little concern to him.

There was a knock on the door. 'Professor Bartenson, are you there? It's Maggie Dell. You said you wanted to see me at eleven.'

Simon opened the door. Maggie was shocked by the way he looked, his face drawn, eyes red-rimmed and flat. 'Are you all right?'

He forced a smile. 'Yes, I just didn't sleep very well last night. I'm sorry to have kept you waiting, Maggie. Please come in. Can I get you a coffee and a biscuit?'

* * *

Sean Hallam was sitting in a battered Range Rover on the hard shoulder of the A1 (M), talking on a mobile that was a long way from being smart. He bought them in bulk, burner phones, for one-time use only. When he needed to make contact, he would text the number then wait for the call back. He looked drab, middle-aged, was casually dressed, and wore glasses, the sort of person who wouldn't draw a second glance and certainly not be remembered. It was a look he had perfected over the years and which helped keep his particular skills in high demand. 'It's been dispatched and processed.'

Amebury spoke quietly and Hallam had to cover his other ear as a large lorry passed. 'What about the local contract?'

'The principal has travelled to the far north. I'm on my way now. Agreement should be reached within a day or so.'

'Good!' The line went dead. Hallam went over the conversation he'd had with Lawson's wife. He said he had picked up her mobile number from the answer phone and was trying to get hold of Giles. His number wasn't on the message. He told her he was an old university friend of his, their year group was planning a 'twenty-fifth anniversary' reunion and he had stupidly agreed to arrange it. He was friendly and chatty and made the wife feel at ease. She told him that Giles had gone to the Lake District on a fishing break. She sounded a nice woman, if a bit eager to get him off the phone. It was mid-morning so she was probably busy. It didn't bother him. He was a bit pissed off that he had wasted a day before they told him that Lawson had gone away. Very few contracts went smoothly though, and, in this sort of job, you had to be able to adapt quickly.

He started the Range Rover and put on Radio Four. He would listen to the afternoon drama. The radio, always BBC: World Service, Four, Four Extra for old comedy, Three and Six when he wanted music. It was his friend when driving long distances and kept his mind and spirit relaxed.

* * *

In Jersey, Giles, feeling out of place and wanting to touch reality, called Patty's mobile but it was switched off. He left a message, trying to sound calm and chatty, but he didn't expect her to listen to it. Mostly she communicated by text. She might call back if she saw he'd phoned, but she was probably focused on her deadline so he didn't expect she would. Neither of the girls answered theirs, but then they never did. If he thought they might have any interest in what he wanted to say, he used WhatsApp. They had a family group that Giles kept promising to keep up with, but he would rather talk than read. He'd have to give in to it one day if he wanted to know what was going on in their lives; or get into Facebook, but that would probably just depress and worry him about the sort of people with whom they seemed to have fun. Still, just trying to contact the family helped and by the time he joined the others he felt less wound up.

The meal that Caron had given them was fantastic, Beef Wellington and then a delicious pudding made from pineapple and melon mixed with cream and coconut liqueur. Not the healthiest option, but it was bloody lovely and worth the guilt. He didn't have to tell Patty. He felt he deserved this extra bit of naughtiness with all that was going on in his life. He looked at Peter and Caron walking ahead of him down the wide hallway, its walls covered with British and American film posters of the nineteen forties and fifties. They were laughing at something Peter had said and had the easy closeness of old friends.

It was hard to believe that he was in Jersey, looking for an ex-convict who might be involved in a murder and staying in the luxurious house of a man who, if not moving on the dark side himself, certainly edged easily around it. Caron was witty, erudite, smart, and quick to pick up and process what was said, responding with clear and clever arguments. Giles enjoyed the chat; the speed and variety of the topics they covered kept his mind spinning but sharp and speedy in response. They had touched on climate change, the UK's new place in Europe, water shortages in Africa, and the place and responsibility of the Church in today's fragile and fractured communities. Caron seemed to be an extraordinary man, as was Peter, who continually surprised him with his chameleon skills and lack of priestly habits. The strangest thing though about Peter was that he seemed perfectly at home here, not just with Caron himself but also in the world he inhabited.

Malo, introduced as Caron's old friend and assistant and who didn't look as though he was there for his domestic skills alone, had served the food, poured the wine, then excused himself to check on progress with locating Bonnere. Caron, Peter, and Giles were now on their way to watch the lawyer's favourite film, Charlie Chaplin's The Great Dictator.

In the small, cosy room, as they settled into the plush seats, Malo came in and whispered to Caron, then went out again.

'A little good news, my friends. Bonnere will be with us in a couple of hours. He was about to take a breath of sea air but was persuaded to join us for a nightcap. We should have enough time to watch this piece of genius. Perhaps, Giles, your search will soon be over.' He waved his hand at someone hidden behind a small window in the back wall. The lights dimmed and went out and the screen began to flicker into life. Giles looked across at Peter, who was smiling happily, then settled down in his seat and tried to concentrate on the film.

* * *

Valerie Loring leaned back in her chair and stretched, screwed up her eyes, then focused on the screen and read through the last few lines she had written.

Unless these preening titans of industry are exposed and the human and environmental atrocities they have perpetrated over the years, in the name of innovation and progress, are brought to...

She stopped. What a pile of shit! She deleted it, put her Mac to sleep, and looked around the room. There was hardly anyone there. What the hell was the time? She glanced at the clock on the wall. Jesus, no wonder the place was deserted. It was just after eleven p.m. She grabbed her jacket from the back of the chair, threw the laptop into her bag and walked through the tangle of screens and phones that in a couple of hours would burst into life with the activity of fresh news and deadlines. She passed the night news editor's desk. 'Goodnight, Tim.'

Tim Godley, a thin man with neat curly hair and a thick hipster beard, looked up from the proof he was reading.

'Finished?'

'No, just writing shit. I'm going to retrain as a masseuse and move to Margate.'

'Good idea! Special rates for old mates?'

She squeezed his arm. 'Only those with something worth getting my hands on! See ya, gorgeous.'

'Night.'

All day she'd had trouble keeping her mind on the fight of the First Nation Communities against the giant Maltby Corporation of Canada. It had faltered and fallen out of focus because she kept slipping into what Peter and Giles had told her. It was always the way her stories developed and grew. If the seed was right it rooted, eased its way into her consciousness, and found space to form. She'd already started to delve and discover and had collated all the prison suicides over the last five years in the UK. It was all on her laptop, but she'd printed out a hard copy. She was going down to the boat tonight and would work on it in the morning. Somehow, spreading the pages out on the floor of her small cabin gave her a better overall picture and she could make notes as they came into her head.

She went down the stairs to the underground car park and got into her ancient Land Rover. It started first time and she drove up the ramp and onto the quiet streets. Everybody took the piss, but it was an old and trusted friend and a lot more powerful than it looked. The only drawback was the noise of the engine and the need for thermals, jumpers, and thick coats in winter when the noisy heater decided to stop working or blew out cold air instead of hot. She would have to replace it but needed to find the time to think about booking it in.

She loved driving at this time of night. Crossing the river on the Richmond bypass she could see down to the village of boats on the Thistleworth Marina. The water glinting from the pontoon lights, shadows hiding the treachery of its tidal pull. It still gave her a strange feeling! She had lived there when she first came to London and still missed the care, warmth, and friendship shown to her by the diverse and colourful boat people. She had loved it and had many happy memories, but when somebody had drowned near her boat, its spell was broken.

The day the body was found, she had been at a party the night before and arrived home around four thirty in the morning and crashed out. Early the next day she was woken by sounds and voices around the boat and had dragged herself out of bed to see what was happening. It was normally very peaceful. The body was in a pool between boats, with the exposed riverbed around it. It was a young guy, Rod, who had bought an old canal barge with his girlfriend and was doing it up to live on. She had gone home late but Rod and a mate had stayed on drinking and smoking dope. The mate had crashed out and the theory was that Rod had been on deck and somehow fallen into the water and drowned, his body caught between the boats as the tide went out. They thought that with the tidal flow at that time of year, he had gone into the water sometime between four and six in the morning. Valerie had been sure she hadn't heard anything as she passed his boat at the bottom of the walkway onto the pontoons. But she'd had a lot to drink! The thought that she might have been able to help had brought nightmares of scratching noises on the bottom of her boat and cries for help. She thought it would go away, but it didn't. It had taken away the security and comfort she had felt living there. After three months of not sleeping or suffering nightmares of the drowned blaming her for not saving them, she sold the boat and moved in with friends until she found her apartment in Battersea.

She'd had to leave her cat Cabbage on the marina, giving her to a couple with two young daughters who loved the little Burmese/Siamese cross and always looked after her when Valerie was travelling. She knew they would all have happy lives together but there was still a jagged tear in her heart for the little cat who used to meet her car outside the marina and sit on her shoulder when visitors came to the small boat. She warned them not to come near, with a scary scream and sharp claws. She was a fierce little thing when roused, but also a warm and loving bundle when they were alone together. Just like her, then!

It had taken her six years to get over the drowning and buy the boat she now used as a workspace and hideaway. It was moored further out than she really wanted, at East Molesey. But her love of the river had returned and she spent as much time there as she could. It was a converted lifeboat called Olive Oil and had cost her the ten thousand pounds she had inherited from a great-aunt. It was tiny with one cabin but had an engine. She could just about afford to keep it and pay the mortgage on her studio flat in Battersea. It meant scrimping on other things, but worth all the sacrifices she made by not buying clothes or a newer car or going out much.

She parked in her space at the lock, walked across the bridge, slippery at this time of year, unlocked the door and went in, switching the lights on. There was a phone on the wall and the message light was flashing. She threw her bag on the bed and pressed the play button.

'Hello, love, give me a ring when you get a chance. Hope you're well. Dad sends his love.' Her mum had this knack of making a few words speak volumes and a shower of guilt sprayed over her. She always rang the boat, would never ring her mobile, and hardly ever switched on the one she had given her last Christmas. She'd ring her tomorrow.

'Val, I think we're on to something. Sit tight, I'll ring you in the morning. Tried your mobile but it was off and guessed you'd be here tonight.' She didn't have a landline at the apartment and only a few close friends and her family had the number here. She smiled at the sound of Peter's voice. It was safe, warm, and easy, and she realised how much she had missed him. Apart from the meeting with Giles Lawson, it had been a couple of years since they had spent time together although they'd kept in touch by text and email.

Valerie was suddenly overtaken by tiredness. She stripped off her clothes and crawled into bed, kicking her bag onto the floor. She put out the light and was asleep within minutes.

* * *

Giles, Peter, Caron, and Marcel Bonnere were sitting around the table in the large kitchen. Behind Bonnere stood Malo and one of the three men who had delivered the reluctant guest to the house half an hour before. Bonnere looked less than happy at this enforced visit and his bloody, bedraggled appearance suggested he'd struggled to refuse the offer. His initial outrage had subsided with Caron's soft, calm, and deliberate questioning. He had now lapsed into silence and was staring at the tiled floor. Stephen nodded to Malo who took out a gun and gently pressed it to Bonnere's head. Giles started to protest but Peter touched his arm and shook his head.

'Well, my friend, have it your own way. I will count to three and then Malo will send you to a better place.'

His eyes never moved from the other man's face. 'One. Two.'

'You're off your fucking head.'

'Three.'

'All right,' screamed Bonnere, 'get the cunt to move the gun.'

'Thank you, Malo, you can relax.' Malo removed the gun and slipped it into his pocket. 'My dear Marcel, I would ask you to remember that you are in the presence of a man of God, so please be kind enough to temper your language. I think perhaps we should move to another room for our chat. Take him into the study.'

The two men helped the trembling Bonnere out of his chair and led him towards the door.

'If you will excuse me.' said Caron. 'Peter, get Giles a drink. There's brandy in the cupboard. He looks a little shocked.'

He went out. Peter got up and crossed the kitchen. Giles followed him.

'For Christ's sake, Peter, who the hell is he? I'm way out of my depth but you seem to take it all in your stride.'

Peter handed Giles a large drink and then poured himself one. 'Sit down.'

Giles sat. Peter stood at the end of the table looking into his glass. Giles waited. He was angry, confused, and scared shitless by what had just taken place. Peter turned a chair round and straddled it, resting his arms on the back.

'I bent the truth a little when I told you how I met Stephen.' Giles started to interrupt. 'No, hang on, let me finish. The artefact bit is true, but I had known Stephen for several years and it was he who approached me. I first met him before I became a priest. I was living in France and had become friendly with someone who, unknown to me, was part of a drugs gang. I was dragged into it when he was nearly beaten to death by someone he'd upset by trying to skim off more than his cut on a cocaine deal. It was a warning that time, but one more slip and he'd be dead. He asked for my help. He wanted to get out of that world but he was trapped in it. He already knew too much for them to let him walk away. I said I would help him.' He chuckled at Giles' look of disbelief. 'It was a time in my life when I wasn't as pure as I am now. Anyway, it was then that I met Stephen. He was a criminal investigator with the Marseille police. His mother was Sicilian, his father Anglo-French, and he had UK, Italian, and French nationality. He was a linguist, so useful to government agencies. I was given his name, contacted him, and he persuaded me to think not only of my friend but also the greater good that bringing this gang to trial would achieve. So, I began working for him and in time I went undercover. I found out that I was good at it and, more to the point, enjoyed the challenge. Sadly, my friend was killed, but that only made me more determined. Over a period of six months we destroyed a multi-million-dollar drugs business. After that I was bottom of the cartel Christmas card list and Stephen decided the safest thing was for me to join him when he went into private practice. So, I did, and for several years, I loved every minute of it. Then a case turned particularly nasty and a woman I was very fond of died. I went off the rails for a while, but through Stephen and a dear friend of his, a monk, Monsignor Bagrielle, I came back to life. Something had happened to me though. A conversion, if you like. I decided to dedicate my life to God, so I joined up. Over the years I became involved in a small faction, working within the Catholic Church, that investigated crimes against the Papal Banner. In reality, its brief was wider and the spectrum less clearly defined. It was and is a fairly secret cabal.'

He stopped and smiled at Giles. 'Do you know the origins of that? It was a name given to five unpopular ministers of Charles II whose initials made up the word 'cabal'. There you are, a bit of useless information to impress your girls.'

Giles moved impatiently.

'The team was run from a secret department in the Vatican and it became my life. It was a good job and gave me reason for getting out of bed. Then I had a bad car accident on an investigation in Spain and was told to take life more as a man approaching middle age. So, I eventually came back to the UK and ended up where you and I met. I have kept in touch with the shadows of the past and occasionally helped out in one way or another, otherwise I am as you find me today. Close your mouth and have another drink.'

He got up, fetched the brandy bottle, and poured a large measure into each glass. 'As for Stephen, apart from you, he is the most honest man I have ever known, although our ideas of right and wrong differ at times. I have in the past trusted him with my life and still would.'

Giles looked at him in amazement. 'Would he have killed that man?'

'I don't know. Probably. Not that Bonnere would be a great loss, from what he told us. I think Stephen would know how far he could push him and, more to the point, it worked, didn't it?'

Giles was still having difficulty taking it all in as one shock leapt on the back of another. This man, one that he thought he knew well, was rapidly becoming an enigma.

Caron came back into the room. 'I'm afraid that an interview with Mr Bateman will not be forthcoming. He has sunk, by now without trace, somewhere off the coast of France, helped along with a couple of bullets to the heart, administered by Bonnere. I am sorry but it looks as if your trip has been wasted. Bonnere doesn't know who was paying him. He received the location, time, and a mobile number, together with his money, at a local café, where various undesirables have a safe box. Never mind, Giles, perhaps your journalist will come up with something.' Peter smiled at Giles who stood up and went over to Caron.

'Are you going to kill him?' Giles said quietly.

Caron looked shocked then roared with laughter. 'Good God, no! I'll hang on to him until you're on the mainland and then pass him on to a friend of mine in the Bureau. I'll see if there's any more I can find out for you, but I don't hold out much hope. At least it gives a bit more weight to your theory.' He paused for a moment. 'I'd take great care if I were you, and if you need anything you can contact me through Peter. Now I suggest you get some sleep and I'll sort out a lift home for you.'

'Sleep?' said Giles. It was the last thing he heard as his eyes closed.

Peter caught him as he fell and smiled at Caron. 'Just a little dose to stop him worrying all night! I always carry it, comes in handy when dealing with troubled souls. Let's take him to his room.'

Giles was starting to gently snore as Caron picked up his legs and they carried him out.

* * *

Hallam's mobile started to ring and he checked his mirror, indicated, and pulled across the lanes on to the hard shoulder and stopped. 'Yes?'

Amebury's voice came through calmly. 'There is a change of plan. The initial northern insurance doesn't run out for another couple of days so it can wait. The package is at the usual dispatch. It needs delivery as a top priority.' The connection was broken. Hallam took the SIM out of the phone, bent it, and threw it out of the window, then started the engine. He drove to the next junction then turned off and went back down the way he had come, dropping the mobile he had just used onto the road. A car travelling behind ran over it.

Simon Bartenson read through what he had written. His neat, sloping script traced his journey from the time he had met Amebury, through Cynthia Orbanon, and the reasons for his involvement as well as detailing all the killings they had set in motion and why those particular victims were chosen. He was ashamed and disgusted that he had allowed himself to become part of this arrogant force of retribution. But it would be finished now, and if they didn't agree to his conditions, he would make sure that they were stopped. He wasn't afraid of anything they might do to him. He had gone past that. He placed the ten pages into an envelope and addressed it to Valerie Loring. She was a journalist who had interviewed him the year before for an article on violent death and the ongoing effect it had on those closely related to the victim. She had impressed him with her understanding and compassion and he had felt able to open up enough to let her feel a little of his grief and loss. He put the sealed package into the larger envelope to be sent to his solicitor with a covering letter of instruction that, on the occasion of his death, the contents were to be passed on to her. It gave him a strange sense of peace to purge himself in this way and a great weariness came over him. He switched off the light and lay down on the large ancient sofa, sinking into its soft, deep cushions, and pulled the thick wool rug over him. As always, just before he went to sleep, he saw Jess's smiling face. He felt her lips brush his cheek and her soft, beautiful voice whispered, 'Goodnight, Daddy.'

As sleep began to wash over him, his tears came, slipping down his face as he let the loneliness and hurt seep out.

* * *

Peter and Stephen Caron were standing at a large picture window overlooking the harbour of St Helier, the lights of the moored boats sparkling.

'It's beautiful,' said Peter.

Caron smiled.

'I suppose I'm used to it. Refill?'

'No thanks.'

'You're getting old, my friend.' He paused, looking out into the night. 'I suggest Giles' family are kept out of harm's way.'

'You think that they're in danger?'

'Three deaths so far, Bateman, Clarke, and Pargeter. Yes, I think it is possible.' He poured out a large measure of brandy. 'What about a holiday in Provence?'

For a moment Peter looked puzzled, then smiled.

'The Sacre Coeur.'

'A beautiful part of the country and they will be safe there. The monks are a hardy bunch and will keep them as their own. You remember Janine Moncleur?'

Peter smiled again. 'It seems like another life. I suppose it is. I'm sure Giles would agree to it, the only hurdle might be his wife, Patty. There's no way she would go without knowing the full story.'

'Then tell her. There will be no cost. I will arrange everything.' Caron put a hand on Peter's shoulder. 'I suggest you call her early in the morning and that they leave tomorrow night. Now, my friend, I will say goodnight. If you need anything, just pick up the phone. Malo will be there.' He turned and walked out of the room. Peter looked at the view again and then followed a moment later.

* * *

David Amebury lay awake, watching the shadows and listening to the music of the city at night. It had been like this the past week. He had managed no more than a few hours a night, surface dozing, and yet he was not tired. If anything, his awareness was heightened. His thoughts had a clarity and insight that he had not felt since the anger and brutality of his youth as he battled his way, ruthlessly, to the pinnacle of multi-national corporate power. It was then, just as he had attained his personal Nirvana, that fate threw him off-balance. His son was taken savagely from him when he had tried to help a friend who was being attacked by two men. They had beaten and kicked him to death, but the friend had survived. It had changed Amebury's drive for wealth and power into an obsession for retribution by cleansing his world of the sort of human trash that infected it. It became an engulfing passion that filled his heart with a hard and cold resolve. Chance had brought Charles Stanley Moncrieff into his tortured life and together they had sought out the remaining members of the group. It had taken time to find and persuade them to consider his proposal. It was months before he had proved to them all that it was the only way to bring some sort of sanity into a world where cruelty, violence, and inhumanity had become a way of life. He had deliberately played on the rawness of their own personal stories and slowly manipulated them into accepting that revenge was the only way to find closure and peace. After retribution against the killers of their loved ones was achieved, the group was bound together by what they had done and the idea of continuing the acts of vengeance for other victims took seed and grew. They were all wealthy high achievers, had a desperate longing for a way to rebalance the world around them, and were tied by the same bonds. The acronym of their surnames' initials had given them the anonymity of AMOEBA, a single-cell shape-changing organism. They had built a powerful and protected organisation. No one, apart from the core members of the cell, he and Moncrieff, knew who carried out their instructions or how they were paid. They had been so successful that they seemed impregnable, but a crack had now appeared that could damage their resolve. Simon Bartenson seemed troubled and vulnerable. Amebury was determined that there would be no weak link. It had to be removed! Nothing could come between AMOEBA and the work it had to do.

CHAPTER ELEVEN

Valerie had woken at around six and couldn't get back to sleep. She had left the heating on and the boat was warm and cosy. It was raining and the pitter-pattering on the roof reminded her of childhood caravan holidays at the tiny seaside village on the Pembrokeshire coast; lying in the bunk-bedded room she shared with her sister, listening to the outside world, safe and secure, comfort just a wall away from where her parents were asleep. It was there, when she was five or six years old, that she had heard the sounds of her mum and dad making love. The low moans had frightened her and she had gone in to see if they were all right. She smiled as she pictured her mother's embarrassment and her father's attempt at covering his rapidly disappearing erection. She had crawled into bed with them and snuggled up tightly to her mum. God, they must have been frustrated.

Suddenly she felt lonely and wished there was someone in her life to share her memories. Her parents' marriage wasn't perfect but had a stability that was bound by love and respect. Perhaps it was her work that had taken her into shadows that shut off trust and commitment. Yet, in truth, although it was tempting, she couldn't really blame journalism. She had always been the same way. It was a familiar and comfortable emotional space. On the positive side, it helped when she went undercover on a story. She was able to easily detach herself from the reality of who she was and become the blank canvas she had to be to create and live that false and temporary life.

She picked up her mug, drank the last bit of cold coffee, and struggled to clear her mind.

'All right, stop now, enough of the psycho shit.' She was surprised at the sound of her voice and looked around as though someone might have heard her. Jesus, she had to stop talking to herself before it slipped out in public. In truth, for her, it was just an extension to the habit of reading the drafts of her stories out loud. It helped distance them and gave her objectivity. But having a conversation with herself was a step into the world of sad and lonely. She filled her mug again, opened her bag, took out the pages of prison suicide reports and spread them over the floor. Right, focus! What would she find? She started at the earliest date and slowly began working through.

* * *

Giles felt dreadful. His head ached and his mouth tasted as though it was coated with three-week-old milk. It had taken him several minutes to work out where he was and another five before the events of the previous day flooded over him. He remembered sleep being mentioned, then nothing else. Had he really drunk that much? What the hell was happening to him? In a week he had gone from the comparative normality of prison life to a place where people were killed without thought and he, for fuck's sake, was expected to accept it, not as the norm, but as a reality that was out of his control. Then there was Peter Satorri! Well, shit, that was another mind-blower.

The door opened and the man himself entered carrying a tray with coffee, water, and what looked like a large brandy.

'Good morning, Giles, I trust you slept well.' He opened the curtains and sunlight flooded the room. Giles groaned and looked at his watch. It was nine-fifteen.

'I feel close to death or madness, possibly both!'

'A trait of the satyristic lifestyle you lead, plus a little help from Mogadon.'

Giles glared at him, confused.

'I slipped you a Mickey Finn. I've always wanted to say that!'

'Why did you do that?' Now he was angry too.

'Stephen thinks Patty and the kids might be vulnerable, so he suggests moving them to a safe house in France.'

'What the fuck are you talking about now?'

'There is a monastery in Provence where they will be out of harm's way. It's just a precaution, and a holiday for them. They will be protected.'

Giles dragged himself out of bed and got close to Peter. 'For Christ's sake! Protected from what? Why should they be vulnerable?'

Peter moved away from him.

'Why do you think Bateman was killed? To stop him talking! Who opened up the suspicions in the first place?' He let it hang in the air for a moment. 'The easiest way is to stop you asking questions.'

It sunk into Giles's confused brain surprisingly quickly. 'Oh, shit!'

'Exactly! I want you to phone Patty. Tell her that Val will pick her up at my flat.'

Giles turned from the window. 'What about the police?' He answered himself. 'No proof and no way of knowing who is involved. Right, I'll talk to Patty, but I'll have to tell her everything.'

* * *

Moncrieff had been trying to reach Jacinta since Sarah Jane died. She wasn't returning his calls and texts and her office had said that she was on holiday and they had no way of contacting her. He had written to tell her the same day but felt the need to hear her voice. It was as though the sound of it might ease the pain that wrapped around him. He had never stopped loving Jacinta and, perhaps, now, after all these years apart, they could find again the comfort of just being with each other. Then he smiled as reality took over. Greed, jealousy, and power had split them. The memory and taste of it was still too strong. Now with the death of their grandchild the final tie had been broken. A line came into his head from a long-ago read book: "All the riches of the world have not the unity and might of a single strand of love returned nor the power to heal of a hand freely given."

His second mobile rang and chased off the memory. It was his secure phone, encrypted and safe. Only the members of AMOEBA knew the number.

'Moncrieff?' Lady Anne Evan-Dyer's affected bass voice rang in his ear. He held the phone away from him.

'Anne, what can I do for you?'

'Cynthia and I need to talk to you.'

'Go ahead.'

'Not now, tomorrow, at Lakeside. It'll have to be early. I've got a board meeting that I can't miss in the afternoon. Shall we say seven-thirty? It's important.'

'Right, I'll be there.'

'Good man! This is just between the three of us.' He had a fair idea what they wanted but this was no time for weakness. Should he phone David? He decided not. He would have to leave early to reach the Kent cottage by that time. He picked up a picture of a smiling Sarah Jane, with I love you, Grandad written in her swirling letters, and felt a white-hot stab of anger in his stomach.

* * *

Valerie had reached the end of her trawl through the reports scattered around the floor by nine o'clock. The rain had eased and a watery sun slipped through the portholes. She had a list of prisons. No pattern there. A little more than half the prison deaths were of those locked up for murder or rape or both and were connected by the savagery of the crimes. The remainder were remand prisoners or non-lifers. Those she discarded. She started to make a list of the thirty-two victims. She realised she hadn't eaten and had just poured out a bowl of granola when the phone rang. She sat on the bed and picked it up.

'Hello, lovely girl.'

'Peter, what news?'

'No "nice to hear your voice"? Ah well. Straight to the point. Bateman is dead, murdered by one Marcel Bonnere, who later today will be delivered to the Bureau to face justice. Bonnere had been holding Bateman for the last few months and receiving instructions by snail mail at a safe drop. If he had known from whom he would have told us. I have a feeling that things could get out of control. Stephen thinks we ought to move Patty and the kids. I think he's right. Giles is calling her. Can you pick them up this afternoon and take them to Tinerton? It's south of Birmingham. There's a flying club there and Stephen's plane will drop us off and pick them up. I'll send you directions. I have to be in London for a day or so, but I think it best if Giles keeps a low profile. Can you find him somewhere?'

Valerie laughed. 'You don't give a girl much time, do you? He can stay here. Look, I've started going through the prison deaths and...'

'Tell me later, sweetheart. Will you ring your contact at the Bureau and explain that we've had to come back earlier than planned? You know, Val, I'd forgotten how much you mean to me. It's good to know you are close again.'

The phone went dead and she put it down, bemused. It rang almost immediately. It was Peter again. 'Sorry, didn't give you a time to meet Patty and the girls. Four at my flat. I'll see you at Tinerton.'

Valerie lit a cigarette. She felt that familiar flutter in her stomach. The hunt was on. She went back to her lists, then checked the time on her phone. Shit, she had to get moving. She'd need to leave by eleven at the latest to get to Peter's by four.

* * *

'Giles, are you out of your mind?' He flinched as Patty's voice challenged his fuzzy head. He felt he was slipping over the edge, so why the hell shouldn't she think he'd gone mad?

'Patty, please just do it. Things are…' He struggled to find a suitable word. 'Unpredictable, and I want you and the kids safe until, oh, Christ, I don't know, it's all over. I've got to go now. Please be there at four.' How he needed her to give him a hug and tell him that everything would be fine and that it was just a bad dream that would disappear with the light of reality. How she would hate him for wanting that. 'You're not a child, Giles, I need you to be a man, not a little boy.' Jesus, how many times had he heard that?

'All right, we'll be there.'

'I love you.'

'Yes!' The line went dead. Giles looked at the phone and threw it on the bed.

'Shit!' he searched for a cigarette. Despite his confusion, he felt a flutter of excitement in doing, openly, what had been forbidden since Patty and the girls decided to take control of his pleasures. That first deep dive into the murkiness of his lungs brought a flurry of nausea and a reminder of why stopping wasn't such a bad idea but, by the third drag, he was beginning to force his body into capitulation and calm.

133

There was a knock on the door and Peter walked in.

'Did she breathe fire?'

'What do you think?'

'But she agreed?'

'Yes.'

'"That which woman has, and man can only dream of..."'

'What?'

'"You have lived too much of the flesh to understand the purity of choice."'

'Can you speak English? My brain is too addled at the moment to follow your disturbed ramblings or decipher which film you're quoting. She didn't like it and she will probably cut my balls off at the first opportunity, but she and the kids will be there, if that's what you mean.'

'Good! Not a film at all. It was Socrates.' Peter looked out of the window. 'I think we're in the middle of something deeper and more dangerous than just the deaths of Clarke and the others. It has a whiff of conspiracy but, whatever it is, it will have to be seen through to the end. We know too much to walk away now. That's why Patty and the girls must go. You can be got at through them. We don't know who is involved and until we do, we can't trust anyone. Stephen and Val will be able to supply anything that is needed. Now, our genial host is arranging an early morning feast, the last breakfast, as he puts it in his heretic way. We had better not keep him waiting or Malo may be sent to hurry us along. Anyway, I'm bloody starving. Are you coming?'

Peter held the door open then followed Giles out.

CHAPTER TWELVE

It was early-afternoon when Hallam parked his Range Rover in the multi-storey car park, locked it, and walked down the three flights of steps onto the half-light, rain-drizzled streets of Hull. He looked at his watch. Two hours!

'Professor Bartenson has a tutorial which finishes at five,' the bored voice had told him when he called. He felt the slight pangs of hunger he always got at this stage of a job and he was impatient to get on with it but would eat before he caught the bus to the university.

* * *

Patty went to the bottom of the stairs. 'Come on, girls, we've got to leave in five minutes.'

'We're coming now,' Sally shouted back.

Once the girls got used to it, they started looking forward to the adventure. Unusually and without questioning, they had accepted Patty's version of the story. It helped that they knew that their father could be unpredictable, but the real reason was that anything that broke the tedium of school was something that was to be grabbed with both hands. The school itself had been a little more difficult in agreeing the request but, in the end, had accepted Patty's plea and gave them permission to miss a week to visit the girls' dying great-aunt in France. Any more than a week would be difficult as they had important tests coming up. Patty wasn't worried about the missed work. The girls could easily catch up. Despite Giles' assurance that it was just a precaution, she was still unsure that it was the sensible thing to do. She had to trust someone she didn't know and, although he was an old friend of Peter's, she felt vulnerable. She must be as deranged as Giles to have said she would do it.

The girls thumping down the stairs distracted her and she quickly checked the kitchen, shut the door and went into the hallway.

'Is Uncle Peter coming too?' Kate asked.

'I don't know. Have you got everything you want to take?'

'Yes, Mum.' Kate and Sally looked at each other. How old did she think they were? She'd be asking if they'd remembered to go to the toilet next! They smiled at each other in understanding.

'All right, I'm sorry I spoke.'

The twins had this telepathic thing going on and she knew they used it to deride what they thought were pointless questions or reprimands from her. They never did it to Giles. He wasn't that much of a challenge.

Patty opened the front door. 'Let's go!'

Valerie was outside Peter's flat. She'd arrived about half an hour earlier with five minutes to spare. Giles' family was late. She picked up her mobile and punched in a number. Nothing happened. 'Stupid bloody thing.' She opened the window and tried again. It worked.

'Basnet.'

'Dave, it's Val, any joy on those names?'

'Would you believe the system's down?'

'Fuck!'

'Couldn't have put it better myself. It should be fixed in an hour or so.'

'Can you bike it to the boat for me?'

'I'll drop it off on the way home, if you like?'

'No Dave, I probably won't be back until very late.' God, he was so predictable. She had just managed to stop the 'fuck off' that would be her default retort. She took a deep breath and told herself that he was doing her a favour and not to piss him off. 'Thanks, but I mightn't be here. Tell them to drop it in the box at the top of the marina in the slot with my name on. It's easy enough to find, there's a big sign on the top of the box saying "MAIL".'

'Righto, babe.' She shuddered. 'Perhaps another time?'

'Yes, perhaps.' Not while I've still got a hole in my arse, mate. 'Keep it to yourself, Dave. It's important.' She had to make sure that he didn't just drop it in when he was talking to his tabloid mates in the pub, particularly Wayne, a nasty little prick on the Sun. It wouldn't be deliberate. He might even think they had some info that could help. But the scavengers he knew were sharp and self-obsessed. A story is a story wherever it comes from, and there was enough for them to start digging. Of course, there was no moral thread that couldn't be shredded for story-first glory.

'Will do! You owe me.'

'Bye, Dave, thanks.' How about I don't rip your jugular out next time you try and get close to me and suggest 'we get mucky, babe'.

Should she ring her mum while she was waiting? No, she didn't have time. She'd only go on about the cost of phoning in the day. She'd never understood that the paper paid the bill and, if she did, she wouldn't think it right to make personal calls. Valerie put the phone back on the passenger seat. She'd try tonight. Just then a car pulled into Peter's drive. She got out and walked towards it as it came to a stop. The doors opened and Patty and the girls got out.

'Mrs Lawson, I'm Valerie Loring.'

'Patty, Kate, and Sally.'

'Hi.' She smiled at the girls.' I'm sorry to rush you but we'd better get a move on. It's a good hour and a half's drive from here. I'll tell you all I know on the way.'

They unloaded their bags and got into the Land Rover, the girls not happy about the lack of covering on the back seats. Valerie passed them a couple of rugs that were in the luggage space.

'Cover the seat and use the other one if you get a bit cold.'

* * *

The bus came to the Hull university stop and Hallam helped an old lady off and handed her the large bag he had carried from her seat. She smiled at him. 'You don't meet many gentlemen these days, thank you, pet.' She looked as though life had worn her out as she shuffled off, stooped and slow.

He watched her go. Age terrified him. He remembered his grandmother as she slowly descended into a dementia that stole away her life and her love for his grandfather. The gentle old man had cared for her and only his grandson had seen those moments when he cried until he exhausted himself and a broken sleep gave him temporary peace. His love for her was complete and he would never have left her or allowed her to go into a home. A week after she died, he took an overdose of sleeping pills and followed her.

Hallam looked at his watch. It was almost time to meet the professor.

He hadn't spoken to anyone on the bus, not even the old lady he had helped off, just smiled at her. It had been too crowded, with the schools just out, for the driver to check the official pass-like card he had waved at him. He had got a childish pleasure from not paying. His mind went back to his early training, having drummed into him that people remembered voices more than looks. He rarely spoke and when he had to, he would change the cadence very slightly. It was always enough.

He walked briskly across the road and onto the university campus. He had a plan of the buildings in his head and he moved amongst the students as though he was part of the life there. He found the building he wanted and walked up the narrow staircase into the gloom of a past age.

* * *

Stephen Caron was flying the small Cessna and Peter was sitting next to him. Behind them Giles was immersed in his thoughts. His whole world was upside down. Why hadn't he left well alone? What had made him ferret about, not happy until he found something? Oh, Christ. What was going to happen? He heard the crackle of the radio from

Caron's headphones but the noise in the small aircraft made it difficult to hear what was being said.

Peter turned around. 'Better strap in, my boy, we don't want you flying through the windscreen if our driver is a bit careless.'

'At least my problems would be over.'

'Stop whining! What would I do without your cheery face with which to share a glass or two? Here we go.' The plane turned sharply and started to descend. 'I've always loved this bit. The most dangerous moment of the flight.' He turned to the front with a chuckle.

Giles strapped himself in. He closed his eyes and crossed his arms. Don't fight it. Let fate take its course.

* * *

Hallam stood opposite the door of Bartenson's room, his back pressed against the wall, his hands, in their latex gloves, hanging loosely at his sides. His breathing was slow and easy. He had watched as the girl left and had got used to the sounds of the building. Each one had a different tone and character. This one wheezed and groaned like an old sow settling down to sleep.

It was time. He closed his eyes and centred the power he would need. His mind took in and accepted the inevitability of what was to come. He moved across and tapped quietly on the door just below the nameplate.

'One moment.' Bartenson's voice was muffled through the thickness of the wood. Hallam waited, perfectly still, balanced, in total control. The door opened and the professor stood framed there.

'Yes?'

The fist struck the centre of his throat, cutting off the rattle of surprise as it crushed the windpipe and snapped his head back, forcing the life out, before Hallam, moving fast, caught the body, pulled it inside, and gently laid the dead man on the worn Persian carpet. He turned the key. It had taken twenty-two seconds. He paused, listening for any sound or reaction outside the room. There was nothing. No change within this building's world except the one living force that had departed it.

From a plastic bag under his jacket he took the length of rope that he had found by the side of the road on his way into Hull from the motorway. 'Always use your initiative and plan around what you have or can find to use.' He made a noose with a large knot, slipped it carefully over Bartenson's head, and tightened it at the exact spot his fist had struck. He looked around the room. You could always find something if you knew what to look for. High up in the corner a pipe crossed from one wall to another. It was thick and, supported as it was on each side, it would be strong enough. He moved the overstuffed armchair that was under it and put an old dining carver in its place. He carried the body over and with seeming ease held it upright on the chair while he threw the rope over the pipe and pulled until the feet were just touching the seat. He tied it off tightly, jumped down and, with Bartenson's feet, knocked the chair to the floor. The pipe groaned at the extra weight but held. The late professor swung gently, his hurt at last eased, his spirit already searching for his darling Jess.

Hallam quickly searched the room. On the desk was a large envelope addressed to Price, Davies, and Pugh.

It was what he was told to find. They knew their man and his predictability. It made sense. He took out a small flat piece of plastic and used it to slit open the envelope and slide out the contents onto the desk. There was an envelope addressed to a Valerie Loring and a covering letter. He put them back into the opened envelope, folded it, and put it into his coat pocket. He noticed the picture of a young woman on the desk and faced it towards the corner of the room. She had the same eyes as her father. It was a nice touch. Attention to detail could mean the difference between success and failure. He stood by the door, listened, waited until he was satisfied, then unlocked it and checked out the corridor. It was clear. He glanced back into the room, shut the door quietly, then locked it again and pushed the key hard through the gap at the bottom. Again he waited and listened then moved quietly and confidently away. It was less than a quarter of an hour since he had entered the room.

* * *

'Twenty minutes,' Caron said.

'Right, and thanks for everything.' Giles undid his belt and stretched. 'I'm exhausted and in no state to placate Patty.'

'Don't be pathetic.' Peter opened the door and started to climb out. 'À bientôt, mon frère.'

Stephen smiled. 'We will meet again soon, Father, take care. I am too old not to miss a good friend. Don't worry, Giles, no harm will come to your family.'

As they walked across to the small airfield buildings it started to rain.

Giles looked at Peter. 'I'm not going to enjoy this. The sight of blood has always upset me particularly my own.'

'I'll take the girls to the bar but, have no doubt, my thoughts will be with you.'

'Thanks!' They entered the small reception area and found Patty and the girls at one of the tables. Peter kissed Patty.

'Hello, gorgeous, where's the intrepid Val'?'

Patty looked drawn. 'Making a call outside, I think.'

Peter held his arms out to Kate and Sally. 'Come, my little sprites, and help me find liquid sustenance.' The girls stood up and he put an arm around each. 'There may be violence here yet awhile and twould harm your youthful eyes to see the like.' The girls giggled and they moved to the bar.

Giles sat down. 'I'm sorry, Pats, I didn't know what I was getting into. I need to know that you and the girls are safe.'

'Have you gone to the police?'

'I can't, this thing is everywhere. It has to be! I don't know who is involved except that people in high positions have been covering up. But I do know that men have died, not directly because of me...' he paused, 'Shit, yes, one was directly because of me. Jesus Christ, Patty! I feel as though I'm living in the middle of a film. But it's not, it's real, and I have to go on with it. If I told you what I knew about our friendly man of God...'

Patty put her hand gently on his. 'I know, Valerie told me quite a lot about Peter on the way over when the girls were plugged into their ear pods and explained what you had to do. What concerns me is that we've had to leave our home, my rush job, which by the way has really pissed the client off, and the kids' school, all at a moment's notice. And we could be in danger and, more to the point, someone is probably going to try to kill you.' She angrily pushed back the tears as they started. 'Giles, I'm scared. Someone rang just after you left. He said there was a college reunion. His name was Mack. I told him you were in the Lake District. He had a lisp. Tell me that everything will be all right.'

The words had tumbled out, bouncing over each other. Giles felt his chest tighten and it was hard to breathe. He tried to relax and speak normally. 'It will, I promise.'

'Now say that without crossing your fingers.'

'How did you know?'

'I'm holding your hand. Give me a hug, Giles.' They stood up and held each other tightly. Over Patty's shoulder he saw Peter and the girls coming back. Kate and Sally looked serious.

'Patty.' She pulled slightly away from him. 'Rasputin and his acolytes are on the way. We've got to be strong for the girls.' Patty nodded. Giles smiled as the girls reached them and cuddled closely into him. It was the first time they had done that in years.

Peter whispered to them, 'See, I told you, not a scratch.' He put an arm around Patty and Giles. 'We'd better make a move. Stephen gets tetchy if he's kept waiting. Val is outside with the car. If the young lovers can tear themselves apart, we'd better move.' Peter smiled but for once it didn't reach his eyes. Only Patty noticed and it chilled her for a moment until she decided she was being too sensitive and had probably imagined it.

Giles watched as Peter led Patty and the girls across to the plane and fought the urge to run after them. He was lost in this new reality of fear and uncertainty and struggling to keep his apocalyptic thoughts in check. What was he going to be hit with next? What other shock was lying in wait for him? His dad had been a bank robber, or his mum an assassin for the military arm of the Methodists? He saw his family climb into the plane, then wave. He waved back, wondering if he'd ever see them again. Peter slammed the door and turned away as the plane started to move. By the time it was approaching take-off he was back with Giles. They watched as the Cessna disappeared into the grey sky. 'Right, that's done, let's go.'

Giles, with nothing to say, followed him into the building.

The Land Rover was noisy and cold as they travelled at a body-rattling seventy-five down the motorway. They were all sitting in the front, which was easier for conversation but shit for comfort. Giles held the picture in his mind of the fuzzy faces of his family as the plane sped down the runway and into the air. He was only half listening to what Valerie was saying.

Peter nudged him. 'Giles.'

Giles started. 'Sorry?'

Valerie glanced across at him then back at the road.

'Who was the OIC on the Clarke enquiry?' she asked.

'Officially it was Peter Alsopp, Chief Constable of West Yorkshire, but it was actually his deputy, Patrick

Duggan, who sat on the Board. Nice guy. I tried to get hold of him after my little bout with Wright but had no joy. Why?'

'Just trying to get a full picture.'

It was very cold in the Land Rover and both Peter and Giles were frozen. Peter reached towards the heater controls. 'Any chance of a bit more heat?'

Loring sighed. 'Sorry, we'll have to live with it. The heater packed up a couple of days ago and I haven't had time to get it done. We should only be another hour or so.'

'Sweet Jesus, Val, we could die of hypothermia before then.' Peter reached into his jacket pocket and took out a large hip flask. 'I suggest a third each to warm the body.'

'You and Giles share it. I'll wait until I get home. Safer for you and me.'

'Then I suggest that we order our own thoughts and not battle to communicate over the gentle purring of your beast.'

Valerie smiled in the darkness. 'A simple "shut the fuck up" would have worked.'

'Ah, yes.' Peter put his arm around her. 'But such brevity would not sate the necessity for the verbal excesses of my ecclesiastic calling. Now, to cheer our hearts and warm our spirit, I suggest a little of Julia and Placido in Carmen. I take it this machine does have somewhere to plug in my phone?'

Valerie reached over them and fumbled in the open shelf and handed Peter a tape. 'It's an adapter, plug your phone in and stick the tape in the deck.' Her breath clouded against the windscreen and she wiped it with her hand. Peter took his mobile out of his pocket and connected it, pushed the tape in, and tapped the play button. He took a deep swig from the flask and then handed it to Giles. The music started. He closed his eyes and leaned back.

* * *

David Amebury spoke quietly into his mobile. 'It's done, no one will query it.' He paused. 'There was an envelope addressed to Valerie Loring. She's an investigative journalist at the Sunday Chronicle. I've asked around and the general feeling is that she's tough, doesn't give up, and is very good at what she does. I know it's short notice but I think we should meet at the farm tomorrow.' He paused. 'Charles, we cannot allow anyone to get in the way. You said you were meeting Cynthia and Anne so will you tell them, and I'll contact Alsopp.'

'Of course, David, but...'

Amebury disconnected, cutting off Moncrieff's response. He felt off-balance and needed a moment to find order. It was something that rarely happened to him and it was disturbing. He was surprised that the confirmation of Simon's death had unsettled him. It was not the decision to kill. That was an inevitable act of protection. The poor man had no fight left in him and his weakness would, in time, have given the others the shadow of doubt that might diminish their resolve. His gentle intellect and quiet strength had been slowly dissipating and he was tortured in his belief that he had become as culpable as those who deserved their fate. Amebury's relief that Simon was at peace now was an unusual feeling for him. Humanity rarely came into the aftermath of his decisions. His response to anything that threatened his position was pragmatic and ruthless.

He had to keep a tight grip on all of them. For now, the others seemed to be still committed to AMOEBA but he wouldn't hesitate to act again if there was more frailty.

* * *

Giles, almost numb with the cold and what was happening in his life, felt a sudden uncontrollable panic as an old enemy burst into his troubled thoughts. A fear of mortality had been with him since he was a small child and he could remember his father understanding his 'nasty thoughts' with a hard slap as he sent him back into his nightlight-buzzing bedroom. Even now he couldn't understand why it had happened and what had driven his father to do it. He would do anything to protect Kate and Sally from hurt and fear.

'Are you all right?' Peter's voice broke in, chasing the monster away.

'Yes, yes.'

'Good. We're going to hit the M25 and I'll be getting out to meet a good and true Christian man and arrange a little celestial help should we need it. You are going with young Val to her retreat on the Thames.'

By the time Giles and Valerie arrived at the moorings, the rain had become torrential and both were soaked as they ran from the car park and crossed the slippery pontoons to Olive Oil. Valerie had taken a large envelope from the mailbox at the top of the marina and had thrown it onto a small table covered in books, papers, mugs and other mess. Then she showered and changed. While she was doing that Giles had dried off and now sat in an old, large, and comfortable tracksuit, a relic of a friend of Val's who had outstayed his welcome. Giles' sodden clothes steamed in front of the small stove. Despite the turmoil inside him, he felt a tremor of excitement at being hidden from the eyes of the world to plot and plan. The small and cluttered space slipped him back to long ago, to nights at his aunt's farm in West Wales where, in the converted dairy, he and his sister fought against and finally tumbled into the happy sleep of today's joy and tomorrow's dreams.

The memories escaped as Valerie came back into the cabin, a cigarette in her mouth, her hair wet and swept back. The outsize sweatshirt she had on made her look childlike and fragile. She ripped open the envelope, took out the contents, read the note attached then screwed it up and threw it onto the floor.

'Dickhead!' She smiled at Giles, 'Not you,' and spread the papers out on the floor. 'Let's see if we can make any sense of this.'

CHAPTER THIRTEEN

David Amebury saw the missed call on his mobile. It was from someone who, unknown to the others, was an integral part of the creation of AMOEBA.

The two had first met thirty years ago. when David had killed three Afrikaners who were about to shoot them after an arms deal in which they were all players had gone badly wrong. Saving that life had been the most auspicious and empowering act of David's early career. Ultimately it was to provide him the pathway to the great wealth and power he now had. The two of them never physically met again after Cape Town but kept in touch. On occasions they had helped each other out in ways that would remain hidden to others but ranged from lawful to unlawful, finance to fatalities. Each knew where the other's bodies, in some cases literally, were buried. It made for a relationship that was symbiotic. It was this relationship that had steeled and shaped David's grief and fuelled his obsession for revenge. His one-time partner was the real power behind the AMOEBA throne and, without the emotional constraints of the others, was the only one who had a clear and objective vision of the strategy and skill that the gameplay needed. He was an expert manipulator who made others believe that they had direction and control of their destinies. Of course, they didn't!

Amebury deleted the number from his mobile and used one of the burner phones he kept in his office safe. It would only be used for this one call.

'It's David.'

'My old friend, AMOEBA has served its time. We must destroy it.' Calm and direct without hesitation, the voice was almost gentle. Amebury's surprise stilted his breathing.

'No!'

'We agreed the decision was always to be mine. I won't contact you again. Make the arrangements. You will not be affected! Now, after all these years, my debt to you is repaid.' The line went dead.

Amebury sat motionless, shocked, his mind whirling with the enormity of those few words. The end of AMOEBA! It was inconceivable, but there was no way out. He had no choice now but to set it in motion. He knew that he was protected but was saddened and disturbed by what he had to do. He was a realist, however, and one thing that he shared with this nemesis of his was an acceptance of the inevitable and an ability, once a path had been chosen, to act quickly without doubt or remorse.

* * *

Peter arranged to meet the two priests at a house in Shepherd's Bush that was owned, through an untraceable shell company, by his former employer, the Vatican-run Intelligence unit. The request to meet and the answer were in notes left in a numbered box at a small newsagents' in Forest Hill. It was the long-time safe drop of Gabriel, the only 'agent' left from Peter's time and a friend he trusted and loved. He hoped that Gabriel, at his age, had not succumbed to just using texts. Knowing him as he did, he thought the safe drop a good bet. Even if he used other ways of communications too, it would always be something he'd keep as a backup. Peter had signed the note with 'L'.

The two of them had been inseparable at one time. They angered and disturbed their superiors by their unpredictable and maverick methods, un-priestly attitude towards life and its temptations, and their sacrilegious choice of code names: Gabriel and Lucifer. They had been good together though. Very good! Not even their serious detractors would deny that truth.

Peter had not seen Gabriel for six years and he felt a tremor of anticipation as he climbed the stairs and opened the door. Two men were on the inside, standing either side of the doorway. A quick movement and he was gripped in a bear hug and lifted off the floor as the door closed behind him. 'For God's sake, Liam, give my ribs a chance or do I have to teach you a little respect for the cloth?'

The big man chuckled, put him down, dropped his arms, pulled away, looked deeply into Peter's face then kissed him on both cheeks. 'Lord, it's good to see you.' His voice was a gruff whisper, the result of a shattered windpipe and too many cigarettes.

Father Liam Orpizeski was the son of an impoverished Polish count who had fled to Ireland when the Nazis seized his lands. He had fallen in love with an Irish girl he'd met at a dance in Dublin. Liam was sixty years old and built like an out-of-condition heavyweight boxer but retained the grace and speed of a champion fencer. He had doctorates in theology and Chinese literature from Trinity College in Dublin, spoke five languages fluently, and 'got by' in several others, all in all, a pretty ordinary priest.

The other man was in his early thirties, very tall, and goodlooking with ice-blue eyes. Father Giuseppe Frinelli was Sicilian and had been working as Liam's partner for the last three years. He'd heard a plethora of stories about the exploits of the two old colleagues. Through his network of 'family' connections the young priest had a web of intelligence-gatherers that crossed the globe. His list of 'contacts' was enormous, influential, and at least sixty per cent of them came from the shady world of Organised Crime. He and Liam worked well together but came from different eras.

Liam took Peter's arm. 'Right, Father, time for a little sustenance, then you can tell your tale and we will make plans.' He led Peter along the hallway while Giuseppe locked and bolted the door.

* * *

In the large kitchen of his house, Sir Roger Alsopp looked at his wife. The anxiety she tried to hide was too near the surface. She snapped her head up to face him.

'Why didn't you say anything? Didn't you think I had a right to know? How can you put me through it again?'

Alsopp tried to be calm. 'There was no point until it had been confirmed.'

'When do you start?' Her tone was harsh.

'Not until the end of next month. I have to go to Kabul for a meeting before then. Don't worry, it'll be all right. I'll be well protected.'

Will I, he thought? It was a hell of a job. He had known two months ago that he was high on the list to head a new Afghanistan team that was advising on policing, terrorism, and public safety. His brief was to design a strategy and train senior officers in the police and military on assessing and gathering intelligence, improving the quality of response in detection and discovery both before and after terrorist attacks. It was a good career move and, for the six months that he would be out of the country, relief from the pressures of the last few years. His growing fear about the insanity of AMOEBA and the knock-on effect of the cover-up deaths to protect the beast they had bred increasingly disturbed him. His anger over Patricia's killing had seemed to dissipate and Bartenson's pointless death had, in some sort of way, convinced him that life after the loss of his daughter had to go on.

'Roger, are you listening to me?' Sylvia's voice was on the edge of hysteria. 'What if they kill you? What will I be left with? Patricia has gone. What would my life be worth? I am still bleeding for her.' She sighed heavily. 'Christ, you're a bastard. I hate you!'

'Sylvia, listen to me…'

'Listen to you. Why should I? Are you going to say anything? You've hardly spoken to me properly since Patricia died. Why the fuck would you start now?' She got up slowly and walked to the door. 'I don't want you near me.'

Alsopp was more shocked by her use of the word 'fuck' than of all the pent-up anger and frustration that he had released in her. She was right. He had hidden himself in his work. The ruthless dedication and immersion in his personal web of crime had become, together with AMOEBA, a type of sanctuary. They were the tools he used to purge the desperate need for revenge. Putting himself in the front-line profile of the Afghan job was an escape. But poor Sylvia, what could she do? He had to try to find a way to ease the darkness that engulfed her. He got up and his body ached with fatigue. He stood for a moment to harness some energy and then left the room turning off the lights.

* * *

There was still a little left in the bottle of Jamesons by the time Peter had finished his story. Liam tipped it towards him.

'Is the Pope a Catholic?'

Liam shared it between them. Giuseppe shook his head and the big man cackled breathily.

'Come on, lighten up, Gio. Now then, what to do? It's a hell of a story but first we have to find the core and very heart of this animal.'

Peter smiled. 'Easier said than done, it's buried deep but whatever we do must be soon.' Liam sat, his jaw pressed into his hand, his eyes narrowed as he frowned in thought. Suddenly he stood.

'Gio, get on your laptop.' He turned to Peter. 'Technology has finally trapped me in my twilight years

155

and, I must admit, it's a damn sight quicker than my lumbering mind.' He turned to a smiling Gio. 'You might well smile, but Peter and I have facts and faces within us that no bit of machinery could ever find. Get all you can on vigilante groups that have been active over the last ten years and a list of prison suicides of convicted killers for the same timeframe. Start with the UK and Europe! We'll need the crimes they committed, and the names of the victims and their close relatives. An organisation of this sort would need a lot of cash to support it. See if you can throw up anybody with money, power, and a reason. Ask around your nefarious family and associates, and, perhaps, get a replacement for the holy water, preferably Irish. Don't look so disapproving, it's a long time since Peter and I had a chance to tell tales and stimulate our failing minds.'

Giuseppe tried to look disapproving but gave up, smiled, and left the room.

Liam put his hand on Peter's shoulder. 'Tell me again about Bateman and the incorrigible Mr Caron.'

* * *

It was after ten when Hallam arrived at the cheap and run-down Paddington hotel and went to his small, scruffy room. No one saw him enter and no one cared. It had been two hours since he had picked up the message from his answer phone in the tiny Spanish fishing village where he lived. There was nothing but the caller's voice, nothing to link it to him at all. The instruction was, as always, brief and simple: Red Sail.

Once inside he took off the cheap raincoat, looked in the streaked mirror over the sink, removed the gum and cheek padding from his mouth, then folded his glasses and put them on the cracked shelf. He sat on the bed stripped of disguise, his grey eyes lifeless and his body weary. He sighed heavily and stretched out on the threadbare pink coverlet. The night sounds of the busy city wrapped around him as he examined the small room. How many places had there been like this? How many cities? How many contracts? Too many to count or remember in detail. There were one or two that weren't that far from the surface, but he didn't dwell on them. If he had, he would never have been able to do the job. He had also managed to qualify taking a life by his own set of standards. The criminal world was simple, those involved knew the risk, but sometimes those on the edges were more difficult. The late professor was one of those. He was led into a dark world through the agony of losing his daughter but his weakness in staying connected to AMOEBA, once her death had been avenged, was what gave Hallam reason. He had helped him to do what he would have done with the courage he lacked: be strong enough to take his own life.

Over the last year, however, Hallam had noticed that his focus was getting less defined and the edge that was an imperative was beginning to slip. That was dangerous! His concentration had to be absolute. It was time for him to stop and live what was left of his life in a place of peace and beauty. Soon he would go home. It was time. He relaxed his body and mind, breathed deeply, and slowly let himself drift into sleep. It was something he had perfected over the years and it now took him less than five minutes to go through the simple routine. Perhaps he should write a small self-help book and make millions from relieving other people of their sleep deprivation.

At midnight his phone vibrated.

'Spinacle.' His voice was muffled and toneless, the lisp pronounced.

* * *

Dave Basnet had done a thorough job. The details on the listed names were comprehensive. Giles and Valerie were sitting on the floor, an overflowing ashtray between them. Giles had, at last, found a good reason to smoke as many cigarettes as he liked and there was no one there who would remind him of the statistics of doom. There were two empty wine bottles lying between them, although one had only been a quarter full when they started. Giles moved them out of sight. Jesus, over the last week he had drunk enough for his liver to give him a kicking or, more likely, give up on him.

He and Loring had split the list in two. One had victims and their known relatives and the second, those that weren't known. Giles was aware of most of the suicides going back five or six years but not the circumstances of the deaths. All of them were killers and, in some cases, rapists too.

A few of the relatives he remembered from the phone-hacking enquiry and some were public figures, often in the business or social focus of the media. They made a separate list of those. But none of it was particularly helpful at first. Some of the victims and relatives were well known, especially to Loring:

1. The daughter of a high-profile actress, who had been tortured, raped, and then killed.
2. The son of an Anglican bishop who had been killed in a fight outside a gay club. The bishop died a year after his son, in a traffic accident.
3. The daughter of a headteacher at a private school who had been found in a wood, strangled and raped.
4. A publisher whose granddaughter was left in a coma after a violent attack and had just died.
5. The head of a multi-national corporation whose son had been murdered.
6. A junior minister whose sister had been killed when she interrupted a robbery at her house.
7. The owner of an exclusive hotel chain whose husband had died after a mugging.
8. The Chief Constable of West Yorkshire, whose adopted daughter had been the victim of an arson attack at her flat.

The final name was a university professor whose daughter had suffered an horrific ordeal of torture and multiple rape before she was killed. He was someone Valerie had met. She had interviewed him for a series she had written on the psychology of the criminal mind and the effect it had on the families of the victims. Attached to the notes was a report of his suicide the day before. Basnet had added a rider.

'He'd turned a photo of his daughter around so he could see her as he died. Sad bastard. If you want to have a chat, call me and I'll come over.'

Giles was tired, his eyes scratchy from the dull lighting on the boat. 'Needs a better light in here.'

'What?'

Giles, not realising he'd said it out loud, sighed and smiled. 'Nothing, just talking to myself, a result of living with three alpha females.' He stretched and lit another cigarette 'God, I'm shattered.'

Valerie tapped one of the names. 'Wasn't Alsopp heading the inquiry into Clarke's death? Or am I making that up? If he did then we might have a connection.'

'He was but got caught up in something else so Patrick Duggan took over. His mind lurched. 'Christ, he couldn't be involved...'

'At least it's something to start with and might lead us...' She suddenly stopped. 'Jesus, shit, of course.' She got up quickly and went to the crowded bookshelves running down one side of the cabin.

'What?'

'Shut up!' She scrabbled through the books. 'Where the hell is it?' She found what she was looking for in a pile on the floor. 'Got it!'

'I could do with another drink.' Giles words ran into each other and he tried to think if they had made sense. They must have done because Valerie glanced over at him.

'There's a box under the seat in the wheelhouse.'

Giles got off the floor uneasily, more pissed than he thought he was. He pulled across the thick curtain that hung over the doorway and went up the three narrow steps into the small wheelhouse.

Valerie sat down again and opened the book. She shook her head. She was feeling a bit woozy too. She forced herself to focus.

'Simon Bartenson gave me a copy of this book when I interviewed him for Criminal Mind. He had written the foreword and I'm almost sure I remember reading a quote from Sir David Amebury that he showed me.'

Giles came back in with a bottle, and unscrewed the cap, and filled their glasses. Loring read down the index and found the pages that related to Amebury. There were five. She flicked through them and discovered it at the bottom of the last page. 'Here it is. It comes from a "Reinstate Capital Punishment" symposium. Amebury was the keynote speaker. I have a feeling it wasn't that long after his son was killed.'

"Until harder and heavier sentences are handed out, crime will increase. There is no doubt in my mind that the death penalty must be reinstated for the offence of murder and custodial terms for rape and crippling injury must carry life, not ten or fifteen years, but life. There have to be sentences in parity with the suffering caused to victims and their relatives, by these animals. This is a priority and a deep passion for me. It is one that I will be pursuing to pressure the government to change its present abject policy of weak and ineffectual punishment. It has to be done before it is too late, before our society becomes totally degenerate and anarchic and law and order disappear."

'Not a man for forgiveness and understanding.' Giles tried the wine. 'This is nice'.'

Valerie could feel the excitement rising. She knew she was on to something. She turned to the publishers' details, sure of what she would find. 'Published by CSM. Charles Stanley Moncrieff!'

'So?'

'Don't be stupid, Giles. Bartenson, Amebury, and Moncrieff. It's a link between three of the names on this list.' She passed him the list of public figures' relatives. Had these rich and powerful victims decided to take reprisals into their own hands? 'Amebury sounded like he wanted to make something happen and, perhaps realizing the government would drag its feet, decided to have a go at it himself.'

'That's a bit of a leap…'

'Is it?' She sat down and picked up her glass. 'Let's take a break.' She put the wine down. 'I'll get some coffee then get into the Chronicle archives and see what I can pull out on this lot.'

'Bit late for that.'

Val checked the time on her phone. 'Yes. Suppose so.' Let's go through it again.'

Giles smiled 'Sure.' He downed the remainder in the glass. 'That's the last for tonight. If I drink any more, I'll be incapable of words, let alone thought.' He tried to stand but slipped and fell.

* * *

Amebury was exhausted. He sat back in his chair and rolled his neck to relieve the tension. He had cancelled the meeting for the next day at the farm and sealed the deaths of his former friends. He felt cold and numb. There was no emotion left. The only remorse he felt was in leaving Julia and knowing that nothing he did would ever bring his son back. He was lost in the infinite void of other worlds. It had been a waste of time and effort. Now that it was at an end, all the pain that had generated his actions surged back. He knew that he wouldn't be able to bear it. His reason for living was over. He was still for a moment then took out a sheet of thick cream writing paper embossed with his name and began to write. The words took shape in his precise and angular script. When he had finished, he carefully folded the single sheet and put it into an envelope. On the front he wrote, 'To my darling Julia'. He placed it carefully in the centre of the bare desk then slowly opened the drawer, took out the small pistol, and lifted it to his eye.

'Goodbye, my darling, forgive me.'

Then he pulled the trigger.

* * *

Giles slowly opened his eyes. He was disorientated for a moment then realised that he was lying on cushions on the floor of a boat, covered by a duvet and surrounded by paper, cigarette ends, empty glasses, and mugs.

The glow from the stove brought a shadowy focus and he saw Valerie Loring asleep in the bed that filled into the sharp end of the cabin. The moment of falling asleep was lost. He began to feel the fingers of paranoia as they traced possible scenarios onto his mind. Had he done or said anything stupid or, Jesus, pounced on Val? The fingers prodded harder. Had anything happened? Should he wake her up? See how she reacted to him?

He almost did but then a sliver of sense dug in. If he had done anything, she would have punched him and there was no blood or pain. His head was beginning to pound. He searched around the floor, found a cigarette and lighter and fired up. It sounded like an explosion in the gloom. His heart was racing. God, please don't let him have an attack of anything here. He would never be able to explain to Patty why he was in a boat with a woman and couldn't remember anything that might or might not have happened. Fatal was okay! It would be a relief. Well, not to Patty and the girls or Val. He breathed deeply and struggled then for a moment the swirl of fantasy lifted and reality calmed him.

He drew deeply on the cigarette, the smoke burning his lungs making him cough. He quickly covered his mouth with the duvet and finally it stopped. He hadn't woken her. Suddenly he needed air that was not the fetid cloud oozing around the cabin. He'd get out of the boat for a bit. The cold air would help clear his head. He crept out past the heavy curtain, opened the door and went out on to the pontoon. For a moment it worked and then he began to realize how fucking cold it was. It took his breath away and his body went into spasms as the icy wind sliced into him. He couldn't stay there so he threw himself back into the boat but got caught up in the curtain in the doorway and fell into the cabin bringing the thick material with him.

* * *

Hallam woke early, his head fuzzy from too light a sleep. He looked at the small clock, luminous in the pre-dawn dark of the room. It was five-thirty a.m. Already the sound of traffic was increasing as the city rose and shook itself awake. As always, at the start of the working day, he lay for a moment relaxing his body and clearing his mind.

Early this morning he had made three calls at intervals of five minutes each. Pre-arranged times, beginning from midnight, a strict routine for whenever he had need of their services. His instructions had been brief. Each one of them knew where to find the 'details' and, when the job was done, they would collect payment in the same way they always did.

He had prepared for this action from the time he had begun working for AMOEBA. Despite all they did to hide the identities of those in the group, he knew all about them, who they were and what they did. He had compiled a small dossier on each of them. Always protect yourself! Make sure that when the time came you would be ready; a step ahead; so, once the die was cast, you would leave nothing behind of your time with them.

He had always known that this day would come and so his plan was already in place. By now everything he had directed would be in motion and unstoppable. Then once his part was played, he would disappear for good.

He stretched and got out of bed. The room was bitterly cold but it wasn't a problem for him. He never seemed to feel the extremes. His body must have adapted to all those years of waiting and watching in all weathers and worlds. He filled the small kettle and switched it on. He waited as it boiled then poured it into the small basin and added some cold. There was a problem with the hot water and they hadn't sorted it out yet. He hadn't complained. Always keep the lowest of profiles. Nobody here would remember the Hallam he let them see. There wasn't even a shadow of the real one!

He washed, shaved carefully, then dressed in a dark tracksuit and began to create his identity. He parted his hair, keeping its natural curliness down with a thick gel, and speckled it with grey. He put in hazel contact lenses, padded out his cheeks, and changed the shape of his eyes with shading. It was enough. Never do more than a subtle suggestion. It was the first thing he had learned about disguise all those years ago. Then everything was possible and the excitement and anticipation of what might be stretched endlessly in front of him. It was all in the past now and over twelve years since he had left the government service and gone freelance. It was a long time in this game and more than a lot of his colleagues had managed. The list of those who hadn't made it into middle age was long and he had lost some good friends. It really was time for him to finish with this sort of life. Just the last act of this drama and then he was done.

He moved his head from side to side, checking his profile. It was good and the change was enough. He was ready. He was again the ordinary guy you wouldn't remember a minute after you met him. Looking into his eyes in the mirror, he allowed his real self to slip into this new mask for a brief flicker. Then he moved away, strapped a long thin knife to his wrist and packed what things he had into a small bag. He stretched latex gloves over his hands and removed all traces of his being there. He looked around one last time and then, satisfied, turned the light off and went out of the tired room, quietly shutting and locking the door behind him.

CHAPTER FOURTEEN

Alsopp spent the night in the spare room. He had tried to talk to Sylvia but she stayed locked in their bedroom, the sound of her tears seeping through the house and filling him with guilt. He had drunk too much coffee. It had not helped. He had slept fitfully and woken late. He spoke to her just before leaving. Her 'I have nothing to say to you' was worse than silence.

He went out to the garage. It wasn't locked. He must have forgotten to do it last night. He slipped the key into the ignition and for a moment sat there, his sadness overwhelming him. He almost went back into the house to try and reason with her but then, with a breath of resolve, he fastened his seatbelt and turned the engine on.

The explosion ripped the house apart and filled it with flames.

Lady Anne Evan-Dyer and Mohammed El Faroud had attended a charity gala at the Dorchester and arrived home in the early hours of the morning. It had been a good evening; they were pleasantly mellow and after making love gently had fallen asleep. They hadn't woken when the bedroom door opened and two shots were fired from the silenced gun, killing them both.

Charles Stanley Moncrieff left home early to drive to London and was just coming around a corner in the narrow lane connecting the driveway of his house with the main road when he saw the motorbike. It was lying on top of the leather-dressed figure, its wheels spinning. He slammed on the brakes and skidded to a stop, jumped out, and ran to the bike. He was undoing the strap on the black smoke-glass helmet when the thin blade was stabbed into his heart.

Cynthia Orbanon had left home early to reach the House of Commons, where she had a meeting with the Deputy PM. She was just pulling out of Dolphin Square when the shot shattered the windscreen and the car went out of control, her body slumped across the wheel.

* * *

Peter and Liam came out into the diverse community of Shepherd's Bush and walked towards the Green. They had been up all night, sifting through everything they had found. Gio had talked to one of his 'cousins' in America, who had got back to him a couple of hours later, with a name in Italy and a codeword that would ensure co-operation. It was almost three in the morning when the Italian had rung back. He said just one word: 'AMOEBA.'

Since then they had been cross-referencing the name but as yet had come up with nothing. The two older men had decided to refresh themselves with a walk and a fry-up while Gio carried on the search. They found a cafe and were now sitting surrounded by workers from a large building project on the site of an old church. Peter finished off the last mouthful of fried bread, egg, bacon, and sausage and pushed his plate away.

'That was fabulous, boy, one of the simple pleasures of life that I'd let slip from an occasional treat to never. Do you want some more tea?' Liam nodded and passed over the large mug. Peter went to the counter and waited while a huge safety-helmeted Pole ordered double helpings of everything. He looked over at Liam, who seemed to fit perfectly with these surroundings.

'Yes, mate?'

'Another couple of teas, please. I'll pay for the two breakfasts as well.'

'Right.' He put down the mugs, which were brimming with the dark, strong liquid. 'That'll be fifteen pounds forty.'

Peter paid him, went back to the table, and sat down. Liam looked at him for a long moment.

'I wonder how long it is since we did this last?'

'Too long!'

'You were right to get out when you did.'

'I had no choice, did I?'

'Even so, it was a good time. I've been thinking a lot recently about going back to a little parish in the West of Ireland and living out what time I have left to me dispensing sympathy, humility, and good wine to my adoring flock. I'm more than a little weary and often out of my depth. Youngsters like Gio are the future of this game,' he chuckled, 'and then, there's times like now, when everything is buzzing and I think right, you old bastard, if you've got to go then let it be with a bloody big bang. So, if you don't mind, I'll tag along this one last time and we'll see what mayhem the old farts can create.'

Peter smiled at him. 'I wouldn't have it any other way.' He got up. 'Hang on here for a minute. I'll give Val a quick call and then we'll make our way over there.' As he went out of the door he tapped in her number on his mobile.

Liam leaned against the wall and closed his eyes in pain.

Peter stood in the small park across the road from the cafe and watched an old couple dancing to music only they could hear. Loring answered.

'Hello, my little water nymph, how are you on this glorious morning? Did you manage to distract young Giles?'

'We found something in the stuff that Basnet left for me.' She told him what they had discovered and he gave her the name AMOEBA.

'It's from a good, if morally suspect, source. Anyway, have a think about it and we should be with you in about an hour.'

'I was about to go to the Chronicle. Who's we?'

'Hang on at the boat and you'll see.'

'All right.'

He started to walk over the crossing. The traffic had stopped but something made him look as the motorbike sped through the stationary vehicles. It shot past in front of him and as he leapt back the machete slashed at him by the pillion passenger just caught his cheek, then it was gone. There was hardly any blood but Peter's heart was racing.

A guy in a small car was stopped at the crossing.

'Are you all right, mate? Bloody idiots will really hurt someone one day playing games like that.'

Peter smiled at the man, 'Yes, I'm all right thanks, just gave me a bit of a fright.'

Peter waved and carried on across to the pavement. His legs felt wobbly as he struggled with what had happened. It wasn't a game. Someone had tried to kill him. It had been a long time since that had happened but luckily his instinct, if a little slow, just got him out of the way in time. As he approached the cafe a thought entered his head that froze the blood in his veins.

Liam was waiting outside. 'What happened to your face?'

'A little nick, that's all, time for that later.' He took Liam's arm. 'We've got to get to the boat.'

Valerie threw the phone on the bed. 'Peter's on the way here.'

The thick curtain was folded on the floor and even with the door shut and the heating full on it was only just about warm enough.

Giles had apologised for destroying her home, waking her, and drinking too much, but she had, after an initial explosion, found it funny and then gone back to sleep. Giles didn't and tidied up as best and as quietly as he could. He couldn't do anything with the curtain but when she woke again Val said it needed replacing anyway. He was determined to pay for it. She had at last accepted his offer and the new one was ordered and paid for online.

Then they got back to work and had just stopped for breakfast when Peter rang.

'They've come up with a possible name – AMOEBA. It doesn't mean anything to me.' Then suddenly it did! Her voice was almost a whisper. 'Oh, Jesus, the names on the list!'

'What is?'

She ignored him, scrabbled around the floor for a pen, found one and ran it down the list. She tried to draw a line through one of the names. The pen had run out. 'Shit'. She found another and scribbled it back and fore. It worked. She went back to the list drawing a line through some names and leaving others. Then paused and looked at them.

'Bartenson – Evan-Dyer – Alsopp – Amebury – Moncrieff – Orbanon…' she said quietly, almost to herself.

Giles couldn't hear what she was saying. God, he was losing his hearing too now.

'What?'

She showed him the list. 'Look! B E A A M O.'

Giles didn't see it.

Valerie rearranged the letters impatiently. 'AMOEBA is an anagram of the first letters of these surnames. Fuck, they're the ones doing this!'

Peter glanced across at Liam then back at the road as the lights on the roundabout changed and the traffic started to move.

'It has to be Stephen. He arranged the car hire and must have had someone track me from there. Cold bastard must be involved in all this.'

Liam saw the shock and pain in his friend and touched his shoulder. His voice was calm and strong. 'There will be time for anger and revenge. We have now to try and think ahead of him. He won't harm the woman and children until he has drawn you and Giles into his web. From what you say, he will be a formidable adversary.'

Peter felt angry at the betrayal and frustration at his stupidity and carelessness. He should have sensed something. He thought he knew this man well. What made him laugh and cry, his strength, his joy of life. Perhaps friendship saw only what it wanted. A chill crept over him and his fingers gripped the wheel. He pressed hard on the accelerator and the car shot forward.

Liam spoke gently. 'Slow down, Peter, I don't want to leave the temptations of this world just yet. There's no one knows our man as well as you do and I have a feeling we'll need all the edge we can get. I'll give Gio a little hunting to do.' Peter slowed the car and tried to control his emotions. He pulled into the inside lane. Liam reached into his pocket and took out a small mobile phone. Out of the corner of his eye he saw Peter's eyebrows raise and a smile start. 'Gio insisted. He worries about me.' He pressed one of the numbers. 'He's good and will mellow well when you and I are dribbling memories at each other and arguing over who bought the last drink… Gio?'

'Where are you?'

'On the way to the boat, we should be there in…' he looked at Peter who mouthed 'Ten minutes,' 'ten minutes. Listen, I need you to check up on…'

Giuseppe interrupted. 'Ring me from a call box.'

Liam's face darkened in anger. 'What the hell for? I'm sitting here with the phone in my hand. What's the point of the bloody thing if I can't use it?'

'Don't argue, Liam, just do it. I'll let you know when it's safe to use your mobile!'

Brief and to the point. Liam shrugged. 'Right, my boy.'

'Be careful.'

'I will.' He closed the phone and smiled to himself. 'The sooner I find my flock the better, young Lucifer. Let's find a call box, if there are still such things.'

* * *

Patty and the two girls had been woken just after six by Stephen Caron. In the background the choral chatter of the monks filled the early morning sunshine with soothing warmth and a sense of security.

'What is it?' Patty's tired voice showed the strain of the past twenty-four hours. She had not slept well and when she had drifted off, she was chased by nightmare images.

Giles' screaming face and a curtain of hanging men, their nooses drawn together and held by Sally and Kate, who danced them in a grotesque ballet. Peter in blood red robes laughing hysterically and singing the last rites as an aria.

The two girls were still fast asleep, curled up together on the hard mattress, their faces relaxed and innocent.

'I'm sorry to bother you so early, my dear, but I'm afraid that we are not as secure here as I would have wished although, be assured, you are in no danger.'

'What the hell do you mean, not secure?' Patty's fear came out as a spit of anger.

'We leave in thirty minutes. Please be ready. '

'I want to speak to Giles.'

'As soon as we are airborne, I will put in a call. Now, please wake the children.' He went from the cell. Patty felt a shiver of apprehension about this gentle, polite, fat man but she reassured herself that Giles and Peter trusted him to take care of them. She got up from the narrow uncomfortable bed and shook the two girls. As always, Kate was instantly awake.

'Morning.'

Sally tried to curl into a ball. 'Go away, I'm asleep!'

'Come on,' said Patty, 'we're off on another adventure.'

* * *

Hallam had been back in the tiny Spanish fishing village since early afternoon. He had flown himself from the small airfield in Dorset to the flying club, eight kilometres from his home. He had carried out his final instructions and, by now, his team would have been 'dispatched' too. Always cover yourself. The two hundred and fifty thousand pounds it had cost to contract out the three men's 'retirement' had been transferred temporarily to a holding account when the contractor had received his orders. Hallam had then killed him! The money would return to his bank in forty-eight hours when it was not accessed, as per the agreement he set up. So many lives ended by him. It was enough. He was finished. Reports of his death had already been circulated on the secret and dark grapevine and no one in the small village knew his real identity.

He poured himself a large glass of champagne and walked onto the terrace overlooking the tiny harbour. It was beautiful here, the small fleet of fishing boats gently rocking as the late afternoon sun dappled the water with shadows and silhouette. The locals had accepted him as a rich man who travelled a lot and he had won their hearts by learning and now speaking fluently the difficult local dialect. Most important of all, he was happy here. For the first time in his life, he felt he belonged. There was a woman too who made him laugh and brought back his youth. Perhaps the relationship would develop into something that would bring pleasure to them both. Time would tell. Later he would meet her at the small restaurant that he had funded and was now one of the most popular on the coast.

Suddenly, to his left, he caught the glint of something in the sunlight and had time only to smile briefly as the bullet threw him back over the table.

CHAPTER FIFTEEN

Basnet had called just after Peter. The news had started to come in, around eleven, of the deaths of Evan-Dyer, Orbanon, whose car had ploughed into a motorcycle, killing the rider and passenger, and Alsopp. David Amebury's suicide and the discovery of Charles Stanley Moncrieff's body had just been announced. Then a man had rung the Chronicle claiming that ISIS had been responsible for the four killings. The Arab-sounding voice had known details that hadn't been released or leaked. 'What the fuck's going on, Val? I could get into deep shit with something as hot as this. You've got to tell me what you're doing. It's withholding information...'

She had thrown the phone down. Her face was white and she felt as though she had been punched.

'Jesus, Jesus, Jesus!'

Giles went over to her. 'What is it?' His heart trembled at the thought that something might have happened to Patty and the girls

She told him what Basnet had said. As he listened a knot of ice formed in his stomach.

'I need a drink. Not wine, something stronger.'

'There's brandy in one of those.' She pointed to a series of bottle-holders built into the wood-covered wall of the boat. Giles went across, searched until he found a bottle of brandy, unscrewed the cap and took a long pull. He offered the bottle to Valerie who took it and drank. The two of them jumped as the boat moved and Liam's face appeared at the door.

'Jesus, Father, would you look at that? That's what I call having a drink. After you, young lady. I fear Lucifer's expertise behind the wheel leaves much to be desired.'

Giles and Loring looked at him in confusion.

'Who the fuck are you?' Val made a move towards Liam, the bottle raised. Suddenly it was in the priest's hand and he was drinking. She couldn't believe what had happened.

Peter appeared behind him. 'I'm sorry, lovely girl, I'm afraid he's never had many manners where the demon drink is concerned. Valerie Loring, Giles Lawson, this reprobate is Father Liam Orpizeski.'

Liam held out a huge hand to Giles and kissed Valerie on the cheek. 'You have beautiful eyes, Loring, and from what I hear from the soiled Father here, you are a good friend to have in times of trouble.'

'You're an even bigger bullshitter than he is,' she said, glancing towards Peter. Liam laughed joyously.

Once they had arranged themselves in the small space, Loring told them about their discovery of the identities of AMOEBA and the phone call from Basnet.

'Sweet Jesus!' Peter snapped.

'The Chronicle received a call from ISIS accepting responsibility. Whoever it was knew stuff that only the killers could know.'

'As I said, Peter, a formidable adversary.' Liam was squashed into the chair at the desk. The boat seemed even smaller with him in it. Giles, still in a state of shock and panic, looked at Peter.

'Who the fuck is he talking about now?'

For the first time since Giles had known him Peter seemed weary and not in control. 'I'm afraid that Stephen Caron is not what he seems.'

Giles went cold. 'What do you mean?'

* * *

Commander Graham Troakes, head of the Counter-Terrorism Force, had just come from a difficult meeting with the Met Police Commissioner, who was now briefing the Home Secretary. He hoped to contain it, although, with the Chronicle involved, they'd have to have slapped a 'D' notice on it before it went online. In this sort of event there were only a couple of hours control without official pressure and threats. The four killings puzzled Troakes. They didn't seem to be connected in any way and so far, nothing more had come from ISIS. There was nothing to tie any of the victims in with Islamist groups, apart from Alsopp who was about to head a team going to Kabul. It hadn't been made public. With WikiLeaks spreading the word, though, the ease of hacking into anything and everything meant nothing. Alsopp was the only one that might lend credibility to the ISIS claim. Even that was a bit of a long shot. Was it feasible that the other murders could have just been random killings? Three high-profile figures all on the same day, in almost simultaneous attacks! It sounded impossible, but his gut was telling him that there was something about this that connected up. Random killing of the rich just didn't sit right with a terrorist view of mass panic. Even the MP was really only a minor political figure.

One certainty though was that they were all professional hits. Clean, direct. The only one with collateral damage was Orbanon and that was more to do with the motorbike suddenly coming out of a mews than amateurs in the mix.

The back of his neck was getting tense. He rubbed it hard. Shit, he could do without this. He was due to start leave in a couple of days but that wouldn't happen now. He'd be lucky to get home for the next week.

The phone rang. 'Yes?'

'There's a Dave Basnet, sub-editor on the Chronicle, he's got some more information and he won't speak to anyone else.'

'Put him through, George… Mr Basnet, what can I do for you?'

* * *

'Merci bien, Père Ricard… ah, oui, toi aussi, au revoir.' Peter put down the phone. 'They left there early this morning. Father Ricard doesn't know where they were going, I'm sorry, Giles.' Peter put his hand on Giles's arm. 'He won't harm them.'

Giles pulled away. 'How can you say that? He's just had four fucking people killed. We have to go to the police. They can't all be in on it and the Chronicle must be able to do something.' He turned on Peter. 'I thought you knew him. You said you trusted him. I knew. I fucking knew there was something wrong with that bastard. I trusted you.' He was getting close to losing it. Valerie moved towards him. 'Giles…'

Liam moved quickly in front of her and put his arm around Giles. 'I suggest, my friend, that you and I go outside and take a little fresh air. I think it will do us good.' Giles struggled but it was pointless trying to break the big man's grasp and he was led out of the boat. For a moment there was silence. As Valerie watched Peter, he closed his eyes, breathed deeply for a moment, then opened them. All the strain had gone out of his face and he was once again in control.

'The power of prayer?' Loring said.

Peter smiled. 'No, a trick I learned a hundred years ago to clear and focus on what is to come. I'll tell you all one day. No time for enlightenment now. We must put our minds to the task. Stephen will know that we'll come after him and will leave a trail that can be followed.' He tapped his head. 'It's in here. There will be a link. They will go to a place that he and I know. I fear, lovely girl, I have led you into a deep and dark space and you have an impossible choice to make. To come with us on our adventure will be dangerous but to stay here could be fatal. You know too much. Stephen has long arms and could pluck you from your nest.' Her mobile rang.

'Loring.'

'Basnet. Just listen. I've been in touch with Troakes of the Counter-Terrorism mob. I told him all I know. They're on their way to you now.'

Valerie threw down the phone again. 'Prick!' She told Peter what had been said.

'It seems your mind has been made up for you.'

Valerie started scrabbling around the desk.

'We don't have time to waste.'

She pulled her iPad out from under a pile of papers. 'It's my story!'

'We'll take the Land Rover.' Peter shouted through the door, 'Liam, there's company on the way.' He moved quickly through the door of the boat, followed by Valerie.

The three unmarked police cars passed the Land Rover as it waited to cross the roundabout at the bottom of Kingston Bridge. As the last one turned left, the Land Rover went straight over towards Teddington. A motorbike, with Comet Couriers on the side, followed it.

Peter was driving, Liam in the passenger seat and Giles and Valerie bounced about on the rugs in the back. Liam was using his phone. He looked behind. 'Black Suzuki 500! Comet Couriers! Q66 MWY! It mightn't be anything but my guardian angel is a little twitchy. Any other bits of news to distract me, Gio?'

'One moment.' Gio went off the line.

Liam turned towards Peter. 'You know something, old friend, I'm looking forward to clashing horns with your man. It will be...'

'Liam?'

'Yes, Gio?'

'Caron hasn't stayed in Jersey. He landed and changed to an executive jet.'

'Did he now, and where were they heading?'

'Give me a break, Liam. The impossible I can do now, miracles take longer.'

Liam chuckled into a cough. 'A little irreverence, Gio? We'll have you human yet.'

'I am almost afraid you will. Now I do have some news. ISIS were not responsible for the deaths and are not happy about it.'

'I'll bet they're not!' He looked back at the motorcycle. 'Well, will you take a look at that?' The motorcycle was veering sharply to the left and mounting the pavement, the rider fighting to keep control. He lost the battle and crashed into the wall of a house. The white BMW 4x4 that had been passing the bike accelerated away and tucked itself in behind the Land Rover. 'You're learning, Gio.'

'I have a good teacher. They'll stay with you until you reach Pington. By then I'll let you know where they have gone. God be with you, Liam, and take care, I don't want to lose you yet. Please ring from a call box next time or get a burner so that...'

'What in God's name is that?' interrupted Liam.

Gio laughed. 'It'll keep for another time.' He ended the call.

Liam winked at Peter. 'I think he'll do. We'll get the plane ready and leave in the early hours of tomorrow.'

To Giles' amazement, Valerie had fallen asleep. His mind was in turmoil and his guilt pounded into overdrive as he realised that when he and Valerie were safe in the boat, Patty and the girls had been taken fuck knows where by Caron. Shit, he would give anything to be able to set time back and for it not to have happened to them. It brought a well of self-pity and he had to fight not to let it escape. Why had Caron done it? Then he was aware that Liam had turned towards him.

'Take these, Giles, they'll help you sleep for a while.' Liam passed a small flask back towards him. 'Wash them down with a little holy water.' Giles took the flask and then the two tablets that were offered.

'What are they?'

'A little concoction for times of trouble. They'll not harm you, just help your mind and body to rest.' Giles looked at the two pills. Two priests had now given him drugs to calm him. The Methodists would have a field day about Catholic sin and manipulation. He tried to shut down the random thoughts and looked at the pills in his hand. What the hell! The worst case would be that he didn't wake up and, in his present state of mind, that didn't seem like too bad an option. He put them in his mouth, took a swig from the flask and swallowed. It was smooth and expensive, only the best booze for holy drinkers.

* * *

Caron's plane landed on the small private airstrip in Sicily at midday. Patty and the girls had passed the short flight in luxury in his customized Blue Falcon jet. He had been charming and witty and the girls had laughed and enjoyed his stories. Despite a niggling concern, Patty found herself warming to him again, although she still kept her exterior cool. He was plausible and hadn't done or said anything to make her concerned, but there was something at the edge of her reason that told her that it was too easy. There was nothing so far, apart from the situation, to feed her suspicions. The move had been explained as a simple precaution so Caron could keep them under his personal care, and the change of aircraft in Jersey as simply a more comfortable ride. Peter had known Caron for years and Giles had said he only wanted them to be safe on the million-to-one chance that something might happen. She decided to try and override her naturally suspicious nature and enjoy the benefits of limitless wealth. God knows when she would get a chance again. More importantly though, the girls seemed relaxed about it all so far, enjoying this surprise break from school and normality. But then, why wouldn't they?

There were two cars waiting for them, a black BMW and a green Range Rover, and three men, two young and one older who was about the same age as Caron and large and powerful-looking. He came to meet them. Caron turned to Patty and the girls.

'This is my dearest friend, Malo. We've known each other since we were first excited by life and he has shared many things with me. He will take you to my house. I'm sorry that I won't be able to accompany you there yet but I have business that needs my attention. I should be able to join you by early evening.' He got into the Range Rover with the two others and they drove off.

Malo smiled at Patty. 'Shall we go?' His voice was gentle, warm, and friendly. He led them to the car and opened the doors. 'There is enough room for all three of you in the back.'

Patty smiled at him. 'Thank you, Malo.'

Kate and Sally got in first, followed by Patty. Malo gently shut the door, looked around, then took out a phone, wrote and sent a text, and heaved himself into the driver's seat. It was a tight fit.

They drove at speed along narrow country roads, although inside the car you would hardly know you were moving. There was no sound of either engine or tyres and the soft blue leather interior was the most comfortable Patty had ever experienced. There was music playing so softly it was hard to distinguish anything but the deep resonance of cello. She was finding it hard to keep awake but she just caught Malo's eyes as he glanced in the mirror.

'Where are we going?' she said.

Malo smiled. 'To one of his houses.'

'One of them?'

'He has several in the area, but Casa Maria is his favourite and he doesn't let many guests stay there. You must be special. I think you will enjoy it. It is only small but very beautiful. We will be there soon.'

Patty noticed for the first time a slight lilt of accent in his fluent English. She took a guess. 'Are you French?'

Malo's eyes twinkled.

'No, I am Sicilian.' There was a pause. 'This is my home!'

* * *

The slight man in the wetsuit pulled himself out of the water and looked around. He was hidden from the river by overgrown trees and reeds and was a good half a mile from the small boat where he had attached an explosive device to the underside of the hull. The Thames there was deep enough for him not to be seen as he set the timer and then swam close to the riverbed until he reached the red marker where he had set up his spot to fish. He stripped off the wet suit and put it and the MiniDive aqualung into the bag that he had carried strapped to his waist. Underneath he had been wearing a black body suit that kept him warm. The dark tracksuit was in the bag full of bait, hooks, and reels, next to the stool and rod. He put it on and packed up the rod. As he walked through the field to where he had hidden the bike, he felt a slight twinge of disappointment that he hadn't caught anything. He carried the bike over the padlocked gate and got on. He checked his watch. Fifteen minutes to go. He wouldn't wait here. He knew that it would be all right. One glance back towards the river and he pulled on a woollen hat and cycled down the narrow path.

* * *

Caron's 'small house' was a two-storey villa with white-painted walls built from old stone and a wide flat terraced roof edged with a balustrade. There were gardens, filled with sweet scent and colour, a mass of flowers and plants cascading down the hillside below a wooden veranda that overlooked the valley. It had taken over two hours to get there and Patty and the girls had been asleep when they arrived at the gates that opened as they approached then closed behind them. Two armed men came out of the trees around the entrance and watched until they disappeared around a bend. They checked the road outside the gates and one of them spoke into the small microphone attached to his earpiece.

Malo gently woke them when they stopped in front of the house. The girls chattered excitedly as the young woman who'd met them at the door led them to their rooms. She told them to call her Gina and that once she'd shown them where they would sleep, she would prepare lunch.

Patty's mobile couldn't find a signal, so she used a landline to call Giles on the number Caron had given her; it had rung then cut off. That rattled her, but Malo had said that it was always a bit tricky here. He explained that the system they had at the house would keep trying the number and when it connected would ring his mobile. He could then link it to any of the phones in the house or mobiles, including hers.

As they walked through the painting-covered hallway and up the wide wooden staircase she felt that she had slipped into a world that could be one of tranquility if she were able to calm her thoughts. She would relax once she had spoken to Giles and perhaps found out a bit more from him about Stephen Caron.

Patty and the girls had their own separate rooms. Kate and Sally's had a hot tub and hers had a steam pod as well. The style in Patty's was gentle and elegant, pastel shades and Degas prints. Malo apologised for the lateness of lunch but said that as soon as they had freshened up, Gina would serve it on the veranda.

Patty sat on the bed after Malo had gone and tried to make sense of the last two days. Their life had been turned upside down. They were a long way from home. Giles was God knows where and she couldn't get hold of him. Caron wasn't there to ask. Only the gentle Malo was there to question and he had a way of answering that didn't really tell her anything. For a moment a sense of impending disaster fluttered around her stomach. Then the phone on the bedside table rang. She grabbed it, realising how much she wanted to hear Giles' voice.

'Giles?'

But it wasn't Giles, it was Malo.

'I'm sorry, Mrs Lawson, but there is a fault on the phone line at the local exchange which is sadly antiquated and needs replacing. They have promised that it will be working again by tomorrow. I am afraid that here you cannot hurry things. Also, the satellite connection has broken down so I cannot get through that way.'

Patty sighed deeply. 'Thank you, Malo!'

She put the phone down, felt a moment of panic and quickly went into the girls' room to check everything was okay. Sally and Kate were in the tub, singing at the tops of their voices along to something loud and indistinguishable on one of their phones. It made Patty feel better. Normality. This lack of consideration for others meant that life was still the same for them, and they would take things as they always did until something upset or distracted them.

* * *

George Keating, on his way to Loring's boat, had been a senior member of the Counter-Terrorism Task Force for five years. A Chief Inspector, he had, at the age of forty-five, got as far as he was going to climb up the slippery police pole. His problem was that he was an instinctive and edgy copper and although his results were often good, the path he took brought him into stark conflict with the bureaucracy and politics of top table management. As it was, today he was in charge of the team that had been sent to pick up Valerie Loring in East Molesey. He wasn't a happy soul. He was exhausted. He'd been OIC on an early morning raid to pick up two terrorist suspects and he'd just got to bed when he was called out again.

'Should be there soon, guv. Newspaper fanny, isn't she?' Hawkins, driving, was crude, dangerous, undisciplined, and fairly thick, but fearless.

'Good!' He didn't feel like getting into a chat about Loring that would inevitably lead to the usual moronic chatter that Hawkins indulged in.

Keating, like his boss, Troakes, felt that there was something that didn't ring true with the chain of hits. It was too tidy.

He closed his eyes and sighed. God, he was tired. He hoped that he'd manage to get some sleep tonight. He was off tomorrow and had arranged his first date in months with a woman from the forensics unit. They'd at last found a day they could both do and were going to eat at a restaurant near where she lived.

At the marina, Hawkins stopped in the car park by the bridge. Keating picked up the radio. 'I'm going to the boat, stay where you are but keep on your toes in case I need you.'

'Right, boss!' DS Kathy Short responded. He liked her. She was a good copper. Keating opened the door.

'Right, let's go.' The two policemen got out and were joined by three from the other car. They walked carefully over the bridge. Hawkins pointed.

'It's on the outside pontoon at the end on its own. She calls it Olive Oil. I wonder if fucking Popeye is there too?'

He laughed happily as they started across the pontoons. Keating had just passed Malaki and stepped onto Olive Oil when the boat blew up, killing him instantly and cutting Hawkins in half, the smile glued to his face for eternity.

* * *

Liam stretched as they pulled in through the gates of the small airfield at Pington. 'Sweet Jesus, you drive like the devil is in you!' He glanced into the back of the Land Rover. Giles and Valerie were now both asleep and her head was resting on his shoulder. 'Well, will you look at that, Father, as peaceful as though they hadn't slipped open the lid of Pandora's box. It seems a sin to wake the little things, now doesn't it?' He turned to Peter, 'Let them rest until we're ready to leave. Come on, it's been a while since I took to the skies but a quick flick through my mind and a glance at the pages of the dummies' guide to flight should suffice. Now is not the time to doubt my memory.'

'I have faith in you, Gabriel.'

Liam chuckled. Peter put his hand on Liam's arm. 'Do you think he'll harm them?'

'You know your man better than me but I think that he has a strange morality and will not hurt a soul that is under his protection.' He opened his flask and took a drink. 'I have to tell you, my friend, that this chase has put a little new blood into my veins and I think that old man and his pearly gates will have to wait a while longer to list my many indiscretions.' The phone rang in his pocket and he took it out. 'You know, I thought we had played our last game together, but there's injury time left... Yes, Gio?'

'Everything all right, Liam?'

'Can we talk on this now?'

Gio laughed. 'Yes.'

'We've just arrived at Pington. What have you got?'

'They landed in Sicily just after twelve. I don't know exactly where yet, probably a private field. My family will be ready to welcome you and will give you all the help you need.'

'Wonderful, my boy.'

'And, Liam... Cardinal Pirotto wants your head on a plate.'

'Tight-arsed little prick. If he bothers you again, tell him I'm in a whorehouse in Florence and have just given his sister a papal blessing. Now, I have to go and learn to fly a plane again. I will call if I need help... and thank you, Gio.'

'God go with you, Liam.'

Liam put the phone thoughtfully into his pocket and told Peter what Gio had said.

Peter was quiet for a moment, his eyes distant with memory. 'I should have known, I spent six months there healing body and soul. Let's go and find this plane of yours.'

They got out of the Land Rover, quietly shutting the doors.

Valerie woke as her mobile buzzed for the third time. For a moment she was confused. Then she remembered and looked out of the window. Where the hell were they now? She must have fallen asleep not long after they left the boat. She realised her phone was still buzzing. She checked the caller. Basnet. Fuck! What did he want now? 'Yes?'

There was an edge of panic and relief in his voice. 'Val, thank Christ. Where are you?'

'Look, Dave, I haven't got time…'

Basnet's loud 'Jesus Christ!' made her move the phone away as he exploded.

'You'd better make fucking time. At the moment you're public enemy number one. Your boat was blown up, two policemen were killed outright and another probably won't make it.'

She started to tremble. Basnet was yelling at her to tell him where she was when she cut the call. She tried to light a cigarette but failed. She started to rock, back and fore and a low moaning came from her. Liam and Peter came out of the shed and walked quickly through the heavy rain to the Land Rover. Peter opened the driver's door.

'What is it, girl?' Liam, getting in the other side, reached across and touched her arm. She started to scream then and struggle. Peter tried to put his arms around her but Liam had moved across the seat and lifted her, like a child, onto his lap and held her. He spoke softly, close to her ear, and soon she stopped.

'I'm sorry.'

'What is it?' He glanced behind at Giles. 'That little sleeping draught must have been stronger than I thought. Just as well. Now, Val?'

CHAPTER SIXTEEN

They had been airborne for ten minutes when Giles started to wake up. He felt terrible, his mouth tasted foul, his head ached and the loud buzz of the little plane started to bounce the pain around. He was strapped into the seat next to Valerie while Peter and Liam were up front. It looked like Liam was flying the plane. He closed his eyes and opened them again. Nothing had changed. He turned to look at Valerie. She looked tense, her eyes red and angry.

'I feel bloody awful. I'm never going to take anything from a priest again.'

Peter turned around in his seat. 'You needed a little peace and rest. Since you've been asleep, things have happened but, sadly, none of them good.'

Liam glanced back. 'We're on our way to Sicily but I fear our man has slipped the bounds of sanity. He has blown up Val's boat and, God save us, two Counter-Terrorism police officers, come to take her in, were sprinkled on the waters.'

'Oh, Jesus Christ!' Giles was barely audible.

Peter put his hand on Lawson's knee. 'I promise you he will not hurt them. I think he's facing his last battle and wants to play the game to the end. AMOEBA is finished! In his eyes I am the cause of its demise and so his adversary.'

'Not forgetting me, Lucifer. '

Giles was slipping into shock. 'You're both mad.' He shook his head hard. 'I really think you're enjoying this...'

Valerie interrupted him. 'Liam and Peter know what they're doing. You have to trust them. We have no choice.'

Giles sat staring out through the small window. Loring had closed her eyes and there was a buzz of whispered voices from the front seats. He felt really rough, dizzy, pains in his chest, and he was sitting next to a journalist who was on the same death list as him. A homicidal maniac who made Stalin look like the Virgin Mary had kidnapped his wife and two daughters, and two priests who had no grip on the sane world were flying him to Sicily. He was plunging away from any sense of reality too. Perhaps that would simplify things. If he lost his mind, then this would all probably make sense...

His ramblings were halted by Peter's voice. 'Giles... Giles!' It brought him back from the edge and he focused with difficulty on the priest. 'Are you all right?'

It took Giles two attempts to get the words out. 'Yes. Just great. Must remember to book again next year!'

Peter smiled. 'Good man! We'll be there in about twenty minutes. Liam's colleague, Father Giuseppe, has arranged some local help for us. I want you and Valerie to stay with them.'

'Bollocks!' said Val sharply. 'It's my fucking story!'

Liam laughed and coughed violently. Peter looked at him with concern as the coughing stopped and the voice rasped.

'Do you think she disagrees, Lucifer?' Liam looked at her for a moment; her eyes held his, determined and daring him to refuse her. Her whole body tensed with anger. 'Perhaps she's right. I don't think she will get in the way so, if she does what she's told, she can come with us.'

Valerie exploded 'Don't you dare fucking treat me...'

Liam turned, all the humour had gone and his voice was hard.

'Be quiet. This will not be an easy ride. Peter and I have done this before and it is not your world, no matter how tough you think you are. You will listen and do what we say, without argument! Is that understood?'

Loring looked shocked at his tone and aware of the power in the man. After a moment she relaxed. 'Yes, I'm sorry.'

Liam's face softened and he smiled. 'No need for that, we just needed some boundaries.' He turned to Giles. 'Young Giles, however, will I think be safer with cousin Vittorio's family.'

Giles glared at him. 'If she's going then so am I. It's my family that this fucking madman…'

'Enough, Giles.' Liam held his look for a moment. 'You will do what we say.' He turned back to the controls and softened. 'Now, if I don't concentrate on remembering how to land this thing, none of us will be going anywhere except to the Good Lord's heavenly home.'

* * *

Angelina Borsellino had known Stephen Caron as long as she could remember and once, way back in the shadows of their youth, they had shared their bodies for a few days when they were both in need of comfort and passion. It had been full of the laughter and joy of their friendship. It didn't last, but had strengthened their love for each other. Over the years they had shared the highs and lows of life and several business ventures that had just skirted legitimacy. These forays had, for Angelina, been a step towards bringing respectability to the 'family' business that she had inherited when her husband had been killed in a car bombing. She'd had to fight like a tiger and be harder, colder, and more ruthless than the men who wished to take over. Stephen had supplied the tool for her revenge. His contractor had cleanly and efficiently killed the four men who had ordered her husband's death. It brought her the respect and acceptance of those who did not at first think she was worthy of taking on Gino's role as don. She took the business to another level and began edging it towards legality. She loved the challenge and it kept her mind agile. It was only recently that she had begun to consider handing over the position to Vittorio and the younger cousins who could move with the speed and diversity needed in today's corporate world.

She had been overjoyed when Stephen had arranged lunch today. She loved his wit, intellect, irreverence, and enjoyment of life; it was only now, after he'd gone, that she felt concern for her old friend. Something was troubling him, something that he couldn't discuss, even with her. She knew well enough not to question him. If he wanted to talk, he would, but she had never seen him like this before and it worried her that she could not help.

There was a gentle knock on the door. 'Come in.'

Edoardo entered, lined and bowed with age but with the shadow of his great strength nestling in the hunched shoulders. He had been with the family for fifty years, first as a young 'soldier' then as bodyguard to Angelina's father. When the old man died, he had become the daughter's shield and was never more than a whisper away from her side. He had once broken the back of a man who had tried to rape her.

'Giuseppe wishes to speak with you. He is phoning from London.'

'Thank you, Edoardo. I'll come now.' She had kept this room a haven for solitude. No mobile phone. No computer. No television. Nothing that could bring in the outside world! Only Edoardo was allowed to enter her sanctuary. The old man bent his head slightly, then turned and went out of the room. Why would Giuseppe want to talk to her? She had not seen him since he had conducted her brother's funeral service. Their worlds were so far apart.

Puzzled, she left the room.

* * *

Dave Basnet had been brought in eight hours after the bomb had gone off, killing the three police officers – the third had not made it through the operation to try and save her. The journalist had protested but the guys who went to get him were in no mood to be pissed about and after a few threats and skirmishes he gave in to the inevitable. He had been there now for five hours and he was tired, his eyes stinging, his head aching from the barrage of questions thrown at him. He had no answers to any of them.

Where was Loring? Who was she with? Who would want to kill her? Was she capable of setting up the bomb herself?

Then the nice and nasty routine!

'Come on, Dave, so you gave her one now and again. Doesn't mean you have to cover up for her.'

'Listen to me, you little cunt, you know fucking well where she is.'

It was a nightmare. The paper knew where he was, so why hadn't they sent someone round to get him out? His tormentors had gone out of the room ten minutes ago. Troakes had stuck his head back in at the door and asked politely if he would excuse them for a moment. He felt like screaming at him that he hadn't done anything, but he didn't.

There was a cigarette packet on the table and a cheap plastic lighter. They had told him that they would ignore the smoking ban if he wanted a fag. He took a cigarette out of the packet and lit it. He nearly choked and stubbed it out. Christ, what did he do that for? He didn't smoke, never had done. He hoped they weren't watching him. Shit, of course they were watching him. That was the point of leaving him on his own to stew. He was almost ready to admit to anything just to get out of there. He had told them, 'Look, guys, she asked me to pull out anything I had on prison suicide, their crimes, relatives, and victims' relatives. That's all I did. I didn't even give it to her. I had it biked to the boat.' Jesus, the number of times he had said that. It was the last time he helped anyone out. From now on, it was look after number fucking one... if he ever pulled himself out of this shit before drowning in it. It was bad enough being here but, when he hadn't done anything, it was fucking unfair to be treated like this.

The door opened and Troakes came into the room and sat on the edge of the table. 'Thank you for your help, Mr Basnet. I'm sorry that we had to take up so much of your time but I'm sure that you would want to help, particularly as it involves your colleague.'

'I can go?' Basnet stood up. He was exhausted.

'Yes!' Troakes smiled but his eyes were cold and hard. 'I don't have to remind you that none of this is to be printed in hard copy or released online.'

'No!'

Basnet stopped at the door and was about to say something, then thought better of it and went out.

Troakes sat heavily in a chair. Jesus, what a mess!

* * *

Angelina felt torn but she had no choice. She had to tell Stephen. Warn him. Even though it was family business, there was too much between them. Gino would have understood. It was honourable. It was strange that she thought of Gino now. Perhaps not, though. The two men had been like brothers and Stephen had helped her through the worst days after Gino's murder and was always there when the pain was at its most intense and she needed to hit out or just be held.

Giuseppe had asked for help and protection for his friends. It was a courtesy to her. Her nephew Vittorio had already agreed to the request and she couldn't make him go back on his word and lose face. He knew about her relationship with Stephen and knew that she would warn him. It had been wrong for Stephen to take the woman and children, but she knew he wouldn't hurt them.

She was tired. It was time to hand everything over to Vittorio. Although he was now the don, she had always been considered the wise head but also the iron fist in the family business. It was a rare and singular privilege granted to her by the other Families. Her only regret was that she would have no one with whom to share her final years.

* * *

Stephen Caron put down the phone. The game was on. Only Liam was an unknown quantity. That put the odds slightly against him. But why play when there is no edge, when you know you can win? Where's the sense of challenge in that? He looked fondly around the large room. One wall was ceiling to floor glass, looking out across the gardens to the valley with its lush hillsides, vines, and olive trees. Inside, the room was decorated with style and huge amounts of cash. The three walls were richly draped in the paintings of Degas, Hockney, and Freud, and lately he had started collecting the unflinching work of Jenny Saville. It was a mix of colours and styles that shouldn't have worked but somehow did; an eclectic collection that matched his moods and gave him the joy of being able to touch and feel the genius of those who created the art that moved him.

He was only truly content and at peace here in this house, surrounded by his carefully created world. It was a place of warmth and safety with a fine balance between the classic and contemporary styles that he admired and was able to afford. A positive pleasure that his wealth allowed him. It was secure, beautiful, and impenetrable, and he relished its isolation and tranquility. The other property where the woman and her children had been taken was a portfolio investment and used as a convenience only, a temporary home for important guests, some of whom were willing recipients of his hospitality and some, those who had something to hide, were not.

Over the years and as his financial footprint grew he had collected property around the world. All were now bound, with the remainder of his wealth, in a trust that on his death would pass to a variety of causes, mostly concerned with those children and young people who were the forgotten of life. Only a lawyer in a small town in Mexico knew the details of the trust, but not the real identity of the man who had employed him to facilitate it when the time came. Sometimes even Caron forgot that the real story of his life began when he was born Carlo Falcetta to a French mother and Sicilian father in Toulouse. It was buried deep in the well of his mind and Carlo's self-inflicted and sad death at the age of twenty was recorded on a gravestone in a beautiful church overlooking the Tuscan hills. The remains in the wooden box belonged to a young man who had dealt drugs and misery and deserved to die. Carlo had been wanted for killing a man in a fight. His parents had disowned him and so he had found a way out.

Not only did this killing begin a pattern of balancing a diverse and contradictory morality, it was the first of many deaths necessary to protect his intricate web of secrecy and corruption as his organisation grew and became powerful. So many shadows of the past touched his life and now threaded through his dreams, that he craved peace, and it was here in this house that he first found it and where it would come to him again.

Now that AMOEBA was finished this was where he would play out this last game too. Afterwards, perhaps he and Angelina could find some comfort together. He should have talked to her today but it was difficult, even with the relationship they had, to open this cache of recent history. She was probably the person he trusted most and who understood him best. Still, she knew now. In the twenty years since Gino's death, although he had always been there for her with financial or moral muscle, he had never suggested making a life together. He knew that Gino would not have minded and would be pleased that they could draw happiness from each other. They both knew loneliness and the chasm of great loss. Perhaps they were too alike and he was afraid of what a relationship together might bring. But now, perhaps, if fate allowed, they might still have a last breath, a few moments together in this evening of their lives.

He poured a glass of Dom Perignon then stood looking out of the window and for a moment tried to let the lush panorama ease his thoughts. His mind raced, however, with the tumbling twists that had surged after he met Peter again. It had made him wonder what might have been. What sort of life he might have lived if he and Peter had stayed close? Would he have found God too? In reality, he realised that, by the time he first met Peter, it was probably too late. He had already signed his pact with the devil. Would it, like Faust, destroy him? Or would this final chapter be payment enough?

Who would he have become if he had not exploited the power and control that enriched his life but ultimately took away most of what was good in him? Would he have been able to find a deeper contentment than the satisfaction and hegemony of great wealth? Would the many years spent only in bringing to justice those who were outside the boundaries of right and wrong have been enough? Why had the excitement of playing both sides of the line of morality and law been such a temptation? He manipulated perception to suit whatever engaged and empowered him most. Why had nothing he achieved ever seemed enough? These were all pointless questions that scattered around his mind but he had no real interest in finding answers; just an unwelcome surge of memory and what might have been moroseness. It was far too late. He had followed these hard and bloody pathways for nearly forty years and that was as unchangeable in this life as the certainty that he was mortal and would soon become one with the next.

He refilled his glass and thought about Amebury and AMOEBA and how that too had been led by fate rather than focus and design. Although even before that had happened, he had begun to question the demons that drove him. He had carefully eased his control and let others take the weight of the monsters he had created and released into the world and whose web encompassed so much carnage; the drugs, the financial miasma, and tentacles of terror he supported around the world. He retained and still ruthlessly ran the visible, legal side of his property and leisure business. Now he needed nothing more than the means to find the peace that was eluding him. In reality, though, he knew his past would always be with him and it increasingly troubled him. He needed to make a change that would bring some quiet to his mind; perhaps even a way to soften some of the horrors of the vivid and terrifying dreams that had tormented and destroyed his sleep over the last years. It was the one thing in his world that he couldn't control and at times the fear had brought a madness and imbalance to his usually pragmatic and clear direction.

When he had spoken to Amebury after his son's death and felt his deep torment and hopelessness, he saw a way that he might help him and perhaps even begin to right some of his own multitude of wrongs, and maybe allow him to find some sort of closure. He suggested a pathway of retribution to Amebury that he, with a darkness of morality and mind, would be able to help facilitate and even fund if it was needed. He owned the house in the Cotswolds and the Swiss company that secured it.

Up to a point it had worked for them all. The collaborators in AMOEBA had found some sanctuary after those who had taken away their loved ones had been removed. After that they had moved on to others who deserved retribution. It had worked well and over a hundred transactions had been expedited. Now, however, it was out of control. Even though he could always justify the killing, it had become too random as the cover up collateral of deaths grew. The killing of the police officers at the journalist's boat was regrettable and careless. Then there was the astonishing co-incidence of Peter Satorri's involvement. It had, at first, shocked, surprised, even horrified him. But then it filled him with an excitement he hadn't felt for years and a desperate urge to win at all costs. It would be a challenge that would test but not defeat him. It would be a game of skill, tenacity, intellect and brutality, with an inevitable end for one of them. To kill an enemy takes skill, but to kill a friend is a different beast and requires detachment, focus and courage.

There was a knock at the door.

'Come!'

Malo entered. 'The woman and children have gone. Alberto is taking them to the airfield.'

'Good! Did she accept the sketch?' He had wanted to give her a small Degas drawing of two dancers that he found particularly entrancing.

'Yes!'

Caron nodded his head. It would be some atonement for their displacement.

He put his arm around Malo. 'Sit down, old friend, we have plans to make.'

* * *

The small plane was met by Vittorio. Liam had bumped it down and taxied to a large shed at the far end of the field. He turned and smiled at his relieved passengers. 'Well, would you believe it? It's not as hard as it looks. A couple of nasty moments mind, when I thought the sins of the good father here might have caught up with us, but my sanctity must have tipped the scales. Now, Val, if you are to come with us, remember what I said. I don't want you getting in the way.'

Valerie bristled but Peter caught her eye and she stayed silent. Vittorio opened the door. He was thickset, in his late thirties, with a mass of tight black curls and piercing eyes that for now sparkled with fun but had a depth where danger lay. He spoke in a Sicilian dialect.

'Welcome to Sicily, Father Liam, Giuseppe speaks of you like a father. It is an honour to meet you.'

Liam shook his outstretched hand. 'And you, Vittorio. Now, at the risk of sounding unsociable, I think we had better move quickly.' Peter climbed out of the plane behind Liam followed by Valerie and Giles.

'Gabriel, it's lucky that you speak with many tongues.'

'It is.'

Giles leaned back against the plane 'I'm coming with you. Patty would want...'

Liam interrupted. 'Patty and the girls are safe and they should be here within the next couple of hours. Vittorio's men will meet them.' He pointed to two men about to get into a car, then turned to Peter. 'Vittorio also has a man in the lion's den. He will be here soon to brief us.'

Peter spoke quietly. 'Ask him if I can have a word with them. You can translate.'

'There is no need, Father, they speak good English.' Vittorio laughed. 'It is always a small advantage to surprise those you have just met.'

Peter smiled. 'It certainly is, Vittorio.' He went towards the car.

Giles felt a great sense of release and this time he couldn't hold back.

Valerie saw the tears start. It would be good for him. She was going to go to him but something stopped her. Strangely, she felt embarrassed, but upset too. What was that all about? Because he cared about his wife and kids! Suddenly she was angry with him for making her feel like that. It gave her a moment of sadness that there was no one except her parents who cared for her but even as that washed over her, she knew it was anger at herself for letting that need surface. It was also untrue. She had friends that rallied around and loved her, but nobody just for her. She pushed the scattering thoughts away, needing to find focus. Soon she did.

Giles, wrapped in his little bubble of relief and guilt, didn't notice her shake tears away as she hurried to catch up with Liam and Vittorio.

* * *

Bartenson's letter, taken by Hallam when he killed him, had been found at Sir David Amebury's home. His wife was too upset to make any sense of it so had asked for it to be passed on to the firm of solicitors whose name was on the envelope. The senior partner, shown the letter addressed to Valerie Loring, had notified the police. Three days later, it had finally landed on Troakes' desk. He already had the information that Loring had asked Basnet for and had found the connection between the dead men and women. They all had relatives who had been murdered! The killers, caught and sentenced, had, apart from one obvious drug overdose death, supposedly taken their own lives. The contents of Bartenson's letter were explosive.

'Jesus!' He picked up the phone on his desk, tapped in a number. 'Is the Commissioner there, Zoe? I need to see him now.' He put the phone down. The repercussions of this could be a political nightmare. He went to the door and opened it. 'Bill, get in here now.'

* * *

Caron was satisfied after Malo left him. It had been good to make final decisions with the one person, apart from Angelina, who was his closest and most trusted friend. He had a clear and careful mind and his words, always well thought out, had clarity. It helped Caron to separate the jumble in his head and he was now focused on the way it would play out. He would be able to shut off any emotional impetus that might threaten his control of the game. There was no place for passion, anger, or remorse. It must be a clean field of combat.

The trickiest part of the concept was to know how he could achieve the right level of play. It had to be clear, precise, and simple. In the end, drawing from Malo's wisdom, it had come to him suddenly and slipped easily into place, like the final piece of a jigsaw. There would be nothing complicated; no high-tech help, but hand to hand with just a simple kill-or-be-killed as the end game. It would be fair and equal, Peter and the old priest against him and Malo. He knew they would be well matched. Peter had great potential as an adversary. After all, he had trained him, but despite his love of chance, he had no real doubt that he would win. He had set the rules of the game. If you understood the way the mind of your opponent worked, there was always a way to simplify the complicated. In this game, he would manipulate Peter to distract, deflect and defeat. He smiled gently. Soon it would start. It was all ready. Lawson's family had been dispatched and would be reunited with him soon.

Then, like a wasp sting, a sudden confusion pierced his optimism. Why had he done that? Was it a mistake? After all, they were his bait to catch Peter. For a moment his anger roared and he squeezed the glass that was in his hand until it shattered. He didn't seem to notice, just stood there frozen, the champagne and blood dripping through his fingers. Slowly, a thought, single and sharp, came and he relaxed, smiled, and held a handkerchief to the wound. Now he had a way out. It was simple but so full of emotional power and reason that it would be irresistible to Peter. Why hadn't he thought of her before? She would give him the magnet and the advantage.

Francoise!

Once he had told Peter the truth about her death, nothing on this earth nor in his spiritual world would be able to stop him coming after Caron.

'Surely you want to keep the pictures?'

Malo's voice, a whisper close to him, broke into his thoughts. Caron hadn't heard him come back in.

A sudden and violent pain seared his head and he slapped Malo hard across the face.

'Do as I say!'

Malo staggered back, surprised and hurt. Instantly Caron's heat and anger dispersed. He rushed to him and put his arms tightly around him. 'Forgive me, my old friend, I am troubled.' He let go and collapsed into a chair and looked at him. His voice was calm now that the moment of madness had passed. 'Sometimes I can't see clearly. I need you to be my eyes for this last battle.' He smiled gently. 'But, if you do not wish to be a part of it, then you are free to go! I've made provision for you. You won't need for anything. I'll miss you by my side but I'll understand and accept your choice.'

Malo looked deeply into his eyes for a moment then a grin broke his leathery and lined face.

'Why would I go without you?'

Caron felt more relief than he thought possible. He hadn't really wanted to face it alone. He smiled as a calm settled over him. He stood and kissed Malo on his forehead. 'Thank you.' He moved away. 'There is work to be done. Let us check that all is well with nature.'

* * *

Sally, Kate, and Patty were sitting in the back of the Range Rover. Alberto, the driver, was in his late twenties, muscular and handsome, with a flashing smile, and both the girls were in lust with him. He kept glancing in the mirror and flirting. Sally would blush and look away but Kate returned his look overtly with what she hoped was a sexy but appealing smile.

Patty punched her on the arm. 'Stop it.'

Kate looked quickly away. 'What?'

Patty had seen the look in her eyes and surprised herself by being shocked. Her little girls were growing up! He was gorgeous, and she felt herself colouring as Alberto caught her glance and winked at her. She looked away quickly, embarrassed. She didn't need this. She was confused that they were on the move again and now, in retrospect, not completely sure she believed what had been said before they left. Early this morning, Malo told her they were going home, apologising again for the disruption in their lives. Circumstances had changed now and the risk to her husband was over. Mr Caron hoped she would accept a gift as recompense. He said he had already given the two girls a cash card with €500 credit to spend on themselves and they were happy enough. Of course, they would be! Their morality, particularly when there were no caveats attached, was still at an easily avoidable stage.

Patty was unsure about the gift. Malo said he understood her concern but there were no strings attached. It was merely to make up for the way they'd been moved around. He said as soon as he managed to get through to her husband, she could talk to him. Malo left then to give her time to pack and be ready to leave in an hour. Now that her short sojourn in the world of the wealthy was ending; Patty decided she might as well enjoy what was left of it. Sally and Kate had had a wonderful time which more than made up for the sudden change in their lives. They hadn't really been given much chance to discuss their 'holiday' before they left but given the possible repercussions if they refused, there hadn't been a choice. She had been worried about Giles and it would be good to see him safe. Would this change him? She would have to wait and see and not put him back where he was before this all began. She needed to take stock too.

The small sketch, covered in a protective bubble wrap, was beautiful! A copy of a Degas drawing. Then, with a shock, she realised that it wasn't a copy at all but original and must be worth thousands of pounds. The initial disbelief gave way to a wash of pleasure that she could own a piece of art history that might even promote a bidding war at auction. For a moment, all they had gone through seemed worth it. One thing Patty had never suffered from was false morality. It was one of the less noble but truthful genes that the girls had inherited and there were times when standards were allowed to slip. She would keep the Degas and probably rip the throat out of anyone who tried to take it away from her.

She suddenly got drawn from her thoughts back into the car. Alberto was singing. Bloody hell, he had a good voice too. He caught her eye again, stopped singing, and smiled.

Patty was entranced by his eyes and felt an exciting warmth but then her emotional seesaw changed balance again and she felt a rush of anger at Giles that shook away the lust. He was impossible! Despite the fact that they seemed to have just found a new balance, he had got them all into this mess without telling her what was involved, she might find it impossible to forgive that. If it was only herself it would be bad enough, but to risk the girls too was inexcusable. It seemed that a short time ago, even if things had been a bit tricky for her and Giles, everything had equilibrium and even family complacency had comfort, however changeable it might be. Perhaps sometimes stuff happened to jar you out of this balance of normality and make you think about what was important and what needed to be real. However, what had happened in the last few days wasn't anywhere near her understanding of reality. It was not something that should be a part of their lives. Suddenly all her earlier thoughts of things not being so bad were shot away in a flash of harsh reality. People had been killed. Giles had been threatened and told that they would not be safe if he didn't give up his search for truth. Even dear, gentle, kind Peter Satorri seemed to have evolved into a character dreamed up by a manic and Daliesque mind.

She glanced at the girls. They were both plugged in to ear buds and oblivious of what was going on in her mind. It was so strong that she must at the very least have changed shape but even if she became a fire-breathing dragon they probably still wouldn't notice her.

She felt the car slowing down as it pulled into the side of the road behind another one. Alberto turned around. 'You will have to change cars here. Your husband is now in Sicily and you are going to join him.'

'What do you mean?' With surprise, she suddenly realised that he was speaking English. Oh, shit! 'I thought you didn't speak it.'

Alberto smiled broadly. 'You assumed I didn't! I lived in London for five years. Now I am sorry, I would love to talk more but I think you had better go. Mr Lawson will be waiting.'

'How do I know that this isn't another bloody change of plan?'

Alberto stopped any more words with a smile and a light touch.

'I promise you this is the end of your stay with us.' Two men got out of the other car. 'Giancarlo and Mario will look after you.' He got out of the car and opened the rear door. The two girls were watching every move he made and practically drooling. 'Please.' Alberto held out his hand and helped the two girls out and then Patty. He looked deeply into her eyes, leaned forward and kissed her hand. 'You have two beautiful daughters, but you are like a full bloom to their awakening buds. Now, if you will excuse me.'

Patty's stomach was turning hoops and Kate and Sally were glaring at her. Christ, if anyone but him had said that she'd have thrown up over them. Giancarlo opened the door of the other car, a large Mercedes.

'Mrs Lawson.'

The three of them walked over and got in. The two men were charming and polite. 'Mr Lawson is with Vittorio's family. Father Satorri said that if we mentioned his name you would be able to relax. He too is in Sicily but has things to do before you meet again. We will be there in an hour.' He closed the door after they all got in from the same side.

Kate glanced out of the window at Alberto and smiled. 'God, he's gorgeous. We could share him.'

'I'm your mother, remember!' Patty was shocked, not at the thought of her daughter and the Italian but the sharing. She wanted him to herself.

'Oh, Mum, you fancied him like mad too!'

Patty looked at the two girls then opened the small fridge in the console. She was getting used to the toys of rich boys.

'Champagne, anyone?'

* * *

The meeting with the Commissioner had lived up to all of Troakes' expectations and hurried arrangements to brief the 'old man' immediately were put in action. The only downside was that Troakes would do the briefing. He would be the one with his neck on the line. It was his personal shitpile. The Commissioner had the New York Police Chief to take to lunch and needed time out to prepare. It was important that these two leaders of law enforcement should have the luxury of good food and comfort whilst others took the flak and were manipulated into responsibility to ensure little culpability at the top table.

The audience with the Home Secretary, who was not known for his patient and gentle nature, had been particularly vituperative and graphic with a rant of what might happen to Troakes if no arrests were forthcoming. The least of which would be his relocation to 'looking after some God-forsaken arsehole of the country full of sheep-buggery and incest.' The interview had ended with the Home Secretary saying that Moncrieff and

Amebury were members of the same club as him and it left a bad taste in the mouth when something like this happened. Almost as an afterthought he said that they had better be seen to take the families of the dead policemen to their hearts and give them a full ceremonial burial. It was the kind of emotional response the people liked and it would be good for the government's flagging popularity if there was a serious slice of authority on show; Troakes could now 'piss off and do what he was paid a fucking good salary to do.' It was only with a supreme effort that Troakes stopped himself from squeezing the life out of the fat little turd.

He arrived back at New Scotland Yard in a foul temper. Jesus! How much longer could he put up with this? Why the hell didn't he just get out, go and work for some rich Emirates prince and earn enough money to cushion his conscience? He supposed, because, at heart he was a good copper and he loved the job. Anyway, his wife hated sun and sand and the grief that she would give him just wouldn't be worth it.

Bill Gordon followed him into his office. 'I've been checking AMOEBA and there's nothing.'

'What about the Grapevine?' This was a central computer in Washington that linked all the world's Counter-Terrorism Task Forces and shared information.

'Nothing. Oh, Basnet rang. He wouldn't talk to anyone but you again. He said it was important and that you should phone him as soon as you came in.'

'Did he?' He sat down at his desk. 'I don't like this, Bill. It's dangerous. If what Bartenson's letter says is true then it links all the deaths. Why kill them all off unless they'd become a liability? If so, who and what did they threaten? And why? Look, go and pick up Basnet and give him a bit of a scare then bring him in for a few words of warning. Send Meg to have a chat with Amebury's wife and then with Bartenson's ex, and get someone to go for a sandwich, cake, and a mug of tea. I'm bloody starving!'

* * *

Valerie watched as the three men looked at the map. Giles had been taken to the farm where he would meet up again with his wife and children. She felt a twitch of envy at the thought of them all together in relieved and happy family mode. She threw it out of her mind. For God's sake, woman, get real. Someone wanted to kill her! That was a reality that was so unreal she couldn't take it in. When Basnet had told her about the boat being blown up, killing the police officers, she had almost slipped beyond saving and she was buggered if that was going to happen again. Also, through no fault of her own, she was probably being chased by the heavy law. In a further slip from reality, she was now standing here listening to two priests and a Sicilian crime boss talking about getting to a multiple killer, who was playing a game with their lives as the prize. On the positive side, though, if she lived to tell the tale, it would be a fuck of a story.

She lit a cigarette. Oh, piss, she only had a couple left. She knew Liam smoked like a haddock and when someone did that, they always carried plenty of spares;

she did normally, but it had slipped low on her list of priorities. She wasn't thinking straight! Why had she phoned the paper and talked to that twat Basnet? He had only given her grief about being picked up and turned over. If he'd even just asked how she was then perhaps she wouldn't have slammed the phone down.

Peter interrupted her thoughts. 'Val.'

She was seeing a different side to him now, controlled, efficient, and cold. She shivered. Jesus, Liam was right, she was out of her depth here. She fought off an urge to ask if she could stay and wait with Giles. It wasn't hard to do. Think of the story!

She realised Peter was waiting for her to engage. 'Sorry?'

'Listen to Vittorio.' The Sicilian smiled at her briefly and looked back at the map. He had marked the outline of Caron's land and there was an inner area covering some fifty acres that had been shaded in.

'This,' Vittorio indicated the shaded area 'is very well protected, but we have a way in.' His mobile rang. He looked at it impatiently. It didn't stop. 'Excuse me a moment. Si?' He spoke for a few moments, then turned back to the others, a bemused smile on his face. 'Signor Caron wishes to speak to Father Satorri.'

Liam chuckled. 'Jesus, would you look at the gall of the man. Quickly, young Lucifer, let us see what he has to say.'

Peter's face hardened.

'Relax, Father, don't let the little divil see he has you by the throat.' Loring watched intently as Peter took the phone and moved away. She glanced at Liam and

Vittorio who calmly went back to the map and talked quietly.

Peter took a deep breath. 'Stephen, it's Peter!'

There was a slight pause, then Caron laughed.

'The warmth of friendship has gone from your voice, my friend. That disappoints me. I thought we had something deeper between us. You knew I would not hurt the woman and girls. I think they enjoyed their stay with me.'

He paused. 'It is strange, is it not, that something as powerful and righteous as AMOEBA could be broken by someone as inconsequential as your friend Giles? But I bear him no malice. I am sorry that I misled you, old friend, but I could not allow you to stop me ending it. I gave it life. Only I could take it away…'

His voice became loose. Peter listened, a sadness coming over him as he began to understand the extent of Caron's deterioration.

'I alone had that right, Peter. No one could be left that would lead to me. It is hard to destroy something that you cherish and that gave you a chance to balance past deeds that were not touched by altruism…'

Peter interrupted, speaking quietly, calmly. 'Come to me now, Stephen.'

Caron's tone changed to ice. 'Be quiet, I will tell you when to speak.' His voice dropped again and a deep weariness darkened it. 'I am tired, Peter. I no longer enjoy the things of life that gave me pleasure. My mind is troubled. It needs the stimulation it no longer finds. I know you will come for me, but it will not be as you expect and you must ask your God to protect and keep you. When it is time for you and the old priest to give up your souls, I will free them swiftly.'

'Let me come alone then. I can help you.'

'No, my friend it is too late. Now listen. I will tell you what I expect of you and why you must come to me.'

CHAPTER SEVENTEEN

Giles was standing outside the small farmhouse as the large car drove up. His stomach was jumping around with anticipation and the remains of the sedative Liam had given him. He felt weak, mentally and physically. If only Patty would put her arms around him and tell him everything was going to be all right. Instead, she would probably smack him in the mouth. His legs almost gave way as the car stopped and a man got out and opened the back door. Giles expected his family to be ragged and, if not bloodstained, at least red-eyed from their tears of worry for him. He couldn't believe it when he saw them. They all looked wonderful. The two girls were bristling with health and Patty looked angry but very beautiful. The three of them stopped and stared at him then Kate and Sally came over.

'Hello, Daddy, you look terrible.' Kate kissed him.

He smiled weakly, hoping that some sympathy would glide across to him. 'I've been out of my mind thinking about you and what might have happened. Are you all right?'

'Yes!' Sally said giving him a smile. She turned to the man. 'Can we see the horses now, Mario?'

He smiled apologetically at Giles. 'I'm sorry, Signor Lawson, Don Vittorio has some Arab stallions that I promised to let your daughters see.'

Well, that's all right then, thought Giles, how could he possibly be more important than bloody horses? They went off and Giles moved towards Patty, who was not looking at him with the warmth that he had hoped. It was more the way you would look at cat shit that had squeezed through your bare toes. But perhaps she was only a bit pissed off with him and would soon soften. He put his arms around her. She was unmoving as he tried to tuck himself into her then pulled away. He tried to be positive. It would be all right once they'd got over this moment of apology and blame. 'I'm sorry, sweetheart.'

Patty was pleased to see him and his pathetic look caused a flutter in her heart but she was so bloody angry at what he had put them through that she couldn't go to him. Not yet!

'All right. Lawson, I want you to tell me all of it!'

* * *

Peter gently placed Vittorio's phone on the table. He found it hard to breathe. His face was drained of colour and his eyes were flat and cold. Valerie gasped and Liam looked up and moved quickly to Peter's side. 'What is it Peter?' Peter was in another place and his voice was raw

'I have to be on my own.' He walked out of the shed. Loring turned to Liam. His face showed none of the concern he felt for his friend.

'I'll give him a few minutes then see what I can do. Now, let's carry on. Please, Vittorio.'

Peter reached the small, wooded area behind the shed, walked until he was hidden from view, then was violently sick. When the retching had eased, tears came, hard and wracking. He clutched his arms around himself as he forced the name out. 'Oh, sweet Jesus, Francoise!' Finally, exhausted he leaned back against a tree. Then the rage came and he roared to release it.

'Now that's what I like to see, a man in total control.' Liam chuckled. 'Oh Lord, Lucifer, for a man of the cloth, you make a terrible fuss.'

Peter started in shock.

'Jesus, Liam, do you want to give me a heart attack too? I didn't hear you.'

'I'm not surprised, the noise you were making. A simple confession would have been easier and less disturbing.' There was a pause as he looked closely at Peter who leaned his head back against the trunk and closed his eyes. 'I take it that this all has something to do with someone called Francoise. I think, if it concerns Mr Caron, you had better tell me.'

Liam's breath creaked as he sat down beside Peter. 'Right then, Father, off you go.'

For a moment Liam's casual response threw him but then he focused. 'All right!'

He paused for a moment, breathed deeply then was ready. 'It was about a year after I started working for Stephen. We'd just identified a powerful drug boss. He was a high-profile local politician in Nice and tied in with the Corsican Mafia. Stephen was asked by the head of the Marseille Drugs Unit to run the operation to take him out of the game. Francoise was one of the team that he pulled together.' He glanced at Liam. 'She was beautiful, ginger hair, small and edgy with grey eyes that saw into your soul and lit you up when she smiled. Even at that first moment something happened between us. Over the next few months we worked together, became close friends, then one night it moved on and we became lovers too.' He closed his eyes briefly then smiled.' She filled my heart. We started living together. It not only gave us a calm and clean place away from the darkness but the strength to go back into that world too. Then the politician started pulling powerful strings and it looked like we might lose him so Stephen decided to put Francoise in undercover. The man was a serial womaniser who used fear and wealth to take and then discard women. His huge ego would make it easy for Francoise to get close to him. I didn't want her to do it but she wanted to bring the bastard down and wouldn't listen to me. It was the only argument we had but she went. I tried to persuade Stephen to put someone else in but he wouldn't listen and promised me that he would pull her out if she was in any real danger. He wouldn't let anything happen to her.' Peter slowly stood and moved away from Liam. The big man was still, silent and showed nothing. After a moment Peter was in control and sat down next to him again. 'I tried to see it as another job. It was what we did. We all knew the risks and what would happen if a cover was blown. There would be no mercy for betrayal. I decided that I was done with it all and that after this job I would persuade Francoise that we should have a future away from this awful world we were involved in. Stephen knew how I felt and sent me on another job in Paris. Whilst I was there Francoise became the politician's lover and part of his inner circle and started to pass back information. Her last message to the Unit was that she was going with him to Mexico to meet up with one of the big cartels there. It was an opportunity and would finally get them what they needed to pull him in. When I got back from Paris they hadn't heard anything from her for a month and then a week later Stephen told me she was back in Marseille and they would pull her out as soon as they knew her location.' He paused for a moment and then continued. 'A week later he told me that they'd found her. He had another source inside the gang who finally came through and told him where she was. I begged him to let me be part of the team that went in and finally he agreed but when we hit the farmhouse they were in, she wasn't there. But they arrested the politician and several other big hitters including one of the Cartel bosses from Mexico. They questioned them about Francoise but they denied knowing who she was. After a couple of days Stephen managed to pressure one of them into telling him what he knew. I don't know what he did. They kept me away from it. He found out that her cover had been blown but that she'd managed to get away.' Peter stopped for a moment and Liam could see a distance seep into his eyes. 'She was found a week later by a digger driver in a landfill site on the outskirts of the city. She'd been strangled, her eyes gouged out, and her tongue slit, the punishment for an informer.' Peter looked at Liam. 'I had a breakdown and without Stephen's support wouldn't have survived.'

He then told Liam what Stephen had said on the phone. Francoise had found out something that implicated him. Stephen had been living a double life, one on the side of law, the other running a rival cartel in Marseille. He had warned the politician and suggested that they got her addicted to heroin. She then became everyone's whore and was used to pass bits of unimportant information to the drug squad. He had then ordered her death. The politician never made the trial. He had been found dead in his cell. His plan all along had been to get rid of his criminal rivals and take over their business. He had succeeded. Giving up Francoise had been merely a tool to gain their trust. 'He was with me when I identified her body and held me when I couldn't take anymore and shut down. I loved and trusted him. I thought he had saved me.'

When Peter finished speaking, he was drained and Liam's face was tight and his eyes hard 'I wish I could say to you that retribution should be divine only. But destroying this animal is something that you must do but only with my help. You and I will go alone.'

Peter looked at him, the pain etched into his face.

'I know it's wrong, Liam. But I have to go through with it.'

Liam put his arm around the priest and pulled him gently into an embrace and held him for a few moments.

'We must go. I think Val may finish us first when we tell her she isn't coming but we'd better face it.' He got painfully to his feet and pulled Peter up.

* * *

Dave Basnet was in the middle of another nightmare except that he was not asleep. Shit, if only he were, then he could wake up and it would all have been a bad dream. How many times did he have to tell different

227

people the same thing? Why didn't they believe him? Jesus, if he could get his hands on that cow Loring! Inspector Munroe smiled at him.

'See it from our position, Mr Basnet. Three of our team have been blown up and they wouldn't have been there if it hadn't been for you. As there's no one else who seems to know anything about it, that just leaves you in the frame, doesn't it?'

Basnet shifted uncomfortably. His bum was numb from sitting on the hard chair and they were in another airless and foetid room.

'Look, I've had enough of this, now, either you charge me or I'm walking.' He stood up defiantly. Eventually the mouse will turn! Barker, the sergeant, a short stocky man with cold eyes, who swaggered as if it would make him taller, walked slowly across and put his face close to the journalist's, pulling him to his feet.

'Is that so?' He butted him hard and Basnet, blood pouring from a broken nose, crumpled to the floor and lay there, moaning.

* * *

Valerie was raging. 'You wouldn't fucking dare!'

Liam smiled gently at her. He loved her spirit and attitude. 'You know I would. Don't fret, you'll get your story.' Valerie started to interrupt. 'Now, just listen before I sit on you. Peter and I have decided that you should be told all so have a little patience. I have plans to make with Vittorio.' He put his arm around her. She felt a child again in the big and comforting arms. She could feel his strength but she fought and struggled to get free and Liam had to hold her tightly. 'Listen to Peter. He has a pain that is harsh and freshly raw. Try and be kind to him. Now, if I let you go, will you calm down, at least until you've heard him out?'

'Yes!' Not said with the greatest commitment, but it was a start. Liam smiled.

'Good girl! Now before you say it, forgive me if that sounded patronising. It wasn't meant to.'

Peter was sitting against the back wall of the shed and a part of her thought, 'Sod you, you can bloody well come to me!'

She went to him.

His eyes, when they looked up at her, were filled with despair and red from crying and there was a hurt so tangible that she could almost touch it. Her heart went out to him and she kissed him gently on the head. She had never seen him like this. He was always strong, in control, full of optimism, suggestion and possibility.

* * *

Troakes was shattered. He had hardly slept since the bombing and had stayed the last couple of nights in the small overnight suite on the fifth floor. The funerals of the three police officers were today and that was bound to bring more pressure from all sides; media and public and, if not from the Almighty himself, then from the verbal lacerations of his self-appointed earthly lieutenant, the God-fearing, fat little Yorkshire born-again bastard of a Home Secretary. Troakes hated the diminutive politician with his disregard for the lives of anyone but those who could keep the slowly drowning government afloat with their water-wing votes.

They'd had to admit that Basnet wasn't hiding anything and let him go. They also had to accept that he was going to expose 'police brutality and the innocent victim'. Jesus, the way things were going, he wouldn't have time to retire but would be thrown to the sharks as he was washed out on a wave of political panic and denial.

He yawned loudly and picked up Meg's report on the interview with Amebury's wife. It was detailed and precise but there was nothing in it that they didn't know. His phone rang. 'Yes?'

'Someone wants to talk to you, guv. Said to tell you it was Emerald.'

'Put him on.' Troakes poured himself a scotch from the bottle on his desk.

'I haven't got much time. So listen.' The voice was soft and lyrical. 'I've got a name for you. Giuseppe Frinelli. He's a priest, working for a high-level Papal security unit inside the Vatican.''

'Jesus Christ!'

'Well, I suppose he would be at the top, but difficult as all hell to get to. That's it.'

The line went dead. Troakes put down the phone, got up and yelled through the door, 'Bill, get me Giorgio Marnetto in Rome and bring me anything we've got on Vatican security teams.'

'You what?'

'Just do it, son.'

* * *

Giles and Patty were walking through a small vineyard nestled amongst olive trees and wild orchids. They had tried to talk it through but there was still ice between them, wedged there by Patty's anger and Giles' guilt at getting them involved. The life of a perennial pessimist is not an easy one. Whatever you think right to do can only bring certain failure and that fabled silver lining of all clouds can only turn into liquid mercury that is forced down your gagging throat by that self-righteous little self that sits waiting at your jugular for the storm of mistakes to bite.

Patty turned to face him.

'What is it, Lawson?' Her voice was not as loving in its tone as he would have hoped for in this moment of truth.

'Promise you'll let me finish before you…'

'Get on with it, Giles.'

'Right.' Oh, fuck.

'Take a deep breath and don't stop until the end,' his courage said as it departed for safer climes.

'That night I stayed on the boat…'

* * *

Valerie wanted to put her arms around Peter. A simple act of comfort for someone who was suffering as he was but one, even with her closeness to him, she found difficult. She wouldn't want it to be seen as something more than it was, an instinctive act of human empathy.

Her mind swirled as she watched Peter slowly find balance again. She was going to have to sort out this little mental barrier before too many more men had passed through her life, not bothering to try and understand or help her find a way to trust. She was also afraid, at this moment, that if she touched his brittleness she would crack and for some jumbled reason she wanted Peter to feel her strength. Why? That was too difficult to answer! Too involved in the past and the feelings she had for this friend who needed her.

'Don't look at me like that, lovely girl. Remember I'm a celibate and bitter man.'

Great, Loring, you hid all that well.

Peter's smile didn't touch his eyes 'A lot worse has happened to a lot more. Still, I suppose, your own hurt has to be selfish. It was a surprise to me too. I thought I had it all safely under lock and key. Sadly, I don't think I'm big enough to treat betrayal with the contempt it deserves. I want revenge! Not a good reaction for a man of God, is it? Perhaps when I reach the point of retribution, I will be free from hate and only pity Stephen and his insanity.'

'Let me come. I'll kill the bastard for you and for blowing up my boat.'

'That's kind of you, Val, but I think not. Until I've balanced myself, Liam is calling the shots. I don't want another life on my conscience, but if you could find me a drink of some sort then my body and soul are yours.'

Valerie smiled at him. She had no intention of staying behind.

'You should be so lucky, Father!'

* * *

Giles told Patty that he'd drunk too much and passed out but when he came round, he couldn't remember anything that had happened. He was on the floor and Loring was in the bed. He stopped but Patty's eyes were locked on his. He had to finish.

'Paranoia kicked in with pictures of what I might have done. Fought with her, said something really stupid, or even tried it on.'

Patty's eyes flashed.

'No! I didn't do any of those things; particularly, try it on. I'm sure she'd not remember or care about my ramblings either.'

Patty looked at him like he'd gone mad. 'What the fuck are you trying to say then, Giles?'

'All that I kept thinking was that, drunk or sober, I would never do anything to hurt you, would never want to do anything. I love you too much.' He smiled, trying to lighten it, but stopped at Patty's obvious signs of confusion.

'Why are you telling me all this stuff that never happened? Or did it? And this is your pathetic way of trying to get out of it.'

Giles had played this really badly. He'd just have to go for honest.

'No, of course nothing happened like that. It just made me realize that without you in my life, nothing matters at all. There would be no future for me. I will always love you and, from now on, do all I can to look after you and the girls, first and last.'

Patty was still and he was sure she hadn't blinked since he stopped talking. He hadn't expected applause but no reaction at all wasn't on the list. The exaggerator imp went into overdrive. What if she'd had a catatonic event, delayed reaction to the difficulties of concern for him and the hardship of what she had gone through, forced into a temporary life of luxury and plenty? What would he tell the girls? What should he do? Slap her? No, even comatose she would retaliate with a devastating punch. She'd hit him once when he was on the loo in the dark and she hadn't seen him and tried to sit down. He'd said 'Hello, you're nice!' He thought it was hysterical to scare her but she had hit him so hard he'd fallen off the toilet and smacked his head on the side of the bath. Perhaps now would be the time to have that almost fatal attack. It would certainly distract, at least until he'd been brought back to life. Despite his fears another thought careered into his slurry of panic. Where the hell were Peter and Liam? If they turned up now, the two mad men of God would probably send her over the edge.

'Come here,' she said softly. He moved towards her and she put her arms around him. Giles breathed with relief. He relaxed and leaned towards her, his eyes closed, touching her head with his. She pushed him away and slapped him just hard enough to show how pissed off she was with him.

Still, Giles moved away from her, in case it was just the build-up to the main attack. 'That was for you spending a night on a boat with a woman who is younger, prettier, and tougher than me, while we were hauled off around the world by a madman who tried to kill her and you and fuck knows who else. And, more than that, for you not knowing how much I love you and would protect you with my last breath.' She paused for a moment. 'And because it hurts that you have never said this to me before.'

She turned and walked away.

'Leave me alone to calm down and then we'll talk.'

Giles watched her disappear into the vines.

'That went better than I thought it would!' He made sure the words didn't slip out so she'd hear them.

CHAPTER EIGHTEEN

Troakes put down the phone. Cardinal Pirotto had not been the easiest of people to listen to or understand. His English was atrocious and Troakes' Italian, learned at night school when he had foreseen a glowing career in Europol, clung to the edge of parody but, eventually, they had communicated. Christ, it was exhausting though. The Cardinal had been less than forthcoming about the scope of his group's activities but the pressure Troakes had been able to exert through the Italian Counter-Terrorism Force had given him enough incentive to disclose a telephone number on which Father Frinelli could be reached. Pirotto had stressed that whatever Frinelli and Orpizeski were doing was not on Vatican business so would the Ispettore keep him in the photo. Troakes had bristled at the deliberate slight of his demotion and was tempted to childishly correct the Italian; but it would be petty for them to try and 'best' each other. And he was pissed off that he had allowed the Italian to get to him. More to the point, who the fuck was Orpizeski?

He looked at the pad on which he had written the mobile phone number. Around it the doodling had become frenetic and he had drawn a priest holding a cross in one hand and a gun in the other. What was more disturbing, though, was that he had given him a short skirt, breasts, and a beard. Christ, the shrinks could spend days on that! He dialled the number. It was answered almost immediately.

'Yes?'

'Is that Father Giuseppe Frinelli?'

'Who wants to know?' The voice was young and the English fluent.

'Commander Graham Troakes, head of the United Kingdom Counter-Terrorism Task Force. Am I speaking to Father Frinelli?'

'You are, Commander. How did you get this number?'

'From an irascible old bastard, excuse my language, Father, called Cardinal Pirotto.'

Frinelli chuckled. 'A good description but one which would not amuse him. I suggest that we meet. Do you know the Kensington Hilton?'

'Off Shepherd's Bush roundabout?'

'Yes. One hour's time in the coffee lounge. I will find you.'

The line went dead. Cheeky sod! Professional, though. Troakes was ruffled to realise that he would have probably talked on the open line. Careless! He put the phone down and smiled. He was looking forward to meeting the good Father. He shouted through the open door.

'Bill, get the car round.'

'God's office want to set up a meet. He's pissing glass at...'

Troakes interrupted.

'Tell them I'm not here. We're going for coffee and confession with one of his warriors.'

'Are you all right, guv?'
'Shift your arse.'

* * *

It was strange. It was as though he knew this time would come and he had to put everything in place. The security that Caron had always surrounded himself with here had, over the last few years, moved from mainly man-based to an autonomous digital system, designed by him and continually updated as the technology outpaced itself. It was, he believed, impossible to breach. It also meant he could secure the estate with a small and trusted team.

There was a twenty-foot-high electrified chain metal fence on the perimeter of his inner estate, edged with an invisible moat of sensors and lasers and a garden of weight-sensitive explosive devices. He had also dotted virtual control ground-to-air security over the rough and wooded terrain that would activate at any unexpected drone activity.

There was, however, one secret way into the estate. It was through this that he would allow Peter entry to the arena for The Game to start. He would know as soon as it was breached.

This 'Achilles Heel' was an underground drainage duct that had been put in a hundred years before he had bought the land. He had not filled it in because he knew it would provide a limited access and that, should he be attacked, would be protection enough. Now he had added a 'locked door'. At the estate end of the duct were explosive pads that would close the net completely.

Through the cameras he'd built into the entry side of the duct, he would know when they had come in. Five minutes after they had exited on the estate side, the pads would activate and send a chain reaction slamming along the pipe. The seal would be complete. He had protected the fence and the legs that straddled the duct with thick steel barriers sunk to a depth of five feet.

Caron had known that Mario worked for Vittorio. He had known from the very beginning and it had suited him to play along with the lie. It was now that this tree of deception would bear fruit. He knew that Mario would disclose this 'secret gateway' to the two priests. He had allowed him to see the original plans when they had discussed an updating of the system. That planned system, however, was nothing like the real one that was in place. Only he and Malo knew that one.

For this Game he had decided to add one final and devastating trick. Sixteen hours after the entry through the duct, the whole estate would be destroyed; whoever won The Game, would also seem to lose it. Caron sat for a moment facing the bank of monitors that lined the walls of his control room. He was content for now, his hands clasped together, his mind ready for what had to be done coldly and without emotion.

He reached forward and touched the gold button in the front panel. A sign above it illuminated lit up. 'Activated – after three minutes this action is irreversible.' As the countdown started, he sat patiently watching as the seconds ticked away and smiled as the three-minute deadline was reached. It was done. His destiny was assured. Nothing could now change the course of his chosen fate.

* * *

Troakes was sitting in the coffee area of the restaurant. Carter had dropped him outside and gone to find somewhere to park. Christ, in the old days, you'd just leave it where you wanted to and God help anyone who touched it. Now it could be clamped, towed away, or even nicked! You had to slog round like a bloody civilian until you found somewhere. It really pissed him off. He looked around. Jesus, why did people want to meet in these faceless places? His inner cynic sneered. Because they're faceless, you moron! His self-esteem was taking a battering and it could only get worse. If he didn't come up with something soon, it wouldn't be only his self-esteem that would be bloody and raw.

A waiter was standing at his side.

'I'm waiting for someone.'

The waiter stayed where he was.

'Look, son, if I want something, I'll...'

The waiter smiled and interrupted him. 'Commander Troakes?'

Troakes narrowed his eyes.

'I'm Giuseppe Frinelli.'

Troakes looked him up and down. 'I expect you are.' He was amused by the priest's humour but the youthful and clean good looks made him feel older than God. 'Sit down, Father, I have a feeling that I'm going to have to go some to keep up.'

Frinelli leaned slightly towards him. 'Not here, Commander. The manager is a cousin and has lent me his office. Now, if you would be good enough to follow me.'

Troakes chuckled. 'Lead on, Father, you're way ahead of me already.'

* * *

The two cars moved away at the same time, Mario, Peter, and Liam in one, Vittorio and Valerie in the other. At the exit to the airfield, Mario turned to the right to go to Caron's estate. Vittorio was just about to turn left when he swore softly and reversed to the shed.

'I will only be a minute, Signorina Loring.' He got out, leaving the engine running, undid the padlock and went inside. It was her chance.

Loring slid across to the driver's seat, checked the shed, put the stick into drive and slammed her foot on the accelerator. The powerful car shot forward and she had to fight the wheel hard to keep control. She glanced in the mirror and saw Vittorio running out of the shed, then the gate was in front of her and she slowed down, carefully went through and turned to the right, following the direction of the other car. Vittorio stopped as he reached the road. As she accelerated, she tried to pull the seat forward but fumbled around unsuccessfully. She swerved as she crept across the road, narrowly avoiding a lorry that roared past her, its horn blaring. She gave up the search for the seat lever and stretched her legs down.

Perched on the end of the seat, her feet barely touching the pedal, a distant memory slipped into her mind. Sitting on her father's lap. How old would she have been? Five, six, certainly not much older than that. She was steering the big old Vauxhall across the disused aerodrome near her home. The memory made her smile. Then the sudden noise of the phone made her jump and it took a moment before she found it. She snatched it up and answered.

'Signorina Loring, please try not to damage my new car. I should be angry with you, but it was my own fault. Liam thought I might need your number in case you got away from me.' He laughed quietly 'I like your spirit. Good luck!'

The line went dead. Pleased with herself up to now, Vittorio's call unsettled her. She began to have doubts about finding the others. What if they had turned off the road? She came fast around a corner at the top of a long straight and saw the other car just going out of sight. She would have to be careful not to be seen. Slowing down, her confidence returned, and she began to enjoy the sense of things being, at least for the moment, under her control.

* * *

Giles was still where Patty had left him. He was sitting on the ground trying to make sense of everything that had happened and wondering how he would be able to get back to any sort of normality; and whether the positive of all this would be that he and Patty would be able to sort out the lists of personality and behaviour pluses and minuses and balance them so they could get back on track, or even find a new and challenging track. In a flash of realisation, he knew he didn't want the same life, didn't want the prison with the pressure and the pain of it all. He wanted to spend quality time with the family and, when the girls went off to university, to explore and enjoy this new life of 'no kids' with Patty. She could carry on doing the job she loved, and he just needed to find a niche, interesting, stimulating, exciting, with normal, nice people and, of course, well paid, for him. Piece of piss really! He began to feel better. There was always something positive to gain from even the worst of situations. Right, with that decided he thought he'd given Patty enough time to adjust to his return and they could begin the journey into their future. Then with a sudden shot of horror, his mind, obviously disagreeing with his choice, spiralled pictures of death and destruction, driving any thoughts of positivity away. The enormity of it all washed him in self-pity and guilt and rooted him where he sat.

* * *

After Mario had dropped them off, Peter and Liam soon found the duct into the estate. It was about a metre and a half round and the end was covered with a rusty grille. It had been hidden by foliage. Once they had cleared it and after using the battery-operated hacksaw that Vittorio had given them on the four corners of the grille, they were able to get it off and out of the way. He had also provided them with food, water and brandy, two hunting knives, gloves, torches, and two Benelli pistols and ammunition, all in a heavy-duty waterproof backpack. Peter went in first. To start with it was an easy crawl but he was glad of the gloves to push aside the brambles that were behind the grille. With the torch strapped to his head, he could see the duct begin to narrow. Then something hard hit him and the torch went out. There wasn't room to get his hand to it and he decided he was happier not knowing what was crawling over him or being crushed by his knees and hands. The duct was about six metres long and by the time he reached the end he was hot, bruised, bitten, and cut by things he didn't want to imagine.

Mario had explained that the duct crossed over the lasers and the beginning of an initial minefield but, once out of it, when they reached the middle of the first wooded area, they would have to take care. There was a second minefield in a figure-of-eight pattern that followed the perimeter fence. Once beyond that they would be safe, at least as far as the outer protection was concerned.

It was a long time since Peter had done anything like this. It had taken him less time than he thought to slip back into his past life and now his anger was not raw but cold and professional and old skills and means were beginning to surface. His only focus was to find Stephen. That was all. There was no space for anything else. His reasoning and reactions had to be of instinct and experience, not emotion.

He crouched by the end of the duct waiting for Liam. The big man's huge frame was causing him some difficulty but finally, breathing heavily and covered in sweat and trickles of blood from scratches, he pulled himself through.

'Jesus, but that was warm and nasty. If that was a taste of hell, I want no part of it.' Peter handed him a bottle of brandy and he took a long swig. 'That's better, now let's move over to those trees and get my breath back.' Liam moved surprisingly quickly as he crossed the small clearing. Peter was covering the duct when he heard a noise. He stopped and moved back to one side.

'Liam, I think we have company.'

Liam came back quietly. The scrabbling was getting nearer and then there was a painful female curse. Peter bent down and quickly pulled back the brambles. Valerie Loring's head appeared and looked round.

'Thank Christ, it's you,' she shivered. 'I don't even want to think what's moving around in this bloody pipe. I don't care what you say, I'm not going back through there.'

Peter helped her up.

'I should have realised that you accepted too easily.' Liam chuckled. 'Ms Loring, I think you might just about be the most persistent and troublesome person I have ever met. How did you get away from Vittorio?' He stopped her before she could start. 'We'll save that for later. Now, let's get out of sight and we can work out what we are going to do with you.'

It was as they reached the trees that there was a rumbling explosion that threw them flat.

Peter somehow managed to get himself over Loring, protecting her body. They lay there for a moment as the stillness returned.

'Well, lovely girl, I think that settles it. You are now part of the merry band, but whether your readers will thrill to your words of adventure is in the hand of God.'

Liam slowly sat up. 'I think your man Caron is set for the hard game. We'd best put our heads together and come up with something a mite clever.'

* * *

Before the meeting with Troakes and Carter, Giuseppe had spoken to Liam as they left the aerodrome and to Vittorio after Loring had taken his car. His cousin had promised to put some men around the outside of the fence but that once they were inside the estate, he couldn't help them. Also, there was news of a family sadness. His aunt Angelina had suffered a stroke. It was a shock. Although she was in her late sixties, she had always been strong and healthy.

* * *

Caron was sitting looking at a monitor in the underground control room. Malo was standing, silently, behind him. On the screen Peter, Liam, and Valerie stood up and dusted themselves off.

'Always the gentleman, Father Satorri.' He turned to Malo. 'Come, my friend, it is time for us to start the game. Are the other charges set?'

'They are all ready and will start countdown in sixty minutes.' Malo was uncomfortable about what he had been asked to do. He had no choice but to stay with Caron and he was afraid for his lifelong friend. He had seen strangeness in his manner and reason and, although aware that there had been changes in him over the last months, it was nothing like the sudden deterioration of sanity that there now seemed to be.

'Come, Malo, we must leave. We don't want to be here when the house falls. The die is now cast, my friend. The game is on.'

* * *

Troakes was shaken by what Frinelli was telling him. Years of locking down emotional reactions gave him a neutral look at moments like this. Carter was sitting open-mouthed after his first, 'Fuck me. Sorry, Father!' Frinelli then led them along the destructive path of AMOEBA and the life and times of Stephen Caron. Finally, he got to the end game, listed the players, leaving out the names of his cousins in Sicily, and explained the details of what led each of them to be there.

Carter had managed to unfreeze his jaw and Troakes was, for the first time in his life, shocked and unsettled. 'Jesus.'

The priest smiled. It made him look boyish. He was the future of this business. It was youth and not old men who would be society's dustmen. If this young man was a sample then the world might just be in safe hands.

Frinelli spoke quietly. 'I have a simple request.' Troakes waited. 'I want you to give me thirty-six hours before acting on what I've told you.' He waited for a response. Carter glanced from one man to the other, completely out of his depth.

'Go on.' Troakes said quietly. Frinelli continued.

'Firstly, you cannot change anything or stop it happening. Peter and Liam will, by now, be on the estate. If they succeed, then you will have them within twenty-four hours. If they do not return, then it is in your hands. I don't agree with what they are doing but I understand why Peter has to do it. As for Liam…' he paused for a moment, 'he is a giant of a man, in size, goodness, spirituality, and heart. He has taught me all he knows about right and wrong and even that which is sometimes unclear. I look on him as my mentor and love him as a father. Peter is his friend and for Liam that is reason enough. It looks as if they have been joined on the estate by the journalist. With your permission, I will leave for Sicily today before the venerable cardinal has me bound hand and foot and thrown before the Holy Father. Mr Lawson and his family are the guests of my cousin and, although he will not allow you to take them away just yet, you will be able to talk to them. I think that your government will be more than happy if this is cleaned up before they have to use their political brushes. It will give them a chance to cover themselves before the story breaks. It is up to you. I will respect your decision, but it won't change my plans. Now, I'll go and get us some coffee, or perhaps a stronger drink might be welcome. I'll bring both!'

He went out of the room. Troakes had a strange feeling. One he hadn't experienced for a long time. He was enjoying himself. It had taken him by surprise but now he was getting the surge of adrenalin. He wanted to stand on the terraces and shout his encouragement. He knew then that he would do what Frinelli asked and by the time anyone found out it would be too late. At least he would go out doing something his way. Carter was looking at him.

'Are you all right, guv? I don't know who's the most barking, me or him, but I want to let them have a go and fuck the consequences.'

'Do you know something, Bill, I couldn't have put it better myself. How do you feel about a trip to Sicily? I'm sure the good Father can add us to his party.'

* * *

Giles had slowly got himself together and made it back to the house. Kate and Sally were sitting outside as he made his slow approach. He stopped as the look they gave him was confusing and then he realised it was concern.

'Are you all right, Daddy?' Kate got up and came towards him. Sally, not wanting to be left out followed. 'Mum said she slapped you.' Kate was trying not to find it funny.

'She did and I deserved it.' He thought he looked contrite and held his arms out 'Come here.'

The two girls looked at him, any concern that might have been there turning to suspicion. 'Why?' Sally said as she glanced at Kate. 'You look strange.'

'He's trying to look pathetic so we'll give him a free pass on upsetting mum.' Kate shook her head sadly. 'And for making us miss school.'

That was too much for Giles.

'Forget it, I just wanted a cuddle, that's all.'

They looked at each other and then at Giles with a sad look. 'Alright.'

Giles held up his hands. 'It's too late now. Where's your mother?'

Kate came up and kissed his cheek, Sally, after a moment did the same on the other side. 'She's gone out on one of the horses. Said to tell you to have a shower before you talked to her.' They both sniffed hard. 'She's right, you smell bad.' They hugged him briefly then pulled away from him. 'There's some clothes in your cabin that should fit you.' Kate pointed to a small building away from the main house.

'Right, I'll do that then. Can I have a proper hug when I'm clean.'

'We'll think about it,' said Sally as they turned and went back to their seats in the sun.

* * *

On Caron's estate, the three had passed the final minefield. The slow, painstaking, and heart-stopping crossing had taken it out of them and they were resting in a small hollow surrounded by bushes, completely out of sight. Much to Peter's chagrin and Liam's amusement, Valerie had found it. She had surprised him. Cool and accepting what she was told to do without argument.

She looked up at Liam. 'I don't suppose you've got any cigarettes?'

'Not a single one. First time for years I've been without. I meant to ask Vittorio but somehow it slipped my mind. Never mind, girl, it will do us good. Now then, Lucifer, what do you think our man will be about?' Before Peter could answer, there was a distant roaring noise and a huge cloud of smoke billowed up. 'Jesus! He seems fond of blowing things up. I hope he's not carrying it around with him. It makes things a little one-sided to say the least.'

Peter was silent for a moment.

'I think he's burning his bridges. He wants us to find him. It'll not be easy. There's a lot of ground to cover, but he'll leave enough of a trail. I doubt that there is anyone with him but Malo. He will want to play cat and mouse with us.' For a moment he seemed lost in his thoughts then he stood up. 'I think we should move on. He'll be headed away from the house and towards the centre of the estate where the wood is thickest.' He stood up and put out his hand to Liam who pushed it away and slowly got up.

The two priests were walking slowly, quietly, carefully, with Valerie between them. Here the foliage was thicker and Liam was using the large knife to cut through it. They had been walking for two hours and Valerie was getting tired and, if she was honest, bored. It was very unreal. Suddenly Liam stopped.

'Jesus, would you look at that.' Peter moved quickly to him and Valerie tried to push her way between them. She couldn't see anything.

'What is it?' Suddenly she wasn't bored anymore. Her whole body tensed and she was scared. Peter pointed towards a bush that looked like any other bush. It was ten metres in front of them.

'Over there, at the top of that patch. The foliage is thicker than anywhere else.'

Valerie had no idea what he was talking about. 'So?'

Liam looked around. At the base of a tree a few feet away from them was a rusty animal feeder just visible above the grass.

'Peter, give me a hand with this.' The two men, after some effort, pulled it free and carried it over to where Valerie was standing.

'Thank you very much, boys, but I've really got nowhere to keep it.'

Peter smiled. 'Just watch and learn.'

They held the feeder between them and swung it back and fore, then threw it into the middle of the bush. For a moment the metal cage just hung there, then it disappeared down through the foliage. The surrounding area crashed in on itself. Valerie jumped back. A large crater had opened up in front of them.

'Jesus Christ!' She stumbled and Liam caught her.

'I would think that in the bottom of that little hole there's something that would not have been good for our health.' He walked towards it, stood at the edge looking down. Covering the bottom of the pit was a bed of different lengths of metal spikes; the longest, about five feet, reached halfway to the surface.

The others joined him. Valerie shivered. 'Can I change my mind and go back? I don't feel too happy about all this.'

Peter put his arm around her. 'Next time, trust your Uncle Peter. Let's get moving. I don't think it will be much longer. He'll let us find him soon.'

Valerie gave a small cry. 'Oh, no!'

Peter stopped.

'What is it?'

She looked embarrassed. 'I've wet myself.'

Peter smiled at her. 'So have I. It's been a long time since I faced being impaled.'

Liam chuckled and suddenly they were all locked into uncontrollable laughter.

Caron heard the sound of laughter and stopped.

'I am surprised that they don't seem threatened by our little games and they know we will hear them. However, their levity will perhaps make them careless.' He stopped for a moment. 'Of course, it could be deliberate. Peter and the old priest are too steeped in their world to not know it would alert us. They will have their own tricks to play. It won't help them. I am ready.' He turned to Malo, as always close beside him. 'They are not far away, old friend, and we have much to do before we send them to meet their God.' Caron's words were hard but edged with excitement. In his heart he knew he was a warrior again. His body, stripped to the waist, was glistening with sweat and he felt the power ripple though him. He felt more alive than he had for years. Age had dropped away and his strength and invincibility had returned. He knew that he was ready for the fight. It would come soon.

He looked up at the sun. It was almost directly overhead. He knew that by the time it rose tomorrow The Game would have ended. He would be able to live again. He turned to Malo. 'Come!'

Malo watched as Caron stumbled awkwardly ahead and his heart was filled with sadness for him. The once unbeatable man looked old and flabby, his face red with exertion and full of insane determination. Malo quickened his step to catch up with him. Although he wanted to persuade him to stop this madness and to just get away, he knew Caron had slipped too far from reality to listen or care. Malo couldn't leave him to face his destiny alone. He had loved him since they were young men and they had shared too many things. When the time came, he would still be at his side as sword and shield and would, without a moment's thought, give up his life to save him.

In his cabin at the farm, Giles was lying on the bed, half asleep, clean and relaxed after spending an hour in the hot tub that was in the wet room suite in the much-more-luxurious-on-the-inside cabin

Patty sat gently on the bed. She looked lovely and the smile almost convinced him that he was forgiven but there was still a distance in her eyes and a wild spark. Giles touched her hand, which didn't entwine with his or respond but at least stayed where it was. 'I'm sorry, sweetheart.'

'Shut up and listen for a minute. I just want to give you something to think about. I know that you didn't know what sort of threat you would drop into our lives but you should have thought and talked more to me, given me the chance to choose what to do and not have it forced on me. If you'd shared with me what sort of madness was possible if you carried on picking at scabs until they bled, I might have been able to help. That's what being together is all about. Sharing, caring, considering and making choices! Whatever happened with us, our little family unit always seemed safe and protected, and even if it cracked occasionally it was easily repairable. You put all that in danger.'

She paused. 'But despite everything that's happened and the lack of trust and your thoughtless leaps into the unknown, what we still have, however fragile it might be, is too important not to save.' Giles squeezed her hand but she pulled away and they struggled for a moment until she freed it. 'I'm not blaming you for the way things are between us. It's my fault too. We both need to grow up, although you have further to go than me.' She paused, looking at him, and he was sure there was a softening. Should he try for the hand again? Perhaps not yet! 'Just one last bit and then I'll stop. If you ever get involved in this sort of shit again though, it won't just be a slap and a sermon. You'll lose us for good. Think about it.' She went out of the cabin.

Well, that's that then! Doesn't seem a lot more to say. If only he'd insisted on going with the others and put off facing her. But, in reality, he wouldn't have been able to do that. He was desperate to see if she and the girls were all right and not damaged by what they'd been through. Obviously, by the look of them all, their only concerns had been in choosing which luxury they should indulge in first. He should have thought it through and then, by the time he saw her, he'd have probably made more sense. But Peter and Liam were adamant that he wasn't going with them, probably because he'd be more of a burden than a blessing. Good word that considering the crazy catholic warriors. Anyway, the end result would have been the same however long he'd managed to put it off. Should he have tried to blame Peter for the whole nightmare? No, that wouldn't have worked at all. He had got Peter involved in the first place and through him Valerie and Liam... and of course Caron. Then his mind, bored with his rambling changed direction. Where were the three of them now? Had they found Caron? Were they all right? He would be to blame if anything happened to them. He was a selfish bastard and hadn't given them a thought since his first little chat with Patty.

There was a loud knock on the door.

'Yes?' Who the hell was that?

The door opened and two men came in. The older one spoke.

'Mr Lawson, I'm Commander Graham Troakes, head of the United Kingdom Counter-Terrorism Task Force in London. If you've a moment I'd like to have a few words.

CHAPTER NINETEEN

Vittorio tapped quietly on the door of his Aunt Angelina's room. It was opened by a nun who had the most beautiful and tranquil face he had ever seen. She seemed timeless, looked flawless, and could have been anything between eighteen and thirty. Her voice was soft and low.

'You can stay for ten minutes. She is very tired but also very stubborn. I will have to trust you.' She looked deeply into Vittorio's eyes. He almost blushed at the way she affected him. He glanced away towards the door.

'She doesn't enjoy being told what to do. I promise not to stay too long. The priest who is coming is her nephew. Will you bring him up, please? She would want to see him but I thought it best if I came first.'

She smiled and her face lit up and a flash of mischief darted across her eyes.

'She showed me his photograph. He is very good-looking.' Vittorio grudgingly nodded. 'She has talked a lot about her beautiful nephew, Father Giuseppe. I will enjoy meeting him.' She turned and walked off. Vittorio felt disturbed. She was one of those women who took your breath away. It didn't seem right to think that about a nun.

'Vitto?' His aunt's voice was weak and slightly slurred. He felt a wave of love edged with a great sadness. It would be hard for this elegant, proud, and pragmatic woman to cope with her new lack of control.

'Yes.' He came into the room and shut the door. She looked old and frail, her body small in the crisp linen sheets. She was sixty-eight now but she had always looked the same to him. Ageless, warm, and strong, she had won respect in the days when life was hard and dangerous and death was a way of moving up the ladder. He leaned over and kissed the sagging cheek. He would know her smell anywhere, safe and comforting. His eyes began to fill with tears but he fought them back. She must not see him like this. The old lady tried to smile.

'Do not think of the shell, Vitto, it is what is inside that counts.' With a great effort she lifted her hand and touched his cheek. 'You are Head of the Family now, Don Vittorio.' She smiled. 'Don Angelina always seemed difficult for the men but I insisted. I was the only female don in Sicily. But with you in charge, it will be better for business and our relationships with the others. You have much compassion and understanding. Only use the weapon when the words fail.' She closed her eyes and for a moment his heart thumped. She couldn't go like that!

The door quietly opened quietly and Giuseppe came in. He looked flushed. It had to be the young nun! Vittorio was pleased that she had affected him too. Gio shut the door and came over to the bed and kissed Angelina's forehead.

'Aunt Lina,' a childhood name that had stuck, 'you look beautiful.'

Angelina groaned and turned her head. 'If only that were true, Gio, but it's so good to see you, even like this.'

Frinelli had to strain to hear the twisted words. 'Vitto, would you let us talk for a moment?'

Vittorio nodded and went out. When the door had shut, Frinelli knelt on the floor, his cheek against Angelina's hand. She spoke slowly trying to make each word sound as it was in her head.

'I wish that there was something I could do to help Stephen, but it is too late, isn't it, Gio?'

There was no point in him trying to make it easier. She wouldn't want that.

'Yes.'

'He was a beautiful man. I loved him very much. He gave me life after your uncle was killed.'

Gio could see that the effort of talking was exhausting her. He kissed her hand. 'Don't talk, Aunt Lina, rest.'

'No, Gio, I want to say something. I am tired and have decided that I want to leave this world without a wasted struggle for life. I don't understand it anymore. Will you hear my confession? It would make me happy.'

He could feel that she was slipping away. He stood up and went to the door and opened it. Vittorio was standing along the corridor. The young nun was laughing at something he had said to her.

'Vittorio, come now.' He went back into the room. Vittorio followed and shut the door. Angelina was peaceful. Were they too late? As they got to the bed she spoke, her eyes were closed but her voice was clear and soft. 'Vitto, come and kiss me.' He did, his feelings threatening to burst through. 'Gio is going to listen to my confession and you must promise not to be shocked. Look after Edoardo. I am ready, Gio.'

The priest leaned closer to her. She said a few incomprehensible words then quietly sighed and left. Gio started giving her the last rites, sadness and loss filling him. Vittorio knelt by the bed, his face wet with tears.

* * *

Valerie saw the clearing in front of her through the trees. The light was beautiful, throwing shadows through the curved ceiling of branches. It reminded her of walks through the woods when she was a child, chasing Bertie, her little Jack Russell, over the rises and falls, streams and bogs of her private world of trees, leaves, and animals. It was never the same going there with her mum and dad. Somehow, they didn't fit in. In front of her, Peter stopped.

'Let's hold on for a moment. I have a feeling he wants us to be here.' It had been over an hour since they left the spiked trap.

Liam sat with his back against a tree. Despite the weariness he felt, there was a flutter of anticipation in his stomach and an eagerness to face what was to come.

'I need to shit!' Valerie hadn't thought, when she had read about situations like this, that the people involved had never had normal bodily functions. They must have kept it all in until it was over. She'd proved that was bollocks.

Liam chuckled. 'Say what you mean, young Val. Go ahead, but don't wander too far and try to keep us in sight.' She looked at Peter. He was watching the clearing intently. She walked back the way they had come and when she thought she was out of hearing, pulled down her jeans and squatted. God, what was the matter with her? Despite the situation and necessity, she felt embarrassed. She looked around for something to clean herself with and froze as the point of the knife touched her throat and a hand covered her mouth. The tip of the blade was pulled across the softness under her chin and she felt the blood start. Oh Jesus, he was going to kill her.

Caron's voice was quiet, his breath rancid on her cheek.

'I am not going to hurt you. I just want to use you as a little bait. You must do what you are told or the scratch on your lovely young neck will become a chasm.' She was pulled backwards. Suddenly the most important thing to her was that she covered herself up. She spoke in a whisper.

'Can I dress, please?'

Caron stopped pulling her.

'Of course, I'm sorry for disturbing you. Please do not try to get away or make a noise.' The pressure was released enough and she struggled with her jeans and managed to pull them over her hips. She could smell the sweat on Caron and the fear inside her was stopping her breath. Caron dragged her until his back was against a tree. He sat down, pulling her with him, and swung his legs around her waist, gripping her tightly, then forced the blade between her lips, lightly touching both cheeks. She jerked slightly then stopped as the pressure increased and she felt the knife cut into her. He was breathing heavily, the air rasping in his chest. Valerie felt a dizziness and then passed out.

Caron held her weight, moved the knife, felt for a pulse and, satisfied that she was still alive, pulled her lolling head back and used the knife to hold it against his chest. Now! He was ready.

His voice snapped Peter's head round.

'Peter, I have the woman. I want you and your friend to come now. If you walk back the way you came, you will see us. Please don't do anything stupid or I will kill her.'

Peter's face filled with rage and he turned to Liam.

'Save your energy. There will be a chance. Anger will make us miss it.'

'Now!' Caron's voice was ragged and harsh.

The two priests ran through the undergrowth until they saw him. Liam's breath was hard in his chest.

Peter stopped dead. His voice was ice-cold.

'If she is dead, Stephen, nothing will stop me killing you.'

Caron spoke, softly and simply as if to a child. 'Peter, my friend, I may have been many things and hidden many truths but I will not lie to you again. She has just fainted. If you attempt to reach me, I will end her life and it will be a slow and painful death.' Peter heard a small cry from Liam and turned to see him fall to the ground. Behind him, Malo stood, a large rock in his hands. Caron laughed then stopped abruptly. 'And then there was one. Now, listen very carefully, Peter. I want you to take your clothes off slowly, very slowly, and then lie on the ground. Malo and I have a little game we wish to play.'

Peter did as he was told and lay face upwards while Malo pushed his arms above his head and tied his wrists together around a narrow tree. At the moment, there was nothing he could do. There will be a chance. He glanced across at Liam. There was blood trickling from his head. Don't let him die.

Caron pushed Valerie to one side and crawled over to Peter.

'I have another little surprise up my sleeve. You remember Cerberus, the hound of Hades, beloved of Zeus. I have my own Cerberus. He will come when I call. I will let a little blood to enrage him. Now, where shall I begin?' He ran the knife over Peter's body, stopped for a moment over his genitals, then carried on. Peter closed his eyes and waited for the agony to start. The point dug into his stomach. 'You are flabby, my friend. I will help you a little with your diet. But first I will call your nemesis. He whistled almost inaudibly. Peter held his breath. The knife cut in and he screamed. The pain was shocking. Was this how it was going to play out, first him, then Liam and Val? He had brought them here. He started to pray. Then the knife stopped moving. There was a grunt from Caron.

Peter opened his eyes and saw Malo pull the knife from Caron's grasp and quickly, without hesitation, cut deeply across his master's throat. There was a look of surprise in his eyes then they clouded over. When Malo turned, he was covered in blood and there were tears streaking down his face. He moved towards Peter, the knife, red with blood, held tightly in his hand. He was going to kill him too. Peter started to pray again but Malo cut the rope that tied him and then went back to Caron, sat down and took the dead man in his arms.

Peter sat up. It hurt like hell but he could move. There was a deep gash and a lot of blood but he would live.

He reached for his shirt, tried to tear it but he didn't have the strength. The knife was lying by Malo's feet. Peter slid over towards it and picked it up. He cut his shirt into strips, tied them together, then balled his underpants and tied it tightly over the cut. Suddenly Liam shouted and Peter heard a roar and saw, almost in slow motion, a huge bull mastiff. It was about five metres away from them. Its teeth were bared and it was growling, its body trembling. Then it went completely still and a split second after started to move. Fear hit Peter and he couldn't make his body obey orders. It was useless.

Somehow Liam got in the way of the huge beast and stopped it in mid-air. Then the two of them were locked together. The noise was terrible. Liam was forcing the salivating mouth away from his neck. He was roaring his own unintelligible words and sounds into the dog's face as it tried to pull away from his grip. Peter dragged himself towards them. He stabbed the knife into the dog's body. It only made the beast more frantic and it tried again to tear its head from Liam's grasp but it couldn't break his hold. They rolled and now it was on top of Liam. Peter had no time to think but sunk the knife into the back of the thick muscled neck. It pulled away and its convulsions carried it around so that Liam was now on top. Somehow the priest managed to grip the head, his fingers digging deep into the jowls and skin on its cheeks. With a roar he used all his remaining strength and twisted the head violently. The mastiff screeched in pain and rage and tried to struggle but it was weakened. Then with a loud crack, its neck snapped and it fell limply with Liam on top of it. Peter scrambled over to him. Liam's face was bloody and there was a chunk of flesh hanging off his chest but his hands were locked on the animal's face. He looked up at Peter.

'Ah, well, young Lucifer, I was stronger than I thought. At least I won't have to suffer the sickness inside me now. Give my love to Ireland.' He smiled, tried to raise himself, then gurgled deep in his throat and died.

Peter had never felt more alone. But his grieving would have to wait. Valerie had come round and seen the horror in front of her and started to scream. Peter went to her and held her tightly. At last, she calmed. He kissed her head.

'It's time we went.'

Malo spoke then, his words tight and strained. 'You must hurry, Father, he has set a charge which will destroy the estate. Go towards the setting sun and find the river. There is a small waterfall there, and at the back is a cave which will take you safely out. It is a way into the estate known only to me. I lived near here as a child.' He looked at the sky. 'You have only six hours. I will stay here with Stephen and help his journey into the next world. I have no reason to live now.'

Peter put what on what was left of his clothes, then knelt by Liam, said a few words of prayer, and kissed him gently on the lips,

'Until we meet again.' He touched Malo on the shoulder, picked up the waterproof bag and led Valerie out through the clearing.

It took them three hours to reach the river and by the time they got there it was dark. They were both exhausted and Valerie was on the point of collapse. On the way, Peter had been in front of her and they had hardly talked, saving all their energy for just moving forward through the thick foliage. Peter felt cheated that he had not killed Caron himself. He knew that he would have done. He was angry with Liam for giving up his life to save them, but he had to keep all that and his grief tightly bound. If he had let go, he would have lost control completely and that would have been the end for them. Val needed him and he had to use all his strength to bring her through this.

The uneven ground aggravated his raw wound and he felt it start to bleed again. By the time they reached the river he didn't know how long he could last before his body went into shock. His mind however drove out that weakness. He repacked the wound and tightened the shreds of his shirt around him. He had lost all idea of time but knew they couldn't have much left.

They walked along by the side of a large stream and then in front, like a mirage, they saw the waterfall tumbling down a wooded cliff. It was beautiful, and in another place and time he would have appreciated it. Now, all it gave him was huge relief.

Valerie collapsed. 'I've had it. I can't go any further. I don't care about being blown up. If I try to go on I'll die anyway.' She was in shock. Later, if they got out, the reality would hit and her recall would hammer in. If they stayed here though it would be immaterial. Peter even considered it for a moment. It would be easy to wait there holding her and looking at the beauty around them until it disappeared along with them. But he couldn't do that.

He touched her face gently. 'You must try, lovely girl, there's not far to go now.'

'No way!'

Peter knelt by her. He took out the brandy, unscrewed the top, and held it to her mouth. 'Drink this but leave me a swallow.'

After he finished the last few drops, he threw the bottle in the river, then put the gun and ammunition back into the waterproof bag and the torch into his pocket.

'Come on, Val, just one last push.'

'I said no, I'm staying here.'

'No, you're not.'

'Fuck off, it's my life.'

'All right, I'll carry you.' He struggled to lift her.

'Don't you fucking dare, Peter!' She had no strength left to struggle and he dragged her over his shoulder and stood with difficulty. He got his balance and started to walk. 'If you call me Jane, I'll kill you!'

Peter laughed. 'Keep that up, Val, and you'll be fine.'

He got them through the waterfall and they were now in the cave. He couldn't feel his hands or feet and knew he must be losing blood. Val had passed out and her weight became just another dull ache that joined the throbbing in his stomach. The floor of the cave was rough, narrow, and wet, and he stumbled several times but managed to keep going, the torch on his head throwing shadows off the damp walls. The ground was getting more slippery and in places where the roof was too low to walk upright or bent over, he wriggled through on his back, turning Val around and holding her on his front. He had long passed the barrier of feeling and just kept moving. He knew that if he once stopped and rested, he wouldn't have anything left to get going again. If it hadn't been for Val he would have given in long ago and accepted his death.

The tunnel seemed endless; perhaps it had been Malo's little joke and it led nowhere. Then, just when he thought he had nothing left, the air began to change. It gave him a surge of strength and he found enough breath left to speed up. It must have been almost half a mile through the cave and the time left must have almost run out. He would be so bloody angry if it happened now when they were so close.

'Please, God, hold it off for a short while.'

Suddenly they reached the mouth of the cave. It came out on a hillside and was overgrown with brambles. He hardly felt them as he struggled through and came out into a full moon-lit night and a blanket of stars. He didn't stop but carried on until his legs finally gave way and he fell to his knees. Loring was still over his shoulder and he leaned forward until his head touched the ground and she rolled off. She moaned but didn't come around. Peter took great mouthfuls of air. His body, now that he had stopped, was screaming. He looked behind him. The fence that bordered the estate was a couple of hundred metres away from them. Would that be far enough? No, it wouldn't. He would have to move but he knew he didn't have the strength to pick her up again. Suddenly from down the hill there was a sound and as it got clearer, he realized it was voices. Slowly and painfully he pulled himself up. He wasn't going to give in easily after all they'd been through to get here.

The two men patrolling the fence with infra-red goggles and torches saw him as he stood and roared at them. They shouted at him that they were from Vittorio, but he didn't hear or understand.

They watched as he fell to the ground. When they got to him, he was almost unconscious but managed to tell them about the bomb. One man took out a radio.

'It's Angelo. We've found them. There are only two, the smaller priest and the woman. They will need a doctor. The whole estate is about to blow.'

There was a crackle then Giuseppe's voice came through the sound of the helicopter.

'We'll be with you in three minutes. There is no sign of Liam?'

'I'm sorry, Gio.'

They had just landed at the farm when the explosion shook the ground and a large smoke cloud rose over the horizon. Gio stood still for a moment and then crossed himself.

'Sleep well, Liam, I'll miss you!' He looked towards the horizon and smiled. 'You were the most wonderful old bastard!'

* * *

Giles was sitting with the two police officers on the terrace in front of the cabin. He was dressed in jeans, a white shirt. and sandals. The clothes, expensive and stylish, were borrowed from his hosts and were too big. He was though looking better than he had for days and was feeling almost human. Patty was still out riding and the girls were in the large swimming pool at the back of the house. Troakes had questioned him for the last couple of hours and Giles had taken him through his journey from Clarke's death.

They stopped as a man came from the main house carrying a tray with cakes, glasses of lemonade, a teapot and cups, and a bottle of wine in a chiller and three wine flutes,

Carter looked on in awe. 'Bloody hell, they don't do things by halves, these fellas, do they?'

Troakes smiled and looked up as Giles went to pour tea. ''Not for me, Mr Lawson, I'll have a drop of the bubbly, the DS will have tea though.'

'Thanks for that, guv, you're all heart.'

Troakes tasted the wine. 'Nice.' He put the glass down. 'All right, Mr Lawson, we'd got to your stay on the boat just before it blew up.' His mobile which was on the table rang. He checked the number. 'I have to take this. Troakes.'

'It's Giuseppe Frinelli, Commander, are you with Giles Lawson?'

'I am, Father.'

'Father Satorri and Ms Loring are badly hurt but safe and on their way to the Sisters of Angelique Hospital. My cousins will direct you there. They will be well looked after.'

'What about Father Orpizeski?'

'Sadly, he didn't make it out.'

There was a brief pause as Troakes took this in.

'I'm sorry, Giuseppe.'

'So am I, but he will rest peacefully and live on in the good he has done.'

'I'm sure he will.'

'I'm afraid you'll have to make your own way home. I have to try and placate "the irascible old bastard" in Rome. I leave in an hour.'

'I'm sure you'll find a way. Thank you for all your help, Father, and safe travels.'

'You too, Commander.'

Giles was waiting impatiently.

'The old priest didn't make it but the other two seem to be okay, or will be, once they've been patched up.'

'Can I see them?'

Troakes glanced towards Carter. 'What do you think, Carter?'

'It'll give us a bit more time before the shit falls, guv.'

'It will at that.' He smiled at Giles. 'Yes, Mr Lawson, you can.'

Giles and Patty stood by the bed looking down at Peter. They had been allowed in for a couple of minutes. Peter was still out of it, covered in tubes and dressings and looked terrible. They stood there silently, shocked and disturbed. Patty took his hand. He smiled at her and moved towards Peter. 'I'll see you back in the UK if I haven't been locked up.' Patty kissed Peter's head.

An old nun, with a lined face and sparkling eyes, touched Giles' arm, tapped her watch, and, with them following reluctantly, went out.

CHAPTER TWENTY

After three days Peter was beginning to show signs of improvement. He had been examined and operated on within two hours of leaving the estate and that had probably saved his life. Apart from a slight concussion, there was a long gash in his stomach lining that needed stitching, and the muscle damage around the wound would heal but it wouldn't be a quick fix. Trickier though was a small piece of blackthorn that had embedded in his knee joint, the infection had started to spread along his leg. They had removed the thorn and given him heavy doses of antibiotics that had now kicked in. His face and body were a mass of cuts and bruises but they would disappear in time. His circulation got better and slowly, agonizingly, the feeling came back into his hands and feet. The medics were amazed at his strength and resilience, considering his age. They were also puzzled and more than a little surprised at Frinelli's remark as Father Satorri was about to go into theatre.

'Take care of him.'

'We will do what we can, but...'

Gio interrupted them. 'He's come through much worse than this, and now he has a new angel on his team he will probably outlive us all.' He touched Peter on the arm and smiled at the confused medics.

For the first couple of days Peter had vague memories of nurses in white habits and doctors in white coats and one beautiful young nun who looked like an angel as she gently washed his face. He had seen nothing of Gio but had a shadowy memory of Giles standing by the bed with Patty, but it might have been a dream. He knew that Troakes had insisted they went back with him.

Peter had been told that Valerie was stable and responding to treatment. Troakes had left him a message saying he would want to see him when he was fit and back in the UK. He managed to get out of bed and walk around his large room and felt that he might live after all. He was a bit shaky and his stomach hurt but he was obviously a lot tougher than he realised. He also had a brief visit from Vittorio who told him that the estate was completely destroyed and that Giles and his family were safely back in the UK. Giles had wanted to stay until he was able to talk to Peter but there was an urgency to get him back before anything leaked out to the media. Gio had been summoned back to the Vatican but would be returning to Sicily soon.

On the sixth day after their escape, Valerie came into his room without knocking. She was pale but looking as though she was finding her feet again. She had been lucky. There might be a faint scar either side of her mouth where Caron had pushed the knife in but none of the facial muscle was damaged and there wasn't a mark on her throat. Peter touched her cheek gently.

'Don't worry, Val, you needed a little something to take the edge off your beauty and it might even add a touch of character and attraction to some who have certain tastes.'

'Fuck off, Father.' She laughed, leaned over and kissed him gently on the lips. 'Thank you.'

'God, Val, that's an unfair way to treat an almost naked man of the cloth.' She sat on the edge of the bed.

She held his hand. 'Do you mind if I don't talk about it yet? I think it has changed my life but I need time to work it out.'

'Me too.'

'What shall we talk about then that isn't anything to do with our little adventure?'

'I could tell you tales of my early life of mischief or we could improvise a quick Mass to try and cleanse your dark soul.'

Valerie grimaced. 'I'd rather face that monster dog again.'

There was a knock on the door and Gio walked in. He smiled at the two of them.

'You both look a hell of a lot better than when I left you.'

'Gio, that's perfect timing. I was about to convert young Val here to the Papal creed. There's more of Liam in you than you would want to believe. How did things go with Pirotto?'

Gio sat on the chair and pulled it closer to the bed. 'He has been pressured from above to move to a loftier position in the authentication of saintly miracles. I think he rattled a few too many bones and abused his position with his own ideology and ego. Cardinal Giorgio has taken over from him. He's an old friend of Liam's and has promised that, unless I sin greatly, he will let me pass on his wisdom to others.'

'Sweet Jesus, I haven't thought about Alberto Giorgio for years. Not since the three of us got stuck in a coal mine in Brazil.' He smiled at their reaction. 'You'll have a good ally there, Gio, and, as to Brazil, that will have to wait for another time.'

Valerie stood up. 'Right, if there's nothing juicy now, I'm going for a coffee. Anyone else want one?'

Gio shook his head 'Not for me, thanks.'

'Nor me, darling girl.' Peter glanced at Gio. 'Mind, a drop of single malt would touch the spot.'

'Not possible unless we can get someone to smuggle it in. I'm going to sit in the rose garden for a bit and find some order in my mind.' She hesitated. 'I'm hoping that I'll be allowed to go home tomorrow. I need to write up the story so it's ready when we can publish what little we'll be allowed to tell.' She went over and hugged Gio and kissed Peter. 'I'll see you before I go, Peter.'

She smiled back at the two priests and went out of the room.

'She's a bit special that one.'

Gio reached into his pocket and took out a flask, unscrewed the cap, and held it out to Peter.

Peter laughed and drank deeply. 'Now, Gio, did Alberto have a few words for me?'

Gio looked unsure for a moment then touched Peter's arm. 'He asked me to suggest to you that you take Liam's place and that we work together. He'll arrange it as soon as you have recovered. He thought if nothing else it might be the final straw for Pirotto and force him into missionary work in some dark and dangerous place.'

Peter looked at Gio in surprise then started to chortle. As the laughter took him over, he held his stomach. 'Jesus, that hurts like the devil.' but he couldn't stop.

CHAPTER TWENTY-ONE

Two weeks later the story broke in the Sunday Chronicle. A six-page spread by the paper's award-winning investigative reporter, Valerie Loring, told as much of the story as was allowed. It began as an exploration of AMOEBA and all those involved, both perpetrators and victims. Then as her involvement grew, it became a thrilling, moving, and dangerous personal story. She didn't mention Peter, Liam, or Gio and his family by name, but Caron and the others were fair game. It was the best piece of writing she had ever done and would go on to win a clutch of awards. She decided to take a sabbatical to write her first book, a psychological thriller about an investigative reporter. She moved to a small village in Greece and lived in a tiny cottage on the beach. There she surprisingly met and began a relationship with a painter who was originally from Sicily.

* * *

The AMOEBA scandal sent shock waves through the country. The Opposition wanted an immediate enquiry into the running of the UK prison service and the screening and selection of prison governors by the Justice Department, plus the screening and selection of Chief Constables and senior officers by the Crime

Commissioners. They demanded the sacking or resignation of the Prisons and Justice Ministers; also, that the Home Secretary took responsibility and, if not relieved of his position by the Prime Minister, be forced to address the House and suffer the media maelstrom. It was, for the Opposition, an opportunity to undermine and perhaps even bring down the Government. Of course, it was tragic for all those involved and they had to be at the forefront of everybody's thoughts and reasons for action. As for the rest, that was just damage limitation, the balance of politics and control of the country.

Two weeks later, the Home Secretary resigned and the Prime Minister just about held on. Under pressure from the Commons and the Public, she surprisingly survived a vote of no confidence by a tiny majority but her position was now very fragile. A new set of laws came in to try and make good the mistakes of the past and slowly and surely it became another battle remembered as they moved on to the next.

Gerald Wright, the Governor at Hill Sutton, was removed from his position but held on to his pension while his connection with Roger Alsopp and a possible one with AMOEBA was looked into. He died of a heart attack three months after leaving the prison service.

Giles Lawson and his family rebuilt their lives. He left the prison service and, after he was fully recovered, started working at a garden centre until he decided what to do with the rest of his life. It meant a drop in money coming in but it was worth it and, serendipitously, Patty was offered a new job with a big salary increase so it almost balanced out. They worked at their relationship and slowly it healed. He made the mistake of telling Patty about some of his hysterics during the ordeal with the girls there and had to endure their laughter and ridicule. At least some things never changed!

Gio Frinelli carried on successfully protecting Vatican secrets but never quite enjoyed it as much as he had done with Liam. He felt the great loss of his friend and that it was his punishment for not having an open enough mind about God and the mystery of the human spirit.

It took Peter Satorri a long time to recover both psychologically and physically. He spent some time in Wales and slowly found his faith again.

EPILOGUE

WEST OF IRELAND

Peter Satorri stood on the hillside overlooking the valley and the small Norman church. It was an early summer's morning and little drops of dew sparkled on the lush greenery. He took a flask out of his pocket and held it up.

'Bushmills, Gabriel, holy water! I have a new lease of life here. I only wish I could share it with you. I make a poor substitute, but I have my memories and these wonderful people make me feel one of their own.'

His phone rang and he looked at the caller ID for a long moment, then smiled and answered.

'Gio, my boy, you pick your moments! I was just sprinkling a little holy water on Gabriel's spirit.'

'Peter, I hope you are well and are caring for your flock?'

'What do you want?'

'Would you believe it is just touching base with a good friend?'

Peter chuckled. 'No.'

'All right. There is a troubling series of kidnaps and killings of priests in and around Mexico City and Veracruz and, as you spent time there together, Alberto felt that you might...'

As Gio talked, Peter took a long drink and then started walking slowly down into the valley.

Printed in Great Britain
by Amazon